T0369132

THE 13 *th* MONTH

THE 13th MONTH

LOUIS PAUL DEGRADO

iUniverse

THE 13TH MONTH

iUniverse books may be ordered through booksellers or by contacting:

iUniverse
1663 Liberty Drive
Bloomington, IN 47403
www.iuniverse.com
1-800-Authors (1-800-288-4677)

ISBN: 978-1-4917-6468-8 (sc)
ISBN: 978-1-4917-6469-5 (hc)
ISBN: 978-1-4917-6467-1 (e)

Library of Congress Control Number: 2015905877

Print information available on the last page.

iUniverse rev. date: 4/8/2015

Also Available from Author Louis Paul DeGrado

Savior

Finalist, *Foreword* magazine's Book of the Year Contest!
Glimpse the future in this exciting science fiction thriller!
How far will we go to save ourselves? Faced with its own demise, humankind turns to science for answers, and governments approve drastic measures in genetic testing and experimentation.

Battle lines are drawn when a religious crusader and the medical director of the largest research firm clash over thousands of people frozen in cryogenic stasis who are being used as human test subjects. Caught in the middle is Kyle Reed, the director of the company, who has been brought back after two hundred years to face his greatest dilemma: support the company he founded or expose the truth behind its plans.

The Questors' Adventures

What do you call a group of boys who set out to explore the unknown? They call themselves the Questors, and they're ready for excitement, adventure, and mayhem. Join the adventure as the boys, ages ten to thirteen, must overcome jittery nerves and active imaginations to investigate a haunted house in their neighborhood. An engaging series for young readers!

The People Across the Sea
Editor's Choice, iUniverse

Within the towering walls of the city by the sea, a dark secret is kept. The city's history was wiped out by foreign invasion, and even now, the city stands poised to repel another attack from the dreaded people across the sea.

A culture based on fear and the threat of invasion has spawned a leader, a council, and the Law of Survivors. Aldran Alfer is now the Keeper of the law and the council leader. He knows the hidden terror that threatens to rip the city apart.

The sons of Aldran, Brit and Caln, find themselves caught in a web of danger and mystery. Brit finds himself on the run from the Black Guard, veiled men who prowl the streets and crush any who oppose the council's will.

While Caln remains in the city, struggling to hold his family's position on the council, Brit heads to the forbidden desert to seek out the Wizard, a man with strange powers who was banished from the city. In the company of the Wizard and a mythical desert wanderer, Brit will find his destiny. He must cross the land of the Sand Demons, fierce predators who stalk the desert, where he searches for a way to carry out his father's plan to lead their people to safety and end the threat from *The People Across the Sea*.

To my mother, Pat, who taught me the difference between right and wrong and guided me with compassion and courage

Contents

Chapter 1

Among All Men

This is an evil among all things that are done under
the sun, that there is one event unto all: yea, also the
heart of the sons of men is full of evil, and madness
is in their heart while they live, and after that they
go to the dead.

—Ecclesiastes 9:3

"There's Jimmie's car. That must be the house," Adnan said from
the passenger seat of the car. "Pull into the driveway; it will
attract less attention."

"Are you sure?" Dr. Claudia Walden asked as she slowly executed
a U-turn on the rain-drenched street. She turned the headlights off
as she entered the driveway.

"I see it too," Kanuik said from the backseat. "This is the place."

"Park behind the cars there," Adnan said, pointing.

"I can't believe I let you drag me into this tonight," Claudia said.
"I'm almost finished with the first season of *X-Files*." The rain was
falling steadily, and she kept the windshields wipers on as she looked
at the house.

"That show has been off the air for over a decade now," Adnan
said.

"I'm a little busy," Claudia said. "I'm spending too many of my nights out with you two."

"Come now, Doctor," Adnan said. "It goes with the territory."

"Besides," Claudia said, "look who's talking about being caught up with the times; do either of you have any plans to ever get a driver's license?"

Adnan looked back at Kanuik and shrugged.

"She has a point," Kanuik said.

The car came to a stop in front of a white and red two-story house. The double-bulb motion light on the outside of the garage came on. As the light streamed down in front of them, they could see a blue Dodge pickup with peeling paint, parked by a small Ford Escort in the driveway. There were lights on upstairs in the house, but the window shades were drawn.

Claudia turned off the windshield wipers and looked toward the house. "So what do we do? Knock on the door and tell them we are a group consisting of a holy man from India, a Native American shaman, a psychiatrist, and a university professor and that we're here because we suspect something evil is about to happen?"

"No," Adnan said, opening his door. Only five feet seven, Adnan was a stocky man who wore only dark clothing, grays and blacks. All that remained of his hair was two streaks of silver on each side above his ears, betraying his age. He pulled his raincoat tight and his hat down low as he leaned on a wooden cane and walked around to the driver's side of the car.

Standing over six feet five, with broad shoulders and long, straight black hair, Kanuik carefully stepped out of the side door and joined Adnan. A long-bridged nose stuck out like an arrow from his face with its broad chin and high cheekbones. With black eyes set deep in his solid face, he observed the scene with precision, accounting for every piece that was out of place.

"Where's your hat?" Adnan asked. "I just got you a nice hat."

"I cannot wear a hat," Kanuik said. "It blocks my power."

In the driveway stood a man wearing glasses and a brown sport coat. He stood at five ten and had brown shoulder-length hair.

"Hello, Jimmie," Adnan said.

Jimmie nodded. He held a small electronic device in his hand that resembled a transistor radio. It buzzed and hummed, and a small screen flickered when he pointed it toward the house. "This is where the signal is the strongest tonight. Should I call Mike and Russ?"

"No," Adnan said. "We will not need the help of any of your ghost-hunting friends tonight." He looked above the house and then back at Claudia as she stepped out of the car and shut her door. "We're too late," he said. "Something bad has already happened. But evil is still here, and it's not going to leave without a fight. Once I open the front door, you better call Detective Jennings and let him know we will need his assistance." He turned to Kanuik. "Let's go."

Claudia pulled out her cell phone and tried to dial while attempting to expand a small umbrella.

"Here," Jimmie said as he grabbed the umbrella and opened it, holding it above Claudia's head the best he could.

"Thank you," Claudia said. She hurried along to catch up to Adnan, with her phone to her ear. "Yes, Detective Jennings, it's Claudia. Sorry to bother you. No, I haven't changed my mind about your offer. Look, we've got a situation." She looked up at Adnan, who approached the door and put both hands on it, as though he could sense what lay inside. He turned and looked at her, shaking his head. "You better bring some resources," Claudia said. "It's bad."

The front door was unlocked, so Adnan pushed it open, and the group entered the house.

Claudia, her long, streaming blonde hair wet from the rain, stood in the doorway, dripping.

"Sorry," Jimmie said, folding the umbrella. He handed it to her, and she put it against the wall inside the house.

Claudia closed the screen door but left the main door open and hesitated.

"What is it, Claudia?" Adnan asked.

Claudia, who stood five ten, shook her blouse and then her head as she flashed her blue eyes toward Adnan. "I don't want to get the floor all wet. It's not polite."

"I don't think these people will mind," Adnan said.

In front of them, a stairwell led to the second floor, and a hallway to the right led to the rest of the house. Down the hall, a light flickered.

"*Ehena tsunigayvl iyulistranv adusde di ay,*" Kanuik hummed low, waving his arms in front of him. His face was stern and dripping wet from the rain. "They've already been here."

"I'm getting a reading from upstairs," Jimmie said, holding out his device.

"I'll check upstairs with Jimmie," Kanuik said. He and Jimmie began climbing the stairs.

As Claudia started to follow them, Adnan put his hand out and said, "No. Please remain close to me." He started down the hallway toward the flickering light, and Claudia followed. Then she stopped.

"Claudia, are you coming?" Adnan said.

She looked down at her hands; they were shaking. She wished she had the ability Adnan and Kanuik did that allowed them to sense the evil. All she had was an uneasy feeling that made her feel sick to her stomach. She crinkled her nose. "What's that smell?"

"Blood," Adnan said.

She'd been around Adnan for more than six years and knew by the way he was acting that they were in for a bad night. She continued down the hall behind him.

The two entered a living room that was dark except for the light from a large-screen television on the wall across the room, opposite of where they entered. Between them and the wall holding the television sat a brown leather four-piece sofa and a black leather recliner next to it. Someone with short hair was sitting on the sofa watching the television, with his or her back turned to the entrance.

Adnan put his hands up in front of him and mumbled a prayer. Claudia watched as shadows moved in the light, but she could hardly tell whether they were reflections from the television or real entities.

"Don't look at them, Claudia," Adnan called out. "Look away!"

Claudia went back into the hallway. It was then she noticed the blood running down the floor, all the way back to the stairs. She had missed this in the poor lighting but could see it clearly now that her eyes had adjusted. She shuddered when she noticed she stood in a large puddle of it. She fought back her reflex to vomit and moved her black-heeled shoes out of the puddle. She gagged a little and tried to regain her composure.

"You can come in now," Adnan said.

She moved back into the living room. Adnan remained behind the couch, watching the television. She followed his gaze and was horrified by what she witnessed.

The television was playing what looked like a home video filmed by someone walking into a bedroom. The visible hand out in front of the camera looked masculine as the camera zoomed in to show a black claw hammer clasped within it. The video camera followed the hand and the hammer as the person entered a low-lit bedroom and approached two people sleeping. Claudia turned her head as the hand rose and the blows began to strike.

She jumped as two hands touched her from behind. She nearly screamed, but the touch was warm and strong. She turned to see Kanuik behind her. He put his finger to his lips as his eyes looked to the screen.

Adnan looked at Kanuik and then at a table by the couch where the claw hammer lay. Kanuik nodded and put his hand on Claudia's shoulder. She took two steps back and let Kanuik silently move forward. He reached into his pockets with both hands. When his hands emerged, they were full of small balls of fire that he dropped on the hardwood floor in front of Claudia in a line. His eyes met her eyes, and he didn't need to speak.

Claudia nodded. She knew she was to stay on the opposite side of the fire.

Kanuik and Adnan went around the couch from opposite sides. Kanuik secured the hammer and threw it over a small counter into the kitchen while Adnan faced the person on the couch.

"David," Adnan said. "David, can you hear me? You are not dreaming, David. Look at me. The shadows around you are real. Don't let them touch you anymore; they are here to harm you. Come back to where I am. Follow my voice." Adnan looked at Kanuik.

Kanuik took out a pipe, lit it, and puffed on it until he had a good amount of smoke going. Then he blew the smoke toward the man on the couch.

"David, look at me. Look at me," Adnan said. He received no response. "Claudia, we may need you. Approach very slowly and do not break the circle."

With Kanuik between her and the person on the couch, Claudia rounded the corner to see a thin, young boy with blond hair, making sure she did not enter the circle of fire. The teen was staring at the screen, with blood in his hair and on his face and hands.

"He's not responding," Claudia said. "Let me check him."

"Okay," Adnan said. "But be careful."

Kanuik moved closer and put his hands on David's so that he was pinned to the couch.

Claudia carefully stepped over the fire and went around to the front of the couch, where she put her fingers up to David's throat and took out a small penlight from the pocket of her blouse and shone it in his eyes. "He has a pulse, but it's very weak, and his body is extremely cold. He's in shock."

"The shadows still have him in their grip," Adnan said. "It is likely that he does not even know what he has done. I will drive them out before your detective gets here."

Red and blue lights flashed outside of the windows. "I better go let them know we're here," Claudia said, "so they don't come in guns first. Kanuik, you need to stand where there is some light on you. Last time you almost got shot."

"I did nothing," Kanuik said.

"You're a six-foot-five Indian who looks like he's straight out of a history book. When you come out of the corners, it's enough to scare anyone. Where's Jimmie?"

"He is still upstairs taking readings," Kanuik said. He moved under the light as Claudia walked to the front door.

Claudia opened the door just as a tall, well-groomed, well-dressed black detective approached it. "Hello, Detective Jennings."

"Claudia," Jennings said. "What do we have?"

"Sorry to call you like this, but there is a disturbed young man inside, Adnan is with him. We found him watching a video, and it appears that he may have killed his parents."

Jennings pulled a gun from under his jacket at Claudia's words. "Please wait outside."

"Kanuik, Adnan, and Jimmie are all inside," Claudia said.

"I'll be careful," Jennings said. He turned to two uniformed officers who stood behind him. "You two," he said, "check upstairs." He headed down the hallway, and Claudia heard Adnan tell him the boy was unresponsive.

Claudia decided to wait outside in her car. Jimmie came out of the house and joined her.

"Too much excitement for me in there," Jimmie said as he sat in the passenger's seat.

Claudia watched the investigators go in and out of the house. The rain had slowed to a drizzle. Three stretchers were taken out of the house, a body bag on top of each one. Adnan and Kanuik exited with Detective Jennings and David, who was handcuffed.

Claudia stepped out of her car as Adnan and Kanuik came toward her. She watched the young boy being escorted toward the police car. He stared ahead, looking as though he were sleepwalking. It wasn't until he came close to the flashing light of the police car that she saw his eyes blink. Then he blinked again, as if coming out of a trance. He stopped walking, tugged at his captors, and looked around.

His voice started low and then grew to a scream. "No, no, no! No! No!" he cried out. He fell to the ground, rolling from left to right and back again.

Claudia reached back in her car, grabbed her bag, and rushed over to the police officers, who were now struggling to contain David.

"He must be on some pretty bad stuff to be this crazy," one of the officers said as Claudia approached.

"Here," Claudia said and pulled out a shot. "This will calm him down."

The police officers restrained David as she administered the drug. He immediately calmed down and looked at her. "Father Frank, save me," he said, and then his eyes closed.

"Thank you, Claudia," Jennings said. "Who's Father Frank?"

"I don't know," Claudia said. "Thank you for responding so quickly."

"I guess it's good we have a doctor around," Jennings said.

"Yes," Claudia said. "I deal with some unstable patients, not all of them locked up. I've found that traveling with my bag in my car has come in useful on more than one occasion."

"Do you have an extra pair of shoes in there?" Jennings said, noticing she stood with no shoes on her feet.

"Oh," Claudia said. "I don't want to talk about it."

"Guess it's a good thing you were here," Jennings said. "Was this a patient of yours?"

"No," Claudia said. "Look, it's been a long night already. Do we need to do this now?"

"I have three dead bodies and a kid who's not talking. There's going to be questions," Jennings said.

"Who was in the third bag?" Claudia said.

"He didn't kill just his parents," Jennings said, "but his sister too. Young girl, by the looks of her."

"Did you see the video?" Claudia said.

"I did," Jennings said. "Looks like this kid taped the killings several hours ago. It'll make this a fairly clear-cut investigation except for a few items—like what were all of you doing here in the first place?"

"If you need to put it in the report, tell them he was my patient," Claudia said. "The truth is, I was with them." She nodded toward the yard where Adnan and Kanuik stood talking to other officers.

"Right," Jennings said. "The two who you've told me have the ability to sense evil. They've been pretty helpful to us and given us a lot of leads. Usually, they're more proactive in the tips. What went wrong this time?" Jennings lit a cigarette.

Claudia extended her hand toward the pack before Jennings could put it away. "Do you mind?"

Jennings handed her a cigarette and held his hand over it as he lit it for her. She took one long puff and threw it down on the ground, stomping it with her pantyhose-covered foot.

Jennings's brown eyes flashed at the waste, and Claudia grinned. "Sorry, I'm trying to quit." She looked back to the house. "I don't know what went wrong, but it seems to be getting worse lately."

"I'm used to being called for the bar brawls, domestic violence, and suicide attempts. This is the first murder. Maybe you should consider getting out," Jennings said.

"No," Claudia said. "Since I've been working with them, I feel that I've really been able to make a difference and help some troubled kids."

"But you just said it's getting worse."

"The evil is getting worse," Claudia said.

"Evil?" Jennings said. "We have a teenager who had problems adjusting, got hooked on drugs, and took out his frustration on his family. Surely you don't think there was some evil force involved with that."

"I didn't used to," Claudia said. "Do you go to church?"

Jennings shook his head.

"If I were you, I'd start thinking about it," Claudia said as Adnan and Kanuik approached.

"Thanks for coming," Adnan said as he walked up to Jennings.

"Damn shame what happened in there," Jennings said. He reached into his pocket and pulled out his lighter, but he couldn't get his cigarette to stay lit as the rain started coming down again. He shook his hand, and droplets of water flew. "What's the use?" He put the cigarettes away. "You know they got those electronic cigarettes now."

"I've seen them," Adnan said.

"A man doesn't look like a man with one of those sticking out of his mouth," Kanuik said.

"I suppose not," Jennings said. He looked to the squad car that held David as it pulled away. "We'll keep him warm and dry tonight, Doctor. With the evidence we've been able to collect, this will be pretty open-and-shut for us. I imagine you'll be spending some time with him, though."

"Yes," Claudia said.

"If you don't mind, I'm going to get out of this rain," Adnan said. He and Kanuik got into the car.

"Thank you, Detective," Claudia said. "Aren't you going to ask?"

"Ask what?"

"Ask that we stay close and don't go out of town in case you have more questions?"

"Look, I've been on the beat for twenty years now and working with you folks for the last six. It's a real mess in there tonight, but usually, your group helps out a lot. Besides," he said, nodding to her car where Adnan and Kanuik were inside waiting, "those two freak me out. I keep worrying they'll put a hex on me or something."

Claudia laughed.

"Please be careful and consider what I said," Jennings said.

"I would if I felt we weren't doing any good," Claudia said.

"I suppose you want me to recommend David be released to you for treatment," Jennings said.

"He will need psychiatric care," Claudia said. "Since we already know the details of the case, it would be best to let me try to help him."

"Come by the station tomorrow," Jennings said. "We'll fill out the necessary paperwork. And maybe after ..."

"Thank you, Detective," Claudia quickly said, cutting him off.

Jennings started to walk away but turned back. "There were drugs in the house. In the boy's room. That probably explains his condition and what he did—no evil forces involved."

"Thank you," Claudia said.

Claudia entered the four-door sedan and shook the rain from her arms. "I hate the end of summer. The weather starts to turn, and soon, all the leaves will fall, and everything will look so barren."

Adnan sat in the back passenger seat and Kanuik behind her. Both men looked forward in silence.

"I thought we were supposed to be stopping this kind of thing," she said. "What's going on?"

"The same thing that's been happening," Adnan said. "They are getting stronger. Our strategy is not working. It's time for a new plan. Did you get the data you were looking for, Jimmie?"

"I got some good readings," Jimmie said. "I'll have to put them into my model and see where we are."

"Did you locate the source of the portal where they cross?" Adnan asked.

"I'm not sure," Jimmie said. "You're not serious about trying to cross through it?"

"The bishop did not like it the last time you recommended your plan," Kanuik said.

"The bishop is sticking to what he knows," Adnan said. "He is not out on the front lines with us. What we witnessed tonight is only the beginning. The shadows were reduced to causing mischief at one time. Now they are influencing murders. We need to stop them at the source."

"We don't have enough information on where the portal goes," Jimmie said. "Besides, didn't you tell me that the last time someone tried to cross over, they died?"

"Look around," Adnan said. "Even Bishop Tafoya wouldn't be able to deny things are getting worse. It's time to try again."

"The boy was likely on drugs," Claudia said.

"Yes, they have been using his weakness for some time," Adnan said. "To push him this far, the shadows would have had many weaknesses and insecurities to work with. A teenager, struggling with his identity. Probably not popular at school. We will profile him and probably find out he was smart, above average intelligence, and

11

he was a quiet kid that no one disliked, but no one made a point to inspire or share anything with him. He'd turned off his family, and they did not respond properly."

"How so?" Claudia asked. "What you just said describes half the households in this city. What would you recommend they should have done to regain his attention?"

"Instead of turning to patience and tolerance and reaching out, they probably gave up. Either they ignored it as a phase he was going through and ignored him, or they might have made it worse by confronting him too much and challenging him or trying to force him. Love must be shown, no matter how hard it hurts. They lost their son long ago when he stopped trusting in them."

"If the parents were the focal point of his rage, why did he kill his sister?" Claudia said.

"That was the shadows exploiting him," Adnan said.

"David wasn't the only one who lost his perspective on reality," Kanuik said. "There were traces of the shadows in the parents' room as well. The shadows never work alone; they are cowards and work in groups. They likely had a grip on the entire family."

"I wish you would show me how you can tell these things," Jimmie said. "Without any technology or instruments, how can you tell where these things are?"

"You don't want to know," Adnan said.

"I guess there's plenty of precedence in history for holy men knowing about evil and stuff, even without technological gadgets." Jimmie opened his car door. "Well, I guess I'll see you later," he said as he exited the vehicle.

"And the drugs?" Claudia asked. "You think they were to blame in any way?"

"Did you see them tonight?" Adnan said. "The shadows?"

"I saw something when we first entered the living room," Claudia said. Shivering, she started the car and turned the heater on.

"You are getting too close," Adnan said. "You will need to hang back more next time, before they recognize you."

"He said something to me," Claudia said.

"Who?"

"David," she said. "Right after I gave him the injection, he said the name 'Father Frank.' And then he went numb."

"Yes, Father Frank Keller," Adnan said. "He's the one I've been keeping an eye on."

"The priest from Fifteenth Street?" Claudia said.

"Yes," Adnan said. "When you go by the police station tomorrow, see if Detective Jennings will give you any information he has on Father Frank and any link he has to David. I will contact the bishop tomorrow and pursue his assistance."

"You're sure about this?" Claudia asked.

"The family that was attacked tonight—I would be willing to bet they know Father Frank," Adnan said. "They might even go to his church."

Claudia pulled the car up to the Kozy Tavern, the place they usually went after being out. Kanuik and Adnan got out, but she remained in the car.

"Are you coming in?" Adnan asked.

"Not tonight," Claudia said. "Remember, I have the first season of the *X-Files* to finish." She put the car in gear and drove away.

✦   ✦   ✦

The Kozy Tavern was located down a district street that had once been a hub of manufacturing but now was a run-down area of vacant buildings. The tavern had very few clients, no live bands, and plenty of space between tables. Adnan walked to a table he was familiar with and sat down.

"They know you are here and are drawing you in like they did last time," Kanuik said. "This time, you are older, and that is the reason they are drawing you in."

"We were all born with a dark side that draws them to us," Adnan said. "I am not afraid of them."

13

"Yes, I know. You are a great warrior, and they will not take you, but that is not how they fight," Kanuik said. "They do not fight in front of you but come through your weakness. Those you come into contact with will be vulnerable. Their goal is to isolate you so you cannot make a difference."

"Then we keep Claudia clear," Adnan said.

"And the priest," Kanuik said. "They know about him."

"Father Frank Keller is no mere priest. He has been put in situations where he had to make life-and-death decisions. His experience has confirmed to him the existence of a power beyond what he can see."

"You think him to be a warrior?"

"I know he is," Adnan said. "He may be stronger than you or I."

Kanuik put his hands on either side of his head and ran them across his face and down his neck. "I have fought the darkness for many years. My group and I started strong—there were five of us; now there is only me. I have found no one to carry on the arrow of truth. I hope that is not the same for you. I will support this man you bring into our group, for your sake."

"You must," Adnan said. "This will be my last try, old friend. I'm afraid my time is growing short."

◆　◆　◆

"I got your text message," Claudia said, entering Bishop Tafoya's office. "Luckily, I didn't have any afternoon appointments."

Bishop Tafoya stood from his desk and walked over to close the door to his office. He politely hugged Claudia, who towered over the much shorter man.

"I called this meeting," Adnan said as he stood from one of the two high-backed, red felt–covered chairs facing the bishop's desk. "It's time we discuss our direction as a team."

Claudia took a seat next to Adnan. Bishop Tafoya walked around to the other side of his desk and sat. She had known him since she was a child. His small frame, balding head, and glasses made him look vulnerable compared to her childhood memories of him. He still seemed strict to her, just like in Sunday school.

"I've seen the tape," Bishop Tafoya said. "It is troubling."

"What's on your mind?" Claudia asked.

"I'm used to using this office and those chairs for counseling," Bishop Tafoya said. "I never thought I'd be having a conversation about members of my diocese going through such a tragedy."

"Members of your diocese?" Adnan asked.

"Yes," Bishop Tafoya said. "I recognized the family name, the Jensons. They are church members. Part of Father Frank's church."

"Father Frank Keller?" Adnan asked.

"Yes," Bishop Tafoya confirmed.

Adnan nodded at Claudia, who continued to be amazed at his intuition.

"We have seen this sort of violence before," Bishop Tafoya said "What's on your mind that you needed to discuss, Adnan?"

"We were too late this time," Adnan said. "Which leads me to believe this was not random. The shadows were not merely taking advantage of an opportunity; they were attacking with intent."

Bishop Tafoya sat up and put his hands on his desk. "Other groups have had this type of thing happen, Adnan. You can't be there in time all of the time. You can't save everyone. You are taking this personally, and that can be dangerous. It opens you up to weakness."

Adnan remained relaxed, completely composed. His right leg was crossed over his left. He spun his hat on his right shoe, which he'd used as a hat rack, and looked at Claudia and smiled. Then he turned back to Bishop Tafoya.

"Do you know the name of every family in your church?" Adnan asked.

"No," Bishop Tafoya responded. "I get reports from every parish, and sometimes they add prayer requests for those families that are in crisis. This family was one of those names. I believe their son had been in counseling."

15

"With Frank Keller," Adnan said, looking at Claudia, who sat up in her seat when she heard this. "David is a member of Father Frank's parish."

"This is about Father Frank?" Bishop Tafoya said. "Not again. I've already told you, it takes years of training to prepare someone. Father Frank is not ready."

"He was a soldier before becoming a priest," Adnan said. "He is a great communicator and is involved with the youth of his church."

"Yes, you are correct," Bishop Tafoya said. "Why him? He didn't always have his faith. It could be exploited as a weakness."

"The weakness is what made him stronger—he has a reason to believe because he's a witness. It's all about faith and conviction. He has both unlike anyone I've ever seen," Adnan said.

"You've been to one of his services?" Bishop Tafoya said.

"Several. I have a strong feeling about him," Adnan said. "He's witnessed an intervention. That leads me to believe that God has a purpose for him."

"Meaning?" Claudia asked.

"Adnan believes that if Father Frank is put in harm's way, this force will intervene again," Bishop Tafoya said.

"Not force, the power of God Himself," Adnan said. "I'm not sure Claudia believes in what we are fighting for."

Claudia hesitated. She ran her right hand through her hair. "Look, all I know is that I can't understand everything that is going on. There may be forces of energy that cannot be seen, but I'm not ready to chalk all this up to faith or an almighty being just yet. There's the question of drug use, mental stress, and psychological disorders that we have only begun to understand."

"Now you sound like Jimmie," Adnan said, "which reminds me— he was supposed to be here."

"I'm glad you are still involving him," Bishop Tafoya said. "It's good to have the scientific perspective."

"He is a skeptic," Claudia said. "He helps keep things in perspective."

"Father Frank is tied into this already; we need bring him in," Adnan said.

"Tied in how?" Bishop Tafoya asked.

Adnan looked at Claudia.

"David mentioned Father Frank's name when he was still, well, not coherent," Claudia said.

"They're calling him out," Adnan said. He sat up in his chair. "The shadows know who he is."

"This sounds risky," Claudia said. "If he's as popular as you're indicating, won't he be missed?"

"We need risky right now," Adnan said. "A game changer."

"All I'm saying," Claudia replied, shifting in her seat, "is you and Kanuik don't exactly socialize with anyone outside of our circle."

"She has a point," Bishop Tafoya said. "If Father Frank inadvertently says the wrong thing to the wrong person, it could expose all of us."

"Maybe it's time to expose the truth," Adnan said. "The public needs to know their role in what is going on."

"They are not ready," Bishop Tafoya said. "There is already a war on religion. All we need is to add one more controversy that casts doubt." He sat back in his chair, his lips pinched together, and closed his eyes for a moment. When he opened them again, he looked at Adnan. "I have already started the preparations to bring Father Frank in based on our last conversation," he said. "I knew you wouldn't let go of this, so I brought in a priest to take over for him in case he needed a leave of absence. You think he will be interested?"

"David and his family were members of Father Frank's church. I'm sure he will want to be involved when the truth is revealed to him." Adnan stood slowly from the chair and stumbled, catching the arm.

Kanuik came forward to brace him, and Bishop Tafoya moved to Adnan's side.

"I'm all right," Adnan said, pushing them away. "Just stayed up too late last night is all." He put his hat on. "If Father Frank accepts the offer, we'll be in the office later today," he said and opened the door.

Claudia smiled politely.

"It's always a pleasure to see you, Claudia," Bishop Tafoya said.

"You too," Claudia said. She walked to the door and waited for Kanuik, who looked at her but moved forward toward the bishop instead of through the door.

"Yes?" Bishop Tafoya said as Kanuik approached. "Is there something I can do for you?"

"Church man," Kanuik said. He pointed to the hallway. "That is your warrior, with whom I have served in many battles. But he is getting old, and it is time for you to make plans for a new warrior to take his place. Father Frank must be made ready. He will look to you, his leader, for confidence. You must be convincing."

"I'll do what I can," Bishop Tafoya said.

"No," Kanuik said. "Father Frank must be ready to face his path. It is a dangerous one. He cannot doubt himself."

"I understand," Bishop Tafoya said. "Thank you for your service."

Chapter 2

Summoned

"Good morning, Ms. Able," Frank Keller said as he opened the door to his apartment complex so that the short, gray-haired neighbor lady could enter. Nearly six feet tall, the dark-haired priest towered over her. "Let me get that for you," he said as he took a bag of groceries from her and walked her to her apartment.

"Thank you," Ms. Able said. "I would offer you some coffee, but I can see you are ready for your morning run."

"Yes," Frank said. "Is there anything else I can help you with?"

"You go about your busy day," Ms. Able said.

Frank smiled and bade her a good day. Exiting the apartment building, he stretched out on the small plot of grass between the entrance and the sidewalk. He spotted his jogging partner, another priest named Mark Uwriyer, coming up the sidewalk.

"Good morning, Frank," the younger, Middle Eastern–looking man said.

"Good morning, Mark," Frank said. He started jogging beside Mark as they headed down the sidewalk.

"Are we going through the park today?" Mark asked.

"I would like to, but I've got to stop in and check on the youth group schedule," Frank said.

"You really are going for sainthood, aren't you?" Mark said.

"What do you mean?"

19

"Youth group, soup kitchen, visits to elderly patrons. It's okay to take a day off once in a while," Mark said. "You know, have what they call 'me time.' Watch some television or something."

"I don't have a television," Frank said. "Let's pick up the pace."

A war-decorated eight-year veteran of the US Army, Frank kept himself in shape by jogging every morning and often went by his church, which was three miles from his apartment.

The men grew silent in their stride until they approached St. Joseph's Church.

"Come on," Frank said. "Let's stop in and get something to drink before we head back. Then I can check the schedule."

He ran up the concrete steps to the back of the long, old brick building in a run-down part of Detroit. He entered a room with a small refrigerator and some tables, with Mark trailing behind him. He took out two bottled waters and handed one to Mark.

"I thought I heard you two come in," a brunette, elderly lady said as she peeked in through the doorway. She was the church receptionist.

"Good morning, Pat," Frank said. "In early doing the bookkeeping, I see."

"Yes," Pat said. "But that's not what I need to tell you. Madeline called from Bishop Tafoya's office and said he wanted to see you today."

"I wonder why she didn't call my cell phone," Frank said as he looked for the youth group meeting schedule.

"Do you have it on you?" Mark asked.

Frank and Mark exchanged glances, and Frank shrugged his shoulders. "I guess I forget about it when I'm jogging." He took the schedule, folded it, and put it in his pocket.

"I'm sure it's to congratulate you on something as usual," Pat said. "Your sermons have become quite popular." She smiled and left the room.

"You up for a visit?" Frank said to Mark. "This might have something to do with you since Bishop Tafoya was the one who assigned you here."

"Sure," Mark said. "Let's get some breakfast first, though."

The two men went back to their homes, cleaned up, and changed before they headed to the bishop's office.

Anxious—that's the way Frank Keller felt as the two walked down the sidewalk and approached their destination. The breeze was steady. He paused on the stone steps and looked at the large, two-story building that served as the bishop's office. On the other side of the building was a grand old church. The two buildings were adjoined by a hallway. The ancient black and white stone building stood solid among the crumbling ruins of the buildings around it, devastated by the collapsing economy.

"I don't understand why you think there might be something wrong," Father Mark said.

"As I said on the way over, Bishop Tafoya usually comes to visit me if he needs something," Frank said. "It's unusual for him to request an audience at his office."

"I think you're overreacting," Mark said. "Still, it did interrupt our morning jog."

"Downtown," Frank said, looking around and shaking his head. "When I was a kid, this used to be the place to go. The place everyone wanted to live. Even the church here was an upscale church compared to the one in my neighborhood. We usually dressed up for church on Sundays, but when we came here, we had to dress even better."

"Really?" Mark said. "Now it's a dilapidated monument to incompetent leadership. The corrupt political system has led the American Dream down the road to crime, poverty, hopelessness, and debt. Fear rules here now."

Frank raised his eyebrows at the younger priest's assessment. He looked at the brown eyes full of challenge and the dark face framed with black hair, complete with a beard and mustache. "I didn't know you were so cynical," he said.

"I'm just quoting what I heard on television," Father Mark said. "But I think they have a point. You Americans have a way to put a bright spot on anything, always partying and celebrating.

But maybe it's time to stop and look at what is really going on around you."

"Hmm," Frank said. "You might be onto something there. I guess it's all about perspective."

"It's a far better place than where I was near the West Bank, I suppose," Father Mark stated. "There, we were always worried about rockets falling from the sky. Shall we go in?"

Dark clouds gathered in the sky above, and Frank paused to look at them as the door opened before him.

"Something wrong, Father Keller?" a woman's voice asked.

Frank looked forward to see a slender young woman in a black blouse with a gray skirt and smiled. "Hello, Madeline," he said to the bishop's assistant.

Madeline smiled back. Her face, enhanced modestly with makeup, paled against the dark, shoulder-length black hair. "I can only assume it's something important," she said.

"I thought it was supposed to be sunny all day today and tomorrow," Frank said.

"Never can trust the weather, Father Keller," Madeline said.

"Please, Madeline, call me Frank. Everyone else does. You remember Father Uwriyer."

"Oh, yes, the one from Israel," Madeline said, smiling briefly. She stepped out and held the door as the two men entered. "I've always wanted to visit the Holy Land. It must be an inspirational place."

"Not if you lived there," Mark said, cutting her smile short.

"After you," Frank said, letting Mark enter first. As he looked down, he noticed Madeline's hands; they were shaking as she held the door. He put his hand on hers and in a soft voice asked, "What troubles you?"

Madeline looked up at the clouds. "The storm is coming." She looked back at Frank. "I've been here for twenty years, and the weather is getting more unpredictable every year, like something is disturbing what controls it."

"Excuse me?" Frank said.

"I'm sorry. I didn't mean to delay you. Please come in. The bishop is expecting you." She stepped aside to let Frank pass.

Frank went down the hall but turned around when he heard Madeline lock the door. She continued looking out the window at the sky.

A look of concern passed between the two men as they entered the bishop's office. Bishop Anthony Tafoya sat behind a large cherry oak desk, eyes closed. The office had two wooden, felt-covered, high-backed chairs in front of the bishop's desk and a pulpit with a Bible on it to the right where the bishop would often stand when he was preparing a sermon. The walls were full of pictures and cards sent to him from people in his diocese.

Frank had seen him in this position on many occasions and knew he was not sleeping but praying. He and Mark patiently waited.

"Father Uwriyer, I need to speak with Father Frank alone," Bishop Tafoya said, eyes still closed. Then he opened them. "If you wouldn't mind, I have several people down the hall in the church that have been waiting for confession, and I am out of time. Would you mind taking the next session for me?"

"Any way I can be of service," Mark said as he exited and closed the door behind him.

"Please," Bishop Tafoya said as he stood and put out his arm, "have a seat. You still look like you're keeping up with your physical fitness. Can I get you something to drink?"

Frank took a seat in the chair on the right. "I'm fine for now."

"You seem nervous," Bishop Tafoya said.

"I'm used to you stopping by my church," Frank said. "I hope there's nothing wrong."

"You are very perceptive, Frank," Bishop Tafoya said. "How is he working out?" Bishop Tafoya looked to the door where Mark had just exited.

"Father Uwriyer is a history buff and keeps up on all the latest archeological finds. He knows more about the historical accuracy of the Bible than anyone I've met. It comes in handy when we are in a discussion with someone who has doubts." He looked down at the ground.

"But?" Bishop Tafoya said.

"He's young and impulsive and lacks patience." Frank said. "Did you know he carries a cross around his neck"—he used his hands to demonstrate—"that ends in a four-inch blade? It's a weapon he says his father gave to him."

"In ancient times, holy men were warriors," Bishop Tafoya said. "We depict angels these days as these peaceful, tender, usually feminine creatures. But that's not how our ancestors pictured them."

"I suppose you're right," Frank said. "Some of the stories he tells me about where he lived … well, it's no wonder his father wanted him to have a weapon."

"You were young and impatient once, as I recall. You turned out fine," Bishop Tafoya said. "You became quite a respected warrior before you came here."

"My intention was not to be a warrior," Frank said. "I went to the military to get money for college and gain my independence. I never imagined what it would lead to. I never thought I'd be in a war. I'm glad those days are over."

"Maybe not as much as you think," Bishop Tafoya said. "You just changed fields."

Frank looked curiously at the bishop, not sure how to respond to his comment. "When I was his age," Frank said, pointing to the door, "I was a soldier in the army, unaware at the time where my destiny lay. He has already decided what path he wants to take, and he will need patience to achieve that path."

"Then I'm glad I put him with you. I could think of no better mentor," Bishop Tafoya said.

"Why *did* you put him with me? There are plenty of parishes that need new, young energy," Frank said.

"Yes, that is true. But I needed to be ready in case I needed to call on you, and that time has come. Tell me, how are you doing?"

"I'm fine," Frank replied. "I am worried about your assistant."

24

"Madeline? Why?" Bishop Tafoya asked.

"After I entered the building, she locked the door and stood there looking out the window as if she were afraid someone was going to break in. I am assuming there is something wrong, and that is why you've called?"

"I wouldn't worry about her," Bishop Tafoya said. "We had an incident last night. A family has had a terrible tragedy. She overheard some of the conversation, and I'm sure it's upsetting her."

"Is that what this is about?" Frank asked. "Do you need me to help this family?"

"Yes, it concerns a family in your parish," Bishop Tafoya said. He stood up from his desk, leaned over, and put his hands on the desk's surface, facing Frank. "I have called you here on a matter of utmost importance." He looked straight into Frank's eyes. "I have known you since you were a young man. I have watched the changes in you as you've become more committed to your faith. But I have never witnessed anyone with so much conviction. Either you have no insecurities about your faith, or you hide it well. I am hoping it's the former because you will need both your conviction and your faith if you take the task I am about to assign to you."

Frank sat back in the chair and then scooted forward. He crossed his legs and then uncrossed them. "I'm ready to help you with any task in any way I can," he finally said. "You just need to ask."

"Even if it took you away from what you currently enjoy doing—preaching and running your own church?" Bishop Tafoya asked.

"Now you have me worried," Frank said. "Just what is going on?"

Bishop Tafoya moved to the front of his desk and sat against it facing Father Frank.

"Father Frank, I am thinking of offering you another assignment. I know last time we talked about you becoming part of my staff, you weren't interested. Is that still the case?"

Frank realized the bishop had given up his appearance of an authority figure by coming out from behind the desk. He still didn't know what the bishop wanted with him or why he'd been summoned, but he decided it would suit him to be open. "Too much of a bureaucracy," Frank said. "I would rather be left alone in my little corner than deal with the hierarchy. Is that why I am here? Are you going to move me? I knew that's why you brought Father Uwriyer in."

"No, no," Bishop Tafoya said. "You have done nothing wrong. Understand, every organization needs structure." Bishop Tafoya walked across his office to the podium and went behind it. He looked down at the Bible that lay there. "For years, I have read from this book and practiced my sermons right here, in this room." He turned the page. "I miss having my own parish. You have the only church in the diocese that has increased enrollment five years in a row. There is an undeniable draw to your message."

"Thank you," Frank said. Then he looked to the back of the office and out a distant window to a small grassy area. He watched the wind blow some leaves off the tree there. "I hate when September comes. Soon, all the leaves start falling. The city is brown enough without all of the leaves falling. It used to really get to me. Then I remember that the spring always comes, and it's so enjoyable to watch everything come back to life." He shifted in his chair to face the bishop more directly. "I believe I am making a difference, but I cannot hide my feeling that things are getting worse."

"How so?" Bishop Tafoya asked.

"Walking here today," Frank said, "I noticed the city is decaying more than ever before. We've continued to close churches in the diocese, and yet the need to reach out and help has never been greater. Crime is ever more violent, and I've never seen so many homeless on the street before. I'm not sure what I am doing is enough."

"I am about to offer you a chance to have a larger impact—to move, how should I say, out of the background and into the front lines. I want to move you up. I want to give you a chance to fight the real fight. I have plenty of priests who are good at prayer, good at leading mass, and good at helping others in need. What I need is a warrior! You have that spirit in you."

"My days as a soldier are over," Frank said. "I am a different man."

"I'm not talking about picking up a weapon," Bishop Tafoya said. "Not in the physical sense. I'm talking about your warrior spirit, the spirit that made you a leader when you played football, that made you lead your team in the war and can help us in our fight. I need you to be a warrior for Christ, for the church, for the cause of good against evil. Are you familiar with this passage?

"'Finally, be strong in the Lord and in the strength of his might. Put on the whole armor of God, that you may be able to stand against the schemes of the devil. For we do not wrestle against flesh and blood, but against the rulers, against the authorities, against the cosmic powers over this present darkness, against the spiritual forces of evil in the heavenly places. Therefore take up the whole armor of God, that you may be able to withstand in the evil day, and having done all, to stand firm. Stand therefore, having fastened on the belt of truth, and having put on the breastplate of righteousness,' Ephesians 6:10–18."

Frank wasn't sure he knew how to respond but sat still in his chair, looking at Bishop Tafoya. "Yes, I have read that passage."

"I can see doubt in your eyes," Bishop Tafoya said. "I assure you, I am not crazy, but I am desperate. There is more going on here than I am ready to reveal. First, I need to know if you are ready for a change, if you are ready to accept that not everything in the world is what it seems."

Frank stood up and walked over to the podium and faced the bishop. "If you are telling me there is more I can do to serve, then I am ready."

"Frank, what I am about to tell you may cause you to doubt my sanity. But it is time you were told the truth."

Frank nodded.

Bishop Tafoya continued. "Have you ever wondered why it seems like moments go slower when they are going wrong, or why bad days seem to last forever? Have you ever experienced a bad dream, a nightmare, that seems so real that you know it must be happening, but you wake up? Have you ever felt pain or loss after one of these dreams that you couldn't explain away or found out that a dream you had was really a vision of something that has come to pass?"

"All of us have moments of déjà vu," Frank said.

"Negative moments," Bishop Tafoya said, "yours or those of others that you are dragged into—those are what I am alluding to. When we are happy or have pleasant moments, it seems we only want them to slow down. But the negative, painful moments, they seem to pass by slower, as though something is manipulating time."

"I guess that's how it can be perceived," Frank said.

"Consider the violence that is going on in the world today, the inhumanity of acts perpetrated by parents on their children, neighbors on their neighbors. How is it that normal people whom we see every day all of a sudden snap and do such malevolent acts? You hear people talk about how they were shocked that the person they knew could do such acts, and at the same time, you often hear of other people who gave warning signs that they weren't quite themselves."

"I believe evil has always been among us," Frank said. "It is opportunistic and preys on us in our moments of weakness and doubt."

"Yes," Bishop Tafoya said. "What if I told you the battle is more in our minds and in our actions than we know? Frank, have you ever wondered why there are texts that speak of demons, of physical forms of evil in the past, but none exist today?"

"History is full of superstition. The lack of knowledge and technology in ancient times contributed to this. In ancient times if it flooded, it was due to gods being mad. Now we know better," Frank said. "If someone got ill in older times or had an affliction, it was blamed on evil. They did not know about or comprehend medicine and mental illness like we do today."

"Yes, you are right in what you say," Bishop Tafoya said. "But what if there was a time when evil walked upright among men in other forms that are no longer here today? They became extinct—lost the battle of existence somehow."

"I suppose I could entertain an idea like that," Frank said. He crossed his legs and put his elbow on the arm of the chair and his hand under his chin. "But why? What's this all about?"

"There was a family in your parish attacked last night," Bishop Tafoya said. "The Jenson family."

"Yes," Frank said. "Their son, David, has been in and out of drug rehab. I've been counseling them, but it hasn't been going well."

Bishop Tafoya stepped away from the pulpit and walked back to the seat by Frank. He sat down and faced him. "David murdered his family last night, in a horribly brutal manner."

Frank sat back in his chair and closed his eyes. He prayed for some time, and the room remained silent. "His sister was only eleven years old," he said.

"We cannot win every battle," Bishop Tafoya said.

He opened his eyes. "I didn't know it was so bad. Thank you for telling me. I will make arrangements to see David; we must try to help him."

"That isn't the only reason I called you here," Bishop Tafoya said. "What if I were to tell you that what happened wasn't just a young teenager acting out? That evil was interacting with humans? That it influenced David's behavior and attacked his family?"

"Are you asking me to believe demons are real?"

"That evil is real." Bishop Tafoya looked around the office until his eyes stopped at the clock. "You are right in what you say—that evil is opportunistic and preys on us in our weak moments. It's in those moments you will learn to defend yourself and the others you protect. I would love to spend all day talking to you, debating and discussing philosophy with you. But we don't have the time. What I need to tell you is that evil is among us, but it is not in a place where we can find it, but hidden in time."

"In time?" Frank followed the bishop's gaze to the clock and then looked back to the bishop.

"I don't think the church knows the specifics, but evil was among men on earth. Some may say it was fallen angels who spread evil in men; others say that we were born in sin. Whatever the case, our free will gave us a choice. Church historians say the first attempt to purge evil from the world was the flood of Noah. The second time He tried was in the time of Enoch. You remember the legend of Enoch's sword?"

"Yes," Frank said. "We studied it in seminary, but those books were not considered accurate accounts."

"Yes," Bishop Tafoya said. "The truth is some of the books not included in the Bible may have been referencing things we could not explain but that make sense in what we face today. When evil was driven from physical form to spiritual, demons that walked upright could no longer do so, except for one period of time in the year, known as the thirteenth month.

"There is debate on when the final battle of good and evil happened, but many believe it was in the time of Christ, when he drove evil forces completely out of men. All that was left of evil then was the ability to influence, but not control."

"Then the thirteenth month no longer existed?" Frank asked.

"Yes, evil was banished," Bishop Tafoya said. "Or so it was thought. But it never really left. It hides in moments of time."

"Hides how?" Frank said.

"I won't go into details. There is someone more qualified than me to do that. You will need a car and some supplies." Bishop Tafoya handed him a list. "Madeline will take care of the car. Father Uwriyer will take over your masses for the time being."

Frank didn't say anything but looked down at the list, which included alarm clocks, batteries, long underwear, a heavy coat, bath salts, and wind chimes.

"Once you've picked up your supplies, here's the address where you'll meet Adnan," Bishop Tafoya said, handing Frank a card with a handwritten address on it.

"Adnan?" Frank asked, looking at the address.

"Yes. That's the only name he's ever given the church. They'll know who he is at the address."

"This is a bar," Frank said.

"You know where it is?"

"This is the address to the Kozy Tavern," Frank said. "My father sometimes headed there after working the late shift."

"Then you won't have trouble finding it. Just go in and have a seat. He'll find you." The bishop placed his hands on Frank's shoulder. "This mission is your decision. If you decline it, our discussion never happened."

"I am here to serve," Frank said.

"I know. That may be the reason …" The bishop hesitated in what he was about to say. He stood up, and Frank stood as well. "God be with you," he said as he reached out and clasped Frank's hands.

"And with you," Frank said. He turned to walk out and then turned back. "What about Father Uwriyer? What do I tell him?"

"That you've been given a mission," Bishop Tafoya said, "and you need his help. Other than that, I'll let you decide how much you reveal to him. There is so much that you don't know, and as it is revealed to you, you will understand the need for caution. We will need others to join the fight eventually. You need to make the decision as to his level of participation. For now, you might just tell him you have a new assignment in counseling and let him take your services for you. I would recommend you keep the rest to yourself. Imagine what it would sound like."

Frank stepped into the hallway to be confronted by Madeline, who stood before him, her right hand outstretched with keys dangling from her fingers.

"Please fill it up when you bring it back," Madeline said.

Frank wondered whether she'd listened to the entire conversation he and the bishop had just had. He reached out and took the keys.

"The car's parked out back, black Buick," Madeline said. "Good luck."

Frank went down the hallway to the church while looking at the list Bishop Tafoya had provided him. The list was handwritten and very neatly done. The bishop had not written it; Frank had seen his handwriting enough to know. He noticed one more item on the list that he'd previously missed—a cat. A note at the bottom read, "Don't skip on any of these, especially the cat."

Entering the sanctuary, Frank found Father Mark sitting in the first set of pews.

"Well, there was only one person in here for confession," Mark said. "I hope your meeting went well."

Frank didn't respond right away. He was still trying to digest all of the information he'd just been given. He folded the list and put it in his pocket. "Yes, thank you for being patient." "Madeline told me I would be taking over your services. Does this have something to do with the family in your parish that was murdered? She told me about that."

"Yes," Frank said. "I will be doing some counseling, it seems. First, I must go pick up some stuff from the store. You remember how you told me you like driving?"

Mark smiled.

Frank pulled the keys out of his pocket and dangled them. "We are going shopping."

Chapter 3

Gathering

"You sure you don't want me to go with you?" Mark said, sitting behind the steering wheel of the black four-door Buick as the car idled outside the Kozy Tavern. The name was painted in black lettering across a faded blue background that adorned the outside of the old, single-level brick building.

"No," Frank said. "I've taken enough of your day shopping and going to the animal shelter."

The shelter the men had stopped by did not typically take in cats. Fortunately, someone had dumped one off at the doorstep that very morning, a tame, spayed female. Frank took it as a sign and, without being charged, adopted the cat.

"I can't forget the look on the shelter worker's face," Mark said.

"What's that?"

"I mean, the cat was abandoned there, and clearly they were going to put it to sleep. Yet two priests show up unannounced and request a cat. Think of the odds."

"I suppose it has a certain element of humor," Frank said. But the way his day was going, the event did not seem as coincidental to him. "Do me a favor and drop the cat by my apartment and give it some of the food we bought. And if you don't mind, set up the litter box."

"You want me to park the car at your apartment?"

"No, it's safer at the church. If Pat is still there, leave the keys with her."

"You sure you don't want me to come with you?"

"No," Frank said. "I don't know how long it's going to take. It's not that far for me to walk home. I'll see you in the morning."

"I would say your new mission is already a success," Father Mark said.

"What do you mean?" Frank said.

"You've saved this poor cat," Father Mark laughed.

Frank shook his head, exited the car, and watched as Mark pulled away. He stood outside the Kozy Tavern entrance, reflecting back to his childhood, and smiled. Suddenly, his phone rang.

He pulled it from his pocket and answered. "This is Frank Keller."

On the other end was his sister Denise, who was older than him by two years and lived in California. "I can't get Dad to answer his phone," she said. "Is something wrong?"

"Dad's fine," Frank said. "I just saw him yesterday. Don't worry. He's in a good place. He's probably just out of his room." The other end of the line was quiet. "Dee Dee, is there something wrong?"

"No one calls me Dee Dee anymore but you," Denise said. "There's nothing wrong. I'm fine."

"Every time you call me in the middle of the day, it's because something is wrong," Frank said.

Denise didn't respond right away but sighed. "I had a bad dream last night."

"See, now we're getting somewhere," Frank said. "What was this dream about that made you so upset?"

"It was about you," Denise said. "You went back to war, but this time, you didn't make it back home."

"That's just a twist on a memory, no big deal," Frank said.

"No," Denise said. "It wasn't like the past. It was the current time, and you were called away, and we didn't know how to get in touch with you. I was so worried in my dream."

"Denise," he said, "I'm fine; Dad's fine. I'm not going anywhere, and I'm too old for the army to want me back anyway. You have nothing to worry about."

"Sorry," Denise said. "You were just on my mind."

"How are your kids?"

"Bobby is fine, but Connor …" Denise sighed. "He's been out late; he screams at us; we think he's hooked on drugs or something."

Frank's mind went into a spin. Suddenly, he was in his counseling room back at his parish with David Jenson and his family. David was the same age as his nephew Connor. David had a drug problem and had started distrusting his parents and rebelling. Frank had tried to work with the family, but they had stopped coming to see him.

"Are you still there?" Denise asked.

"Yes," Frank said. "Of course."

"Well, I was hoping you might have some advice since you deal with troubled youth in your church."

"Yes," Frank said. "Make sure he knows you love him and will support him through anything he needs, but ask him to remember who he is. Don't push him away, whatever you do. He needs to know you care."

"But we can't accept his behavior," Denise said. "It's downright destructive at times."

"I'm not asking you to accept it," Frank said. "Just be ready to forgive him and support him. He's just going through a phase that's testing his character. His memories of what you've done for him are still there. Don't replace them with negative ones."

"We were thinking of getting him into counseling," Denise said.

"That's good," Frank said. "Maybe you should all go. It's a family crisis, not just a Connor crisis. You need to be involved as a family."

"Okay, I'll consider that," Denise said. "Next time you see Dad, let him know we are praying for him."

"Look, I'm kind of in the middle of something right now and need to go. I'll call you later."

Frank looked at the phone before he put it away in his pocket.

Suddenly, the mission he was on became more personal. David and Connor had similar issues, and he wondered whether he would discover something that could help his sister. He headed to the Kozy Tavern and entered through a heavy, thick wooden door.

A few heads rose from the tables as he entered. Smoke filled the air, but not the usual annoying cigarette smoke of a normal bar; this was the sweet aroma of an expensive pipe tobacco. He looked across the old tables and the vinyl-covered chairs and stools that gave the bar a classic appearance.

He felt he'd stepped back in time, to when he met his father here after work. The pool tables, though showing more wear and tear, were still in the center of the room, and the cue sticks were still in the same corner. There were mirrors across the top of the far wall and to his left across the top of the bar, which looked unchanged, as though frozen in time.

Although the bar looked unchanged, the customers who used to frequent the place were not unchanged, and it didn't look like many new customers had discovered the place. Looking across the room, he found the source of the aroma; at a table against the wall, in the farthest spot from the door, sat a dark-skinned man with long hair, smoking a pipe. Puffs of white came forward from the pipe as the man's solid eyes stared right at Frank.

"My goodness, you've grown," a voice said, startling him. Frank looked upon a short, stocky man behind the bar with shaggy silver hair on his head. The man, who looked to be well into his sixties, chewed on a cigar that wasn't lit.

Frank walked up to the bar. "I beg your pardon?"

"Sure, I recognize you. Your grandfather worked at the factory down the street. You and your grandmother used to come here and wait for him to get off the graveyard shift."

"Chic?" Frank said. "Could it be?"

"I guess it's been a long time," the bartender said, reaching out his hand and smiling. "But you still remember my nickname. Have a seat. I didn't know they let you go to bars."

"No, bars are not off-limits, but I don't think you catch many clergy in a bar."

"I've been to a few services of yours," Chic said. "I've heard a few sermons in my time, and you have a way with words. Your father would be very proud." His eyes narrowed. "You didn't quit or anything like that?"

"No," Frank said.

"Good." His face relaxed.

"So you've been to my church," Frank said as he took a seat at the bar.

Chic put a dish of peanuts in front of him. "Sure have. I wouldn't say I'm a regular. Mostly holidays and stuff like that. Not many boys from your neighborhood grew up to be something proud to talk about. Now what brings you to my place?"

"Actually, I'm here to meet someone. Maybe you can help me—his name is Adnan."

Chic stopped wiping the glass he was cleaning. "Is that so?"

"Yes," Frank said. "I wasn't given a last name. Do you know him? I mean, I was surprised myself when I was told to meet him here since he's associated with the church."

"I know him," Chic said. He took out a shot glass, filled it full of whiskey, and put it in front of Frank. "On the house. Adnan should be along any minute. It's good to see you've turned out so well. Your grandfather would have been proud." Then he turned around and began putting glasses away.

Frank thought about asking Chic what he knew about the man he was meeting but decided not to press. Inside he was starting to hope the entire day had been a bad dream. He wanted to believe he was being tested in some way, and the ridiculous list was just a way to see if he would follow instructions without questioning.

He turned around and looked out from the bar. The entrance was centered in the middle of the northern wall, with the actual bar, where he sat, to the left of the entrance. A row of tables formed a rectangle around three pool tables, none which were in use at the time. The wall farthest from the door had three tables along it, but it looked as though there should be four: the center table was widely spaced from the other two, and it was at this table he'd seen the dark-skinned man smoking a pipe. He still sat at the table but had been joined by a lovely lady; she wore a white blouse and floor-length black skirt and had her blonde hair tied up in a bun. The two glanced at him several times as he scanned the room. He nodded politely.

Frank turned back around to the bar and was surprised to find that a man had come up to the bar right beside him.

"Sorry if I startled you," the man said.

The man looked to be in his sixties, his skin tone indicated that he was probably Indian or Middle Eastern, and he had long, silver hair streaming down from a dark gray homburg hat. He was dressed in black slacks and a gray shirt, a black evening coat, and city shoes but no tie. He leaned up against the bar but was not seated.

"I didn't see you there," Frank said. He put his hand out to greet the man. "I'm—"

"Father Frank Keller," the man said.

"Adnan?" Father Frank asked.

The man tipped his hat. "At your service." He took a seat at the bar. "I'm glad you found the place."

"It wasn't hard," Frank said. "My grandfather and then my father used to work at the factory down the street before it closed. We would come here to meet them at the end of their shifts."

"Factory?"

"Auto parts," Frank said. "Before they all started coming from overseas."

"Well then," Adnan said, "you are among familiar surroundings and, I assure you, among friends. But you probably found this to be a strange place to meet."

"A little," Frank said. "I didn't expect I'd be spending much time in places like this anymore."

Adnan tapped his hand on the bar and swung around, looking out at the surroundings. "Why, this is a first-class joint, a relaxing atmosphere with an aura about it. Men gathered here to share stories, start quests for glory. There is a sense of brotherhood that doesn't exist in places like these any longer. The noble atmosphere has given way to one full of sex, violence, and drinking these days."

He looked at Frank, who smiled and pulled on his collar a little.

"Yes, well, I apologize," Adnan said. "Bishop Tafoya didn't tell you I am not a priest, at least not in the definition of your church. I have found this place to be a nice little getaway, a place to unwind. Mr. Karson here," he said, motioning to Chic, "has always been generous to our cause."

"Mr. Karson?" Frank said.

Chic turned around and looked at Adnan. "Now don't you start," he said, shaking his head. "I might be your elder, but don't be reminding me."

Adnan chuckled, which put Frank at ease.

"Tell me," Adnan said, "what did Bishop Tafoya tell you?"

"I'm not sure I can describe what I was told. He mentioned that you were working on a case that involved a family from my parish."

"Yes, the Jensons," Adnan said.

"Bishop Tafoya mentioned that you fight evil somehow and thought I might be able to help. In fact, he was quite insistent."

"It's normal to be confused," Adnan said. He picked up a tall, slender glass containing a brown liquid that Frank assumed was liquor.

"Confused?" Frank said. "That's putting it lightly. I am told about a tragedy that happened in my parish and asked to give up my work for a mission that starts with getting the items on a ridiculous list, and now I'm sitting in a bar. Can you tell me what happened to the Jensons? Bishop Tafoya made it sound extreme; he said that they were targeted by evil somehow. I want to help, but I have a lot of people depending on me. I would hope to be back to my normal duties as soon as possible."

Chic put a few ice cubes in a glass, filled the glass with water, put it in front of Frank, and then headed down to the other end of the bar.

"Stay or go—it's your decision, Frank," Adnan said. "What you have been doing at your church is making a huge difference. But I am certain you are meant to work with us."

"Us?"

"I will introduce the others shortly. As I said, you help many people in your parish, but you still see suffering and injustice in ways you cannot explain, correct?"

"True," Frank said.

"Does it bother you?"

"It's the struggle we all deal with, to have faith and believe in God's plan despite the suffering we see around us."

"What if I told you I know the secret to why that suffering takes place and gave you a chance to change it? Are you ready to take on a task to help others? Do you feel the calling to make a change?"

"You're not a priest?" Frank asked.

Adnan shook his head as he took a drink.

"Then what are you?"

"I was a scientist," Adnan said. "Genetics, biology, some meddling in physiology."

"Science and religion aren't usually sitting at the same table these days," Frank said.

"I was in research—DNA, evolution of humankind. It was there that I found it, the Creator."

Frank didn't respond.

"The first clue was in the mitochondrial DNA; it linked the human race to a single mother. Then there was the bottleneck in evolution, linked to a great flood. And finally, everywhere I looked, intelligent design. I realized, any scientist that could claim all creation is just random was insane. There are patterns, intricate designs, a purpose, and a goal. Just like you," he said, gesturing toward Frank, "I changed direction, turned toward faith."

"Like me?"

"Yes," Adnan said. "I know the priesthood wasn't your first choice. Now I am asking you, are you ready to step into a new world with your eyes open, realizing that doing so may change everything you currently know about the world around you?"

"If I can serve and make a difference, I am willing to take the chance," Frank said.

"Even if it means you may not be able to go back to the life you know? You must be committed to this possibility."

"What if I get started and decide it's not for me?" Frank said. "Is it my choice to go back?"

"It all depends," Adnan said. "It is not I who will hold you back. But once I show you the truth, you may decide it's better to stay."

"If I don't?"

"You go right back out that door, and I will tell Bishop Tafoya we don't need you. He'll think nothing of it. Only you will still have the doubt, those nagging questions that have kept you here this long."

Frank looked down at the glass of whiskey in front of him. He put his fingers around it, lifted it slightly, and pushed it back away from him. "What's next?"

"It's time for you to meet the others," Adnan said. Picking up his glass, he went to the table where the man and woman who had been watching Frank were sitting.

Frank took his water and followed Adnan to the table. The man and lady stood up as Adnan and Frank approached to greet them.

The woman, tall and slender, wore glasses, and Frank estimated she was in her early forties. She was about his height in her heels, which would make her a few inches shorter than Frank without her shoes.

The dark-complexioned man had long, straight black hair and an iron face. His black eyes had a piercing, evaluating quality. Frank put out his hand as the man offered his. As he expected, the hand was strong.

"This is Kanuik, a fellow warrior and holy man," Adnan said as Frank shook hands with Kanuik. "And this lovely lady is Dr. Claudia Walden."

"I didn't know Native Americans were so tall," Frank said, noticing that Kanuik stood over six feet tall.

"Kanuik is from the Cherokee tribe. Members of his tribe descended from northern Israel and were visited by the Knights Templar. They inherited some of their traits, including their height."

"Oh," Frank said. "And you are a doctor?" he asked, turning to the woman. Frank couldn't help but stare at Claudia as she sat down. The confidence in her eyes and the beauty of her face drew him in.

"Doctor of psychiatry," Claudia said. "I specialize in treating the mentally ill. Please, you can call me Claudia."

"Sounds like the start of a joke," Chic said, walking up to the table. "An Indian, a priest, and a psychiatrist walk into a bar."

No one smiled or laughed.

"Sorry," Chic said, shifting the cigar in his mouth. "Are your other friends going to come in tonight?"

"Jimmie and his group are on other business tonight," Adnan said.

Frank was about to ask who Jimmie was but was interrupted.

"Can I get you anything?" Chic asked.

"Just some space tonight," Adnan said.

Father Frank followed Chic's gaze around the bar. There were only a few people in the place, gathered far away from where the group sat.

"Humph, that won't be a problem." Chic shook his head and went back to the bar.

"Now that you've met our group," Adnan said, "you may be asking, 'Why me?' Claudia, would you do the introduction?"

Frank sat back in his chair, expecting Claudia to speak about herself. He was surprised when she began talking about him instead.

"Father Frank Keller, never married, son of an automotive manufacturing manager, grew up not far from here. Three-point-oh grade average through high school but IQ much higher, indicating he was often distracted from his schoolwork. Part-time job in construction, football player, played defensive end, and was the star of his high school team between sacks and fumble recoveries. His father lost his job during the second round of layoffs; the plant he

42

worked at subsequently closed down when Frank was in his senior year. Then Frank Keller had a football scholarship but instead of taking it joined the US Army to become a helicopter pilot. Served in Operation Desert Shield and Desert Storm in Dhahran, Riyadh, Iraq, and Kuwait City. Survived the scud missile attack in Dhahran and was awarded multiple service medals. He left the military after eight years and joined the ministry. His father, also named Frank, is at Sacred Hills nursing home. He has a sister, Denise, married with two boys, lives with her husband in California. His mother passed away before she could see the new path he'd chosen."

"During his education," Adnan said, picking up the narrative, "his seniors immediately noticed his discipline, commitment, and charisma. Due to his positive relationship with the local community and his reputation as a school football hero and a decorated vet, the church, with declining membership in this area, decided to station him here. To their credit, the decision has yielded them a prosperous parish. Attendance is up, and Frank represents the most successful parish in his diocese and all of the surrounding area."

When Adnan stopped talking, Frank looked at Kanuik.

"What?" Kanuik said.

"I figured it was your turn," Frank said.

Kanuik stood from his chair and walked to one side of Frank and then the other. "Hmm," he said and then sat down.

"His eyes and mannerisms suggest patience and commitment and that he is secure with himself, but our talking about him has made him uneasy," Claudia said.

Frank moved forward in his seat and put his hand around the glass of water but did not drink.

"He has power," Kanuik said. "I can see it in his aura, but he is not the peaceful man that his outer appearance suggests. He has much strength, that of a warrior."

"Understandable," Adnan said.

Kanuik looked at Frank. "There, I have had my say."

"Thank you," Frank said.

"Frank," Adnan said, "as you can see, we know a lot about you, and we can assume more. But I would like you to tell the group your story."

"What is left to tell?" Frank asked. He felt uncomfortable being analyzed. But he had nothing to hide or be afraid of.

"Priests are not supposed to be such big, powerful men," Kanuik said, his accent thick. "Why did you become a holy man?"

Frank took a drink of water. "From the time I was a kid, my parents took me to church. It wasn't something I questioned. My mother was a stern woman, and going to church was not something she took lightly. But as I grew up, I started to notice things around me—death, bullies, evil, injustice, the things that make anyone question the truth: if there was a God, why did He let so many cruel and bad things exist? My mother passed away my senior year of high school—cancer. No amount of praying helped. My father was not himself the rest of the year. I had a few options when I graduated but wasn't sure what I wanted. The military seemed the right choice at the time. It gave me independence and money for college. My faith was already in question by this time, with my internal doubts reinforced by the examples of the society around us.

"I was a young man. I thought I knew who I was at the time and had a plan of where I wanted to go. That all changed when I was sent to Saudi Arabia. Imagine everything you were about to do being put on hold. I had never felt so out of control over my own life and destiny. I started praying. I prayed every day. I could not believe my life could be relegated to such a small significance. I thought I was destined to do something greater.

"One night, we had come in from the field—that's where we usually stayed, camped out at some undisclosed location. We had come in for hot food and showers. It was nighttime, and we were loaded on the buses to go back to our location. Everyone was celebrating because it was the first time in a month we'd gotten mail. Everyone was opening their packages of cookies and letters, looking at pictures of the Christmas they'd missed. I sat by a friend of mine, newly married, who'd missed the birth of his baby at home. I sat near the window in this large bus, looking down at the pictures he showed me. He looked out the window, and his eyes froze with fear. I looked out and spotted what looked like two shooting stars heading toward our location.

"They were not stars; they were missiles. It happened fast, but I started praying. We watched the defensive Patriot missiles launch. One struck its target, but the other missed. I closed my eyes. I felt something in that moment, something close to me, something stronger than me. When I opened them, everyone was yelling at me to get my chemical gear on. And I did."

"But the missile never struck the ground," Adnan said.

"No. It was never found," Frank said. "It was never explained. Moments later, a barracks was hit by another missile as we headed out to our location. The missiles were real, no doubt."

"That's quite a story," Claudia said.

"That's not where it ends," Frank said. "The next morning, I was shaving. We had outdoor sinks set up with mirrors. None of us had slept well the night before, all realizing the reality of war and the threat of death. A siren went off as I was running the razor down my left cheek. I closed my eyes and prayed again. The same feeling of strength came over me as the night before."

Frank turned his head to the right and pointed to a scar on the left side of his face. "The flash and explosion startled me. I cut myself with the razor here. A piece of the missile fell at our location, but no one was injured. Through the rest of my tour, I was in several close calls, but I never feared. It was like I knew something was watching over me and I wasn't meant to end there."

"You've had the same feeling since?" Adnan asked.

"Many times," Frank said.

"What led you to the church?" Adnan asked.

"I wanted to make a difference," Frank said. "I wanted to reach out to the youth and share with them the strength I had found, an unexplainable strength that could come from only one source."

"What did your family think about your decision?" Claudia asked.

"My father was proud," Frank said. "My mother would have been ecstatic, but she passed away before I finished high school. I don't have any brothers, and my sister doesn't understand. She wanted me to marry her best friend. I dated her in high school and even saw her once after, but I wasn't sure I wanted a relationship. After the military, well, my course in life changed."

"And that is why you came back here, Father, to your community," Adnan suggested.

"Yes. To work with youth. It's through teaching them that I can make the most difference."

"Yes," Adnan said, "I've heard about this work. Whenever the police have trouble, they send the problem children to Father Frank, and he is able to convert them to a better path."

"They say I have a gift," Frank said.

"Maybe it's not that simple," Adnan said. "Don't sell yourself short. You have an amazing ability."

"I just wanted to help," Frank said. "The younger generation is our future, so they say, but I don't see anyone truly investing time in them. Debt is being racked up; school standards are being lowered. I see our youth slipping away every day."

"I can see how many young men would see you as a role model, a cool priest. You have tasted a life not many in your fellowship have been offered. Why the Catholic Church? There are many others without such strict policies."

"The Catholic Church is the only one that creates a bond beyond material things—the oath of poverty, the complete reliance on your brethren, and the complete commitment to the faithful. There is a sacrifice to serve. I mean, no offense to the other practices, but what are they truly giving up to serve when they live just like the rest and run themselves more like a business and an entertainment center?" He paused. "Why so many questions?"

"Don't worry, Frank," Adnan said. "We are just trying to get to know you."

"What Claudia didn't tell you is that my father suffers from Alzheimer's and doesn't always know what's going on around him. His condition is getting worse."

"I'm sorry to hear that," Claudia said. She reached across the table and touched his hand. Frank pulled back, not used to the show of affection.

"Did you get all of the items on the list the bishop gave you?" Adnan asked.

Frank nodded.

"Good," Adnan said. "You will be relieved to know we are done with our questions."

"Then I have few of my own," Frank said. "First, why all the secrecy?"

"People want their privacy and security," Adnan said. "Can you imagine us going out and advertising that there is a war against forces of evil but not being able to produce a shred of physical evidence to the nonbelievers?"

"Okay," Frank said. "Then why the late hours?"

"We work where and when we are demanded, which is the late hours," Adnan said.

"It is about time to go right now," Kanuik said.

Adnan nodded to Kanuik. "Give us a minute." He turned back to Frank. "Please consider all we have talked about tonight. If you are interested in learning more and about how you can help, meet back here tomorrow at seven in the evening. Be well rested."

Adnan sat back in his chair. His eyes closed just like Bishop Tafoya's did when he was praying. Kanuik took out his pipe, filled it with tobacco, and lit it. Soon, smoke came forth and crossed over the table to where Frank sat. Kanuik's eyes were fixed on a point off in the distance. Only Claudia met his eyes as he looked around the table. The interview was over, he understood.

"This is the part where I leave so you can talk about me," Frank said. "I get it." He stood and headed toward the door. "Good night, Chic," he said, waving.

Chic returned the wave.

+   +   +

Adnan sat with his eyes closed. He breathed in and out deeply and focused his thoughts on his mission and his faith.

"What are your thoughts?" Kanuik asked.

"The force inside of me was unusually quiet," Adnan said. "But it is gaining strength, and we are running out of time."

"Then let's go," Kanuik said.

They stood and headed to a door at the back of the bar that led downstairs to a hallway. They went to a small, circular room lit by a single light. The room had a brick floor and brick walls. It looked older than the tavern above. There were religious symbols painted in white and blue on the walls around them.

Adnan stood at the center of a circle carved in the floor while Kanuik filled the circle with oil. "Use the fire as a last resort," Adnan said. "Oh, and make sure you open the vent."

Kanuik reached to a lever on the wall and pulled it down. Above Adnan, a small metal door opened, and a fan spun on the other side, pulling the air out of the room below to a vent in the roof.

"Ready?" Kanuik asked.

Adnan's face turned red, and veins popped out on his forehead. His fists were clenched, and his arms, hanging down at his side, began to shake. His eyes opened and rolled back in his head but then became focused as he stared forward, and his body began to calm.

A dark form materialized from his chest; it started small and then grew bigger. The outline of a head and torso without arms became apparent and moved away from Adnan's body as though trying to escape, but its legs and feet seemed lodged within him somehow. It went back toward him and then moved to the edge of the circle on the floor. It did this multiple times and started increasing its speed.

Adnan shook and jerked forward, as though the shadow coming from him was physically bound to him, and each time it pulled, he moved in the same direction. The severity of the pulls increased until Adnan jerked back and forth enough to nearly fall. Then he reached his hands in front of him, and although the form did not appear solid, he grasped it somehow and held it. The shadow did not approve. It turned back toward Adnan and flung itself toward him.

Adnan shook and buckled. "Damnation from hell!" he yelled. "That is what you are. You shall not win this night." He crumpled to his knees, and the form engulfed his head, like a fog surrounding him. When his eyes opened, they were black. Adnan's body shook violently, and he began to levitate a few inches off the floor.

Kanuik stood with matches in hand, ready to light the oil he'd poured in the circle surrounding Adnan. He began chanting and walking around the circle.

Adnan started shaking and convulsing. This lasted for an hour as Kanuik stood outside of the circle. Finally, Adnan went to the brick floor and stood with great effort. The shadow coming from him was visible no more.

"Adnan?" Kanuik said. "Where are you?"

"Somalia," Adnan said. He collapsed to the floor. Kanuik lit the match and threw it to the floor, lighting the fire around him as the dark form emerged. It was larger than before, and only a small portion remained attached to Adnan as the thing approached the barrier of the fire and searched for an escape. Adnan appeared unconscious as the dark form continued to circle, finally stopping at the spot where Kanuik stood.

"There is no place for you to go," Kanuik said. The form slowly drifted back to Adnan and disappeared as Adnan stirred.

"Kanuik?"

"I am here," Kanuik said.

Adnan's eyes opened. He was still on the floor. "I thought I told you to use the fire as a last resort."

Kanuik moved across the flames that were dissipating and leaned down to help Adnan to his feet. "That thing is getting stronger," Kanuik said. "It almost broke free."

"It is not stronger," Adnan said. "I am getting older, my friend."

"Then let's kill it before it kills you," Kanuik said.

"That thing is our ticket to the other side," Adnan said. "Don't worry. We drained enough energy out of it tonight that it will be easy to control—if our Israeli allies are correct, and Father Frank is one that was touched by an angel."

"They believe he can control them?"

"No," Adnan said. "They believe he can use his strength to cause them to flee. When they back away from the portal, I will pass through, and they will let me pass because of this thing inside of me. You will see. The time is almost right."

Chapter 4

That's What We Do

A loud crashing sound woke Frank from his slumber. He rose from his bed and searched his room but saw nothing that could account for the noise. The clock by his bed indicated it was almost six in the morning. He listened to the noises of the apartment around him, to the traffic on the street below, to the voices talking in the distance. Remnants of a dream sat heavy in his head. He'd dreamed about being in the army, in his helicopter in the war, but not exactly in the war. There were changes. He remembered seeing others, but the young men around him were not the same men he'd served with, and he could see himself, but he wasn't young; he was his current age.

Sounds came from the living room of his apartment; something or someone was moving around. He shook his head to clear it from the dream and focused on the task at hand. He looked around for a weapon and settled on a letter opener on his desk. Weapon in hand, he went to the door of his bedroom and slowly opened it. He looked into the living room but saw no one. He stepped out into the hallway.

To his left, the hallway led to a bathroom, the only one in the apartment. Just ahead of him was the living room adjoined to a kitchenette. He could see the entire room from where he stood, with the exception of the coffee table that was on the other side of the brown leather couch. He looked at the front door. It was closed. The windows were intact. He approached the couch. On the opposite side was a space for a television, but Frank did not have a television. Instead, a plain wooden rocking chair sat in the space, with a book he intended to read atop its seat.

Suddenly, there was a flash of movement from the other side of the couch, and something jumped up to the top and faced him! "Oh, it's you," Frank said with a sigh of relief. The cat shook its tail back and forth as it looked at him and then put its claws forward and started scratching the couch.

"Nooo!" Frank moved forward quickly and picked up the cat. "Not there. Don't scratch that." He walked around to the other side of the couch, put the letter opener down on the coffee table, and then sat down on the couch with the cat on his lap. He noticed a glass of water he'd left out spilled on the kitchen counter. He held the cat up to face it. "Looks like someone was thirsty and needs a scratching post."

The cat didn't respond but purred when he put it back down and started stroking its back.

"Guess that was you making that racket," Frank said. He carried the cat into the kitchen where Mark had set down a combination food-and-water dish for the cat. Both sides were empty. He set the cat down. "Guess you must be hungry and thirsty," he said, righting the toppled glass, from which water was still dripping off the counter onto the floor.

He filled the water dish and poured food for the cat before cleaning the spill on the counter and floor. He changed into some jogging sweats and headed toward the door. The cat jumped on the top of the couch and watched him, tail moving back and forth like a metronome.

"I see," Frank said. He went into his bedroom and came back out with a blanket, lifted the cat, and put the blanket across the top of the couch. The cat kneaded the blanket a few times and then sat down and purred.

"So you like to be at the high point where you can see everything. I get it. Just behave yourself while I am out."

He went down the stairs of his apartment complex and out to

the street to wait for Mark. Adnan's words came back to him: *Be well rested.* "I can always take a nap later," Frank said to himself as Mark came up, and he started his jog. Exercising always helped him relax, and getting out in the open air stimulated his thoughts. He normally used the time to discuss his sermon, but today, he was not preparing a sermon. Instead, his mind turned to the events of the previous day.

"Thanks for feeding the cat," Frank said.

"No problem," Mark said. "I parked the car by the church, and Pat has the keys if you need them."

"I won't need the car today," Frank said. "You feel rested enough to go through the park today?" The park was the longer of the two different routes they ran.

"I would love to," Mark said. "But I'm covering for you today, and I have a meeting with the church staff at nine to go over the schedule."

"Sorry," Frank said. "Hopefully, I won't be out for long."

After the two parted, Frank ran to the park. He thought about his sister in California and his nephew Connor. He found himself considering again that his nephew was the same age as David Jenson. Connor seemed to be going down a similar path as David, although Frank hoped not as violent. Frank crossed into a small park and waved to a homeless man sitting on a bench, wrapped in an old army field jacket and wearing ripped jeans and a worn leather cap. He had seen the man there on many occasions; his presence was a sign of the times.

Adnan, a scientist, he thought. How did Claudia and Kanuik fit in? He wondered what he would be stepping into by returning to Kozy Tavern. He'd made the decision to go back and learn more. He came upon another bench and felt winded, so he slowed his pace and sat down. He closed his eyes, breathing in the air, listening to the sounds around him. This early in the morning, there was very little noise, so he enjoyed the peace until he sensed a presence beside him.

Frank opened his eyes to find the homeless man he'd passed on the bench beside him. Surprised that the man could have covered the distance in such a short period of time without Frank noticing,

Frank quickly scooted down to put some distance between himself and the man.

"Out early today, Father," the man said. "Yes, I know you, priest."

"I'm Frank, Frank Keller." He held out his hand, but the man coughed and laughed.

"Pray, Father; pray that all is not lost." The man handed him a square package wrapped in a bag and walked away with a considerable limp on his left side.

Frank waited until the man was out of sight before he unwrapped the item to find it was a book with a worn cover. "Hmm," he murmured. He took the book in his hand and continued his run back to his apartment.

Upon entering, he saw that the cat hadn't moved. After a shower and a change of clothes, he sat down on his couch and picked up the book the man had handed him. "Savior," he said, reading the title aloud. Then he turned the book over and read the back cover. "Battle for the soul of humanity," he said to the cat, who purred and flopped its tail back and forth. After reading the first few chapters, he fell asleep on the couch and woke midafternoon.

* * *

Frank walked down to the Kozy Tavern and arrived by five o'clock. He looked down at his watch. "Two hours early." He didn't want to seem too anxious, so he walked up and down the street several times, crossing in front of the bar, and then strolled down the opposite side of the street in the small, run-down business district, made up mostly of pawn shops and liquor and convenience stores. He finally rested on a bus stop bench where he had a view of the front door of the Kozy Tavern. No one had walked in or out in the nearly two hours he'd been outside watching. He looked down at his watch, which he could barely see in the streetlight, the evening having grown dark. "Ten to seven. I guess I'll see what's going on."

Frank headed across the street and into the Kozy Tavern. He

waved to Chic, who was at the bar. Adnan sat alone at the table, in the same chair he had occupied the night before, a chair that faced outward to the rest of the bar.

Adnan's eyes were closed, but his position was erect, which indicated he was not sleeping but meditating. If not for his change in clothes, which were black but a different style, Frank easily could have thought he'd stayed the night in that same place. His gray homburg hat and cane were hung on the chair beside him.

"Did you sleep well, Father Frank?" Adnan asked, opening his eyes as Frank walked up to the table.

Frank took a seat across from him. "No. I did not."

"Was it because of our conversation last night?"

"It was because of the lack of conversation," Frank said. "I still don't understand what I am doing here or what this is really about."

A noise in the background distracted both of the men. When Frank turned, he saw that a set of wind chimes hanging in the middle of the ceiling was ringing. Four men were playing pool, and two of them were arguing. Frank turned back to Adnan, who had turned pale and looked as though he was about to vomit.

"Take this," Adnan said and handed Frank a small, six-inch-diameter mirror with a handle that was encased in silver.

"It looks expensive."

"Please, don't break it," Adnan said. "Did you get all of the items on the list?"

"Yes. About that ..."

Before Frank could continue, a crashing sound came from behind Frank—a fight had broken out. Adnan was jarred from his seat as though something had pushed him from behind.

"Do not move from the table," Adnan said. "Try not to turn around, but watch what happens from that mirror."

Frank looked in the mirror and watched as Adnan approached the pool table where the two men were fighting; the other two players steered clear. Frank blinked his eyes twice as he spotted a dark form like a wraith coming out of Adnan's chest. He looked up at the bar mirror but could see the dark shadow only in the mirror Adnan had handed him. The two men fighting also had shadows swirling about their heads that looked somewhat human in shape, but that lacked defined arms and legs and moved unnaturally. Frank turned to look for the reason the things were appearing, hoping to find a trick in the lighting. Again, he could see nothing until he looked back into the mirror Adnan had provided him.

Adnan had now reached the men who were fighting. One had broken his pool stick hitting the other man, who was bent over. The first man looked to hit the other again and had raised his hand to strike when Adnan took his cane and waved it in front of the man.

"That is quite enough," Adnan said, causing the man to pause and look up at him. "That's it—think about what you are doing. Do you really want to hurt this man who just moments ago was someone you were drinking with?"

Frank stood from his chair, ready to help Adnan, but continued to watch what was happening in the mirror. The dark forms were no longer swirling about the men, and the one from Adnan had receded and was still.

"Let's get out of here," the man holding the broken pool stick said, throwing it down on the pool table. Three men left the bar. Chic came over and helped the man who'd been struck to a chair.

Frank sat as Adnan came back to the table. He still had his hand clutched around the mirror, and Adnan noticed and nodded.

"Sorry about that," Adnan said. "I was going to wait until later to show you, but the opportunity presented itself."

Frank shook his head. "What was that? It looked like some type of wraith."

"That was your first exposure to the shadows," Adnan said. "You followed my instructions?"

"Yes," Frank said.

"We call them shadows because they usually bring out the darker side of those they associate with; they are attracted to the sin that we all harbor inside. I'll need that back," Adnan said, taking the mirror and laying it on the table where he had again hung his hat and cane. "You'll be able to see them without the help of the mirror soon enough. Until then, we need to take some precautions."

"Precautions?" Frank said. "You mean to tell me those things are real, and they attack people?"

"We will get to that. First, let's talk about the list," Adnan said. "What we are dealing with will take us out onto the streets and to places where it will get extremely cold, even when it doesn't seem it should. That is the reason for the long underwear and coat. There are often power outages when we work; that is the reason for the candles. The shadows have problems with flames, not so with light. They cannot cross fire. The wind chimes"—he pointed to those hanging from the ceiling of the bar—"indicate they are present and will go off even in the absence of any air moving. The alarm clocks will be used to keep our subjects and ourselves from falling into a trance of sleep that is not sleep. Every time you are around the shadows, you will want to cleanse yourself after. That is where the Dead Sea salts come in."

Frank looked around behind him and kept his voice low as he leaned in and whispered, "And the cat?"

"The cat is there to protect you. It is a guard against evil. We don't know why, but evil will not manifest itself in a cat's presence. Many ancient cultures seem to have known this and worshipped cats. Amazing how much they knew about the world then that we are just discovering now."

"Cats?" Frank raised his left eyebrow.

Adnan smiled. "Now do you believe evil exists among us?"

"I'm not sure what I witnessed," Frank said. He still couldn't understand why he needed the mirror to see the things but didn't want Adnan to know his doubts. "But I am not naïve. What I have seen in the world leaves little room for doubt. At the same time, I want to believe that God is all-powerful and that what exists has a reason."

"Which leads you to wonder, if God is all-powerful, why doesn't He just destroy the evil then?" Adnan said. "There are some who believe in the theory of opposites—that without evil, we wouldn't know good. Without hunger, we wouldn't know how to be filled," Adnan said.

"Do you subscribe to this theory?" Frank asked.

"Not sure," Adnan said. "I think there is a need for some way to compare, but that doesn't mean there have to be equal amounts. Justifications like these are why I have strayed from religion. When the church wants to, it knows God's will. When it can't explain why bad things happen, it says no one can know God's will. Other religions use the same tactics of fear and repression to force their beliefs on others, even at the price of murder in the name of their religion. This is in no way different from siding with evil and its goal of spreading fear and despair."

"Let me tell you what I believe," Frank said. "I know that Christ existed. That is proven. I have witnessed a power I cannot explain, a power of good. I believe this power to be in all things and constantly around us. And the more people that believe in this and tap into this power, the greater the moments they can make happen."

"You have discovered the energy of God and have answered your own question," Adnan said.

"What question?" Frank asked.

"The one that brought you here," Adnan said. "What do we want from you? If you join our group, what is it that we do?"

Chic came up to the table. He put a tall glass of ice water in front of Frank and a tall glass of what Frank assumed was whiskey in front of Adnan. "Can I get you anything else?"

"Do you have any bread tonight?" Adnan asked.

"One loaf of my special garlic bread coming up," Chic said and headed back to the bar.

"We fight evil," Adnan said. "The evil around us is a form of energy. You spotted that in the mirror; it's made of a special glass that can see the energy. Here is where science and religion agree: energy cannot be destroyed, only transformed." He took a drink from his glass. "Perhaps, as the great Creator, God is unable to destroy what He has created."

"Are you saying that He created those things that I saw?"

"No," Adnan said. "Not those things exactly. But an energy that has intelligence and has become unguided."

"How come I needed the mirror, but you did not?"

"This mirror allows the user to see the shadows without them knowing. Once you believe they exist, you should be able to see them, but that comes with risk, and you have to be careful."

"Careful how?"

"I will teach you," Adnan said.

"If they are energy," Frank said, "can't we counter that energy or stop it?"

Adnan smiled and nodded. "All we would have to realize is that all the things we perceive as bad are not. Death, for instance, in the right context is simply a transformation of our energy."

"Just as we've been taught," Frank said.

"It is a concept," Adnan said. "Understand that the evil around us only influences. It's a parasitic force that exists in the world because man is cruel to man. Our insecurities and fears fuel this energy, allowing it to remain and grow and feed."

"I've always believed we are not as helpless to change what is around us as we assume. I think God isn't waiting to intervene; He's waiting for us to make the right decisions!"

"You are quite passionate," Adnan said. "I can see why you are so successful in your parish. You really believe in the message you are spreading."

"Bishop Tafoya said something about evil being vanquished, but somehow it came back in moments of time," Frank said.

"Yes. The battle now is between energies, including the negative energy you just witnessed," Adnan said. "There is no influence where there is no intent. We attract evil by our intent, and then it tries to influence our actions."

"You fight that influence?" Frank asked.

"That and the force behind it," Adnan said. "We are not the only warriors out there. There are many. But I'm afraid to say we are losing ground. There are more people slipping away than we are gathering. And with every step they take to allow evil in, the more powerful it gets, until it consumes whole moments of time. And not just moments with a single individual, but with entire groups."

"I'm still trying to grasp it myself," Frank said. "You mean these things influence us like we are in a dream?"

"I suppose to some people it may seem like a dream. But it is a delusion they are put into by the influence of the shadows. They may not understand the reality of what they are doing. Sometimes, what they think may be just a bad dream is reality. Once the shadows have hold, they can steal moments of reality and warp them so they are perceived differently. These become the short instances where we have a lapse in judgment. It opens a portal for the evil that was banished in the past and allows it to steal more time."

"To what end?" Frank asked.

"We don't completely understand the motives ourselves or where they come from," Adnan said. "We just know evil is an energy; a force trying to impose its will."

"How can you fight something like this?" Frank said.

Chic walked up to the table and put another glass of water down in front of him, along with a loaf of fresh bread and a knife and butter. He gave each of the men a small plate. Frank drank the water until the glass was nearly empty again.

"Thank you," Adnan said. He sliced the bread in thick pieces and handed one to Frank.

Frank sank his teeth into the warm bread, which tasted delicious. He looked up at Chic and nodded. "This is really good."

Chic smiled and walked away.

"The evil will use any experience against you that it can. If you have any baggage from the past, any weakness, it will exploit that," Adnan said. "It will become what you are afraid of it becoming. It will make you feel helpless and condition you to a path of hate, depression, and desperation."

"Are you saying it can control me?" Frank asked.

"Influence," Adnan said. "'Control' is a strong word, and there are a lot of lawyers and judges who would disagree with us taking that side. No, it's not that simple. You see, the evil is a force that influences our moments, tries to make us change our values. By doing so, it steals more time from us and conforms us to its reality, where it is stronger. The more time we give it, the more powerful it becomes."

"How do we fight it?" Frank asked.

"By stepping directly in front of it." Adnan put his left hand palm up on the table and chopped down with the other hand. "You are consciously fighting it every day with your actions of influencing the young to do the right thing. We must continue to strive to place values at the forefront. Values such as the respect for life. We must teach principles that influence the behaviors of kindness and understanding and preach lessons of strength to help those with insecurities."

"That doesn't sound so hard," Frank said.

"That's the battle behind the scenes—what you've been doing. Now you are going to the front lines, the very moments where the vulnerable are approached by the dark forces. You will use your faith to fight these moments. You will use that same influence you employ while giving a sermon to try to help people make the right decisions. Believe me when I say this will take courage. You cannot be weak, and you cannot be afraid, because those you will be helping are fragile, and as soon as they see you are weak, they will doubt. In that moment of doubt, you will have lost them."

"This evil force is around us all of the time then?" Frank asked.

"Think of it as a shadow," Adnan said, "always lurking just outside of the light, waiting to get more exposure. Unlike a wraith, the shadow is an entity that does not exist without a host. The more energy it gets, the more the shadow becomes real. Many think the darkness feeds on fear. It is not that simple. It feeds off of insecurity and those who initiate fear, those who feed on the weak, with intent to harm or take. 'Blessed are those who have regard for the weak; the Lord delivers them in times of trouble.'"

"Psalm 41:4," Frank said.

"There are many such scriptures throughout the Bible," Adnan said. "Even the ancient codes of the knights and chivalry were adapted to such causes—to protect. By protecting the weak, they fought the influences of evil."

Frank reached for the last slice of bread. He offered it to Adnan, who put his hands out in front of him and shook his head.

"Ah, here come the others," Adnan said.

Frank looked to the door and saw Kanuik and Claudia standing there. They didn't head toward the table; instead Adnan stood and put on his coat. "Come on, it's time to go." He collected his hat and cane and headed to the door.

Frank finished the bread, drank once more from his cup, and quickly wiped his mouth and face before following Adnan.

"Is the car ready?" Adnan asked.

"Yes," Claudia said.

They walked outside to a black four-door sedan. Adnan and Kanuik took to the backseat, and Claudia went to the driver's seat.

"You don't mind sitting up front?" Adnan said.

"Not at all," Frank said as he took the front passenger seat.

"Jimmie?" Claudia asked.

"He and his team are already out there," Adnan said.

"Team?" Frank asked.

"Yes," Adnan said. "Jimmie is a professor at the university, but on the side, he runs a group that researches paranormal activity. They have equipment that helps us measure the energy we've been talking about."

"So we drive around until these two sense something or Jimmie calls," Claudia said. "That's how we know where we are needed."

Frank's mind churned with the day's events, and he rubbed his forehead. Claudia offered him some aspirin, and he accepted.

As the car hummed along the city streets among the night traffic, Frank and Claudia chatted. "You really don't have a television?" Claudia asked.

"Not for years," Frank said, yawning. "I prefer to read or experience life, not sit and watch it on television."

"A novel idea, Frank," Adnan said.

Frank yawned again.

"I think our new recruit is not used to being up late," Adnan said.

Frank smiled and looked back. "Actually, I'm used to being up late, but I'm usually more active than this."

"Don't worry—we'll get to our destination soon enough," Adnan said. "Before we do, let me give you some instructions. There's a reason we work in pairs. You will stay close to Kanuik and me. That way, you will not get stuck in a moment. When we engage the shadows, you are to remain still and silent. Just observe."

"I feel I should be loading a weapon or putting on a flak jacket or something," Frank said.

"Don't worry," Adnan said. "I want you to watch what we do. Even if it looks like we are in trouble, stay in your area and don't interact with them."

"Them? You mean the shadows, as you call them?" Frank said. "But I don't have the mirror."

"You might see them without the mirror, unless you think all that stuff back at the bar was smoke and mirrors."

Frank had his doubts, but he decided he would keep them to himself until the night was over.

"As long as you don't interact with them, they should leave you alone," Adnan said. "You are somewhat protected by your profession. They generally prey on easier targets."

"I thought I was here to assist," Frank said.

"Yes, but let's give it some time," Adnan said.

"Do not be in a hurry; you will put us all in danger," Kanuik said.

Frank didn't speak for several minutes. He looked at Claudia, who gave him a reassuring smile.

"Do you know where these things come from?" Frank asked.

"We don't know," Adnan said. "But when you are in the moment, you can look around, and sometimes you can see a doorway made of light. Jimmie—Professor Barnes, that is—has instruments that have allowed us to detect this energy. He believes it is some type of portal that allows them to enter and leave. We work in groups of no less than two. If one of us gets too caught up in the moment, the other one stays aware so that they can pull their partner out. When we can find the doorway, one of use guards it to keep more from coming through while the other one takes care of the ones already through."

"How do you guard it?" Frank asked.

"There are certain talismans, prayers, and chants we use."

"And caught up in the moment?" Frank said. "What does that mean?"

"It's like being in a daydream," Adnan said. "You are awake, but not fully conscious. You can stay in this state if you enter the illusion of the person the shadows are trying to influence."

"Can these things be destroyed?" Frank said.

"We think so. Sometimes, when the person they are influencing is tied in to them and denies them, they appear to vaporize. It takes a while sometimes."

"If there is a doorway, has anyone tried to go through it to see what's on the other side?" Frank asked.

The sharp glance he got from Claudia let Frank know he'd stumbled on a sensitive topic.

"It has been tried," Adnan said. "A great warrior attempted it once, but he did not survive."

"It would take great medicine to pass," Kanuik said. "I have been at these crossings many times. Just like we stand guard on our side, they have sentinels that guard the door on the other side so that we cannot pass to where they come from. Their forms cannot solidify in our world, but we may not be able to cross into theirs."

"No one knows if we can cross over," Adnan said, "which is why I think it's about time to try again."

"You don't know what's out there," Claudia said.

"That's exactly why we should see; it's time to find out." Adnan's usually calm tone was elevated now.

"No, it's exactly why you should not," Claudia protested. She pulled into a convenience store and parked. "I have to go to the ladies' room." She looked at Frank. "Some of the people we deal with are permanently damaged after these interactions, including those who try to help. They never come back to reality." She exited the car and headed into the store.

Kanuik stepped out of the car and pulled out a small pipe and lit it. Frank glanced in the rearview mirror and saw Adnan sitting quietly with his eyes closed.

Frank closed his eyes for just a moment, and he drifted off to sleep until the vehicle moved when Kanuik got back in. Frank looked toward the store and noticed that Claudia was now inside making a purchase at the counter.

"Feel free to step out and stretch your legs if you need to," Adnan said.

"I'm okay," Frank said. "I'm just not used to being out late."

"Let's hope our night is productive and that we aren't keeping you up for no reason," Adnan said.

"How will we know if it's productive?" Frank asked.

"You will be tired but unable to sleep after what you've seen," Adnan said. "Don't worry, though. You'll get used to it. That is, if you decide to keep working with us."

When Claudia came back to the vehicle, she was carrying a bag of snack. After settling into the driver's seat, she handed an orange juice to Adnan; a Dr. Pepper to Kanuik, who smiled when he received it; and a coffee to Frank. "I had to guess, but I put in two sugars and no cream."

"Thank you," Frank said as she started the car and pulled out onto the street. Frank sipped his coffee. It was too hot, and he burned his tongue. He yelped and cringed, and Claudia laughed at his reaction.

"I hate when that happens," she said.

Frank shared the moment of humor and laughed. Then Claudia's cell phone went off. She pulled over and answered it. Frank could hear a male voice on the other end telling her about something that was going on and that she should come quickly.

"That was Jimmie," Claudia said. "He has a hit downtown by a dollar store."

Adnan stepped out of the car and tapped on Frank's door. Frank got out and switched places with him, taking a seat in the back.

"So," Frank said, trying to start a conversation with Kanuik, "how did you come to start working with Adnan?"

Kanuik finished cleaning his pipe and put it back in his jacket pocket. "We were in combat in Somalia. We were there with the Christian Ethiopians trying to help. A warlord there was slaughtering people, and we decided to take the fight to evil. There was a group of us, including some missionaries and some soldiers. Adnan saw the shadow that had the warlord and thought he could break the bond. Adnan got close to the warlord. Convinced he was a holy man who had power, the warlord accepted. We tried for days to tell this man he did wrong by his people. But he did not change. Adnan thought he had a better way to help and could break the shadow's grip. When it exposed itself, he reached out and touched the shadow." Kanuik paused.

"That's when he found he had the ability to resist them," Frank said.

"No, he wasn't as successful then as he is now. The first time he touched one of the shadows, he fell ill, but the evil stopped," Kanuik said. "For twelve days exactly, the warlord stayed in his camp and had his men start building better shelters for the people. They weren't allowed to attack. No raping or pillaging. Adnan's legend spread, and we moved on to another warlord, thinking we had found a way to win and could do so again. Then, on the thirteenth day, the day we moved to the next village, the warlord's forces surrounded that village. They took no prisoners. Killed everyone, even the children, the missionaries, and the few soldiers who had stayed to protect them. I fought my way free. Adnan stayed to confront the warlord."

"What happened?"

"The warlord's men beat Adnan. Left him for dead. I found him just in time and moved him to a safe location. We were the only survivors in our group. The rest were dead. Since then, we have been together."

Kanuik's story brought silence to the group. All three passengers stared out the windows at the sleeping city. Once in a while, a cab or police car would pass by, but for the most part, the streets were empty. Frank watched as Claudia kept a steady gaze in front of her, looking in the rearview mirror on occasion. He wondered how many nights she'd spent doing this.

"This is it," Claudia said. "There's Jimmie's car."

The group exited the car in front of a closed dollar store along a street of small outlet stores and restaurants, all of which were closed. Three men approached them.

"Frank, this is Professor James Barnes," Adnan said.

"Frank Keller," Frank said as he reached his hand out to a young, slightly overweight man with long, black hair tied back in a ponytail. He wore a dark brown sport coat and dress jeans.

"Call me Jimmie," the man said as he shook Frank's hand. "These men are my crew. This is Russ Mothner, a baggage handler at the airport by day and a paranormal investigator by night."

Frank shook hands with a balding man his height who looked to be in his late forties.

"And this young man," Jimmie said, pointing to a tall, lanky redheaded man, "is Mike Delgado; he works for the cable company."

"Pleased to meet you," Frank said.

"Let's review the rules," Adnan said. "We cannot have any of what we are doing end up on your websites or television shows. That's the agreement for letting you tag along."

Jimmie, Russ, and Mike nodded.

"What do you have?" Adnan said.

"In there." Jimmie pointed between the store and another building. "There's an alley that runs behind all these businesses, used for deliveries."

"We thought our instruments were malfunctioning," Mike said, holding a small electronic device that had a wand and a light that flashed when he moved the wand in particular directions. "Then we realized, the force wasn't stable, but something was going up and down the alley."

"It stopped just moments ago," Jimmie said. "Whatever it is, it's behind this store."

"I thought you said we should stay out of the dark alleys," Claudia said.

"I did," Adnan said. "But this is where the evil is tonight." He looked at Frank. "And we need Frank to see what we are up against. Remember, Frank, you are only an observer tonight."

Frank waited as Adnan and Kanuik led the way between the buildings, taking a right turn into the alley that ran behind them. He noticed Kanuik had a cane exactly like Adnan's. Frank walked alongside Claudia and Jimmie, and Mike and Russ lagged behind.

In the back alley, they encountered trash dumpsters, wood pallets, and back doors with bars on them. They stopped under a dim light, where Adnan looked ahead. "There," Adnan said, pointing.

Five men were gathered at a wall, their backs turned to Frank and his group. The men wore similar black leather jackets and jewelry that Frank knew to be common among street gangs. Frank felt his heart rate increase; he was unprepared for a physical confrontation. He remained close to Claudia.

Kanuik approached the group from behind with Adnan staying a step back from him. One of the men turned and noticed Kanuik and stepped toward him. When he did so, Frank could see that the men had surrounded a young girl who was up against the wall.

"You don't want to be here now," the man said. "You should leave." Then he noticed Adnan, Frank, and Claudia and tapped one of the other men, who turned around as well.

"Detective Jennings, please," Claudia said. Frank turned and saw that she had pulled out her cell phone. "We have a possible rape in progress," Claudia said and gave the location of the group.

Frank turned his attention back to Kanuik, who was being approached by three men while the other two held the girl against the wall.

With a flash of his hands, Kanuik grabbed the closest man and threw him to the ground. Two others attacked, but Kanuik dodged their attacks and landed his hands on them in a manner that didn't strike them but that used their own momentum against them, and they too were thrown to the ground. He waved his cane like a weapon in front of the men.

"You do not want to be doing this," Kanuik said. "Go now." He pointed down the alley.

Frank looked at Adnan, who closed his eyes, and then at Claudia, who had her hand in her purse. Jimmie and his group were moving close to Kanuik.

The two men let go of the girl, and she slumped down to a sitting position against the wall. They helped their friends off the ground, gave Kanuik a scalding look, and started walking down the alley in the direction Kanuik had recommended. Claudia stepped beside Frank; she had her right hand firmly around a Glock 19.

"Sorry, but you never can be too careful," Claudia said as she engaged the safety and put the handgun back in her purse. "Don't worry. I have a permit. I learned how to use it after working with so many violent cases."

Frank and Claudia joined Adnan, who headed toward the girl. She was unconscious and slumped over, with just her head up against the wall.

"Jimmie, get your readings fast," said Adnan. "Then you and your group should probably leave unless you want to answer a bunch of questions when the police arrive."

"Got it," Jimmie said. His device clicked and sputtered sounds. "See you back at the tavern," he said to Adnan. "Come on, guys. Let's get out of here." Jimmie and his crew left the alley.

Adnan looked at Frank. "What are you thinking now, Frank? You are thinking we just saved this girl from a gang of hoodlums. They were

69

tempted by the moment, and evil was about to take that moment. But what you are not seeing is that the evil wasn't just in them. It was also attacking this girl. Its goal was the ruination of her and these men."

Kanuik went over to the girl, who had long black hair with green streaks in it and who was dressed in a black leather skirt, a short, low-cut pink top, and leather boots. She was no more than twenty years old. Blood was present on both inner thighs, and she appeared to be unconscious until he approached, and then she stirred.

"Here," Frank said, offering his coat. "She's got to be cold."

"Stay back, Frank," Adnan said. "Give us a moment."

A flame came from Kanuik's hand and landed on the ground, followed by another and then another, until she was surrounded by a circle of small burning balls of fire. The flames reached about a foot high, and Frank could feel the heat.

Frank didn't understand the words Kanuik spoke and assumed they were in his native language.

"It's holy fire, Frank," Adnan said. He moved closer as the girl sat up only a few feet from the back of the building. He stayed outside of the fire and started praying.

Frank moved closer and tried to get a good look at the girl's face. He wished he had the mirror from the bar.

Kanuik reached his hand out in front of Frank. "Do not break the circle," Kanuik said.

Frank looked back at Claudia, who stayed farther back and just looked on.

"Do you see them, Frank?" Adnan asked. "They know we're here. They know you are here."

Frank looked on and suddenly spotted movement. The dark form that hovered around the girl on the ground was not quite human-shaped, but its outline shifted from the size of a child to as tall as Kanuik. It moved like it was made of water. Almost transparent in some areas and darker in others, the upper torso, minus arms, was very humanlike. It stood behind the girl, who opened her eyes and sat up against the wall.

Frank backed away as the girl's haunting eyes locked on him. He jumped when Claudia touched him on the shoulder from behind. He turned and looked at her.

"Sorry," Claudia said. "Didn't mean to scare you. Do you see it?"

"Yes."

"Don't worry," Kanuik said. "It will not break the circle of fire. Don't be afraid of it, or others like it will come."

Adnan started speaking to the girl. "Can you tell me your name? Do you know what time it is or where you are right now?"

"Lisa," the girl said. She looked around the alley in a daze. "Who are you? Where am I?"

"We are here to help you," Adnan said. "But stay where you are for now. Frank, Lisa is not herself today. Those men were not attacking her on their own; she had succumbed to an evil influence before, and that is what got her into this situation. The men were being influenced—remember, our enemy is opportunistic. We must try to influence Lisa and get her to see her decisions were not correct and how close she was to death. The evil is still feeding off of her; it cannot exist in this moment without her. Its goal was to influence those men as well and increase the energy it feeds off. Her downfall was the shadow's goal."

Frank watched as the dark, legless form circled around the girl's body and around her head. She didn't seem to notice it. Adnan stepped to the edge of the fire. When he did this, the shadow came forward to where he stood and stopped abruptly as if there was an invisible wall between them. Then it circled back around Lisa and disappeared behind her. When it came out again, it emerged from her chest, and there were more with it—three or four total from what Frank could see.

He noticed a single, dark form similar to those coming out of Lisa also coming from Adnan. The one from Adnan came from his chest and seemed to be trying to pull him forward as it moved from Adnan to the other shadows in a tugging motion.

Adnan stepped into the circle and put his hand out to touch the girl, who immediately looked up at him and gasped for air as though she'd been suffocating. Frank moved closer but was careful to stay outside of the flame. He watched as a section of the shadow reached out from the larger form and moved toward him. The flames leaned outward as the figure stretched toward the fire, but there was no wind. Kanuik stood close and continued to chant but did not breech the circle. The alley grew darker as the lights around them seemed to be drained of power, and all around them went silent.

Frank could hear himself breathing, but it didn't sound normal. His breathing and heartbeat had slowed. He spotted a gray cat coming down the alley, but it did not move naturally; it seemed to be walking in slow motion. Water dripped off one of the buildings in a trickle, and he heard the drops slow and nearly come to a stop. The cat passed behind him, and he turned and saw its eyes glow and reflect the light of the fire. It stopped on his left side, suddenly curious about what was taking place.

Adnan did not move. He still had one hand on Lisa and his other on the cane that he used to steady his position as he leaned on it. The dark figures circled around him and lunged at him, causing Adnan to jerk violently and cough.

Frank sensed Adnan was in trouble. He moved closer, summoning his courage. "Leet mee help," he said. His words continued to sound awkward and slow as they left his mouth in a long, low mumble. "Lisa, I am Father Frank, from St. Joseph's Church in the neighborhood. We are here to help."

Adnan reached out with his right hand and clutched the dark form around Lisa, which immediately ceased its swirling motion.

The flames flashed, and Frank felt a momentary heat against his legs. He stepped forward to help.

"Don't break the circle!" Kanuik yelled to him, but it was too late. Seeing the distressed girl coming out, Frank reached across the flames to help her. She looked at him directly and crossed in front of him. The shadow flowed out of her body as though Adnan had it by the throat and kept it in the circle. One of the shadowy creatures attacking Adnan turned and came toward Frank. Its movement was slow, but Frank couldn't seem to move fast enough to get out of its path. He suddenly felt lethargic, and everything around him blurred. The shadow continued to float toward him. A hand reached out from the humanlike shape and grabbed at the girl.

Frank felt the command leave his brain, but it took his foot what seemed like minutes to step over and place him in front of the creature to block it. Lisa made it completely out of the circle.

The shadowy figure twisted, and a mouth opened and growled as the shadow lunged at Frank. Hitting him in the chest, it disappeared inside of him. Suddenly, he could not breathe. He felt flesh tearing from his arms and neck. He quickly prayed and shouted at the same time. "You have no power over me!"

Frank closed his eyes. The pain left and was replaced by thoughts of desire and power. He envisioned being a bishop himself and ruling over the diocese. He envisioned standing in front of thousands of people and telling them things that were not true, yet they gave money to him anyway. He opened his eyes to find that no one was in the alley but him and Claudia. She looked attractive, and he struggled to keep his eyes from wondering over her curves.

Frank felt a large hand grab his shoulder from behind. His eyes were open as the vision before him collapsed into darkness. He was pulled backward suddenly and fell to the ground. When he could see again, Kanuik stood over him. Time had righted itself, and his motions and breathing were normal.

"You are lucky," Kanuik said. "Sit here for a moment."

"I'm fine," Frank said, trying to get up. But he found he was too dizzy to stand and sat back down on the concrete.

"You are not fine," Kanuik said. "That was foolish. Adnan told you not to interfere. You have burns on your legs from the fire."

Frank looked at his arms, where he thought he was burned. The pain had been severe from the shadow touching him, but there was no mark or indication of the contact. Then he looked at his legs, and just as Kanuik had said, he had burned the back of both ankles where he'd crossed the circle of fire. Frank turned to see Claudia behind him with Lisa.

"You're safe now, Lisa," Claudia told the girl as she wrapped her coat around her, before looking in Frank's direction. "Are you okay?" she asked.

Frank nodded from his position on the ground.

Claudia took the girl and walked back in the direction of their car. Blue and red lights flickered from the alley entrance.

Adnan stood in the ring of fire. Several dark creatures were in the ring with him. Adnan's body moved from side to side, his eyes closed like he was in a trance. His body left the ground, and he levitated but never fell. His cane hung around his wrist. One of the dark forms broke away from him and went to the perimeter, only to be met by Kanuik, who stood on the outside and chanted words Frank did not understand.

Adnan reached out his hand, and although the creature was only a shadow, Adnan again seemed to grasp it somehow and pull it back from the rim. The forms slowly grew smaller and faded, as did the ring of fire Adnan stood in. It was nearly out when he met the ground. His eyes opened, and he walked to Frank. He put his hand out, and Frank took it and stood.

"Now you see without the mirror," Adnan said. He headed out of the alley toward the car.

"Come, we are done here," Kanuik said, and he and Frank followed Adnan.

When they exited the alley, two police cars were parked by the store, and Claudia was speaking to one of the uniformed officers. A tall, young black man dressed in a suit and tie was also speaking with her; Frank noticed a badge on his hip pocket. The man glanced at him as Kanuik helped him to the edge of the sidewalk. Two paramedics helped Lisa and put her into an ambulance.

"Look at her arms," Adnan said. "See the puncture wounds. She probably comes from a broken home. The evil has been at work with her for some time."

One of the paramedics came over and looked at Frank's legs, cleaned the wounds, and wrapped them with gauze. When she was done, she handed Frank another pack of gauze. "You must keep the wounds clean and replace the gauze in the morning. You should be fine if you keep the area clean."

Frank nodded as he heard the instructions. Everything registered, but Frank was watching the events around him as though he was not fully there, but rather was watching a movie from inside of the screen it played on while others were on the outside. The detective asked him a few questions, and afterward, Frank couldn't remember his answers. He took his seat next to Claudia as she started the car and drove back toward the Kozy Tavern.

Frank looked down at his digital watch, but the display screen was solid black. He removed it from his wrist and shook it. The display came back on for a moment, but the hours and minutes raced like a stopwatch and then went blank again. He looked at the car's clock display. Three hours had passed, although they had been in the alley for what seemed like only thirty minutes.

"Like I said, they steal moments of time," Adnan said from the backseat. "When you entered the circle, you were in their moment."

"I don't understand," Frank said. "How can this be real?"

"The evil is among us right now," Adnan said. "In the subways, in the street, in our homes. Always tempting and trying to get in. Within seconds, decisions are made. Once it gains a foothold in a person's reality, it will start feeding and influence more moments."

"These things are parasitic," Frank said.

Adnan nodded.

"How can you tell when they have a hold on someone?"

"We can tell by changes in behaviors, the types of decisions a person makes, or the path their life is on. The other way is more spiritual," Adnan said. "There's a whole network. Not just on this continent and not just your religion. We met at a conference that was open to all religions. The concept was to try to get all of the world's religions to unite for a common goal: to win this fight."

"What happened?"

"The conference was a failure," Adnan said. "There were some small groups that did unite, and now we do some stuff out of the mainstream."

"You and Kanuik are one of these groups then?"

"Yes," Adnan said. "We've worked loosely with the church. We depend on them for resources and funding. The church priority is to help families. If evil goes after a family, it can affect more than one person. It's believed that the family structure promotes security and belonging and is the best resistance."

"I'm sorry," Frank said. "This is a lot to take in."

"That is why not everyone knows about what we do," Adnan said. "It's an ancient battle, and the church thinks we have the upper hand because demons no longer walk among us upright in physical form."

"You don't think that?" Frank said.

"No," Adnan said. "I don't."

They exited the car and started toward the Kozy Tavern.

"Isn't it closed?" Frank said.

Adnan smiled and pulled out a key to open the front door. Frank didn't ask any questions but went straight to the restroom and washed his face in the coldest water the sink could produce before walking back out to the bar. To his surprise, Chic stood in his usual place behind the bar, where he was facing Adnan and Jimmie, who were seated at the bar. Claudia was near the front door on her cell phone, and Kanuik passed Frank as he headed down the hall to the restroom.

Frank went to the bar, and stood beside Jimmie. Adnan was one seat over and was drinking a dark liquid from a tall glass. Before Frank could open his mouth, Chic put a shot of whiskey in front of him. Frank put out his hand, and this time the fingers didn't hesitate. He closed his eyes as he felt the liquor burn his throat on the way down. It was a good burn.

"Can I get you anything else?" Chic said.

Frank shook his head. He looked at his reflection in the mirror behind the bar. He didn't look good. His skin was pale and his hair disheveled.

"I guess I wasn't the only one having a late night tonight," Jimmie said as he patted Frank on the back. "We started the night over on Ninth Street, the old brewer's pub that's supposed to be haunted. That's what you need, Chic. If your place was haunted, it might draw some customers."

"I don't need any of those types," Chic said.

"I'm one of those types," Jimmie said.

"Well, we'll make an exception in your case," Chic chuckled.

"So, Father," Jimmie said, "how did tonight compare to your experience in the war? Did you ever have to look in the face of evil over there?"

"Take it easy, Jimmie," Chic said. "It's his first night."

Frank didn't answer. He leaned his back up against the bar and stared out at the empty pool tables. Claudia finished talking on her phone and went to the table where Kanuik had just sat down. He had a towel and was drying his hands. Jimmie put his glass down and headed over to the table. He stood and spoke with Kanuik and Claudia for a moment and then left the bar.

"As I mentioned before, Jimmie works out of the university and has access to a lot of resources the rest of us don't have," Adnan said. He moved one stool over to sit closer to Frank. "I've found his help useful. He puts a more analytical spin on things."

Frank remained silent. He turned around and sat down. His stomach was roiling from the shot of whiskey, and his head was spinning from the night's events.

"Now you've seen what we're up against," Adnan said, sipping his drink. "Problem is, that was one alley of millions in the world. There are many of us fighting, but it's a matter of opinion who is winning."

Frank looked in the mirror at Adnan and behind him to the door. The mostly empty place seemed to him the proper setting for their conversation. Chic kept busy cleaning and organizing, the cigar shifting back and forth in his mouth. He turned back and looked at

Frank for a moment as though he wanted to say something but then went back to his business cleaning.

"Now you know what we do: we fight evil," Adnan said.

Frank looked at the empty glass in front of him. He thought about the cold touch of the shadow and how it had affected him. He wondered how Adnan was able to stand direct contact for so long when for Frank it had such an adverse effect.

"I didn't know what to expect," Frank said. "I didn't know it would be so … physical."

"In older times, it was not so difficult," Adnan said. "People had faith. It's all about influence. That's how we know God exists; there is an undeniable common core of values and feelings we all have. It's not right to murder, to steal, to hurt others; we all desire relationships and love. But we have lost our way."

"You think we've lost our way?" Frank asked.

"The fight has changed. We used to be able to tell people, 'God wouldn't want you to do this' or 'Jesus is with you.' We were able to invoke holy symbols. They are less effective these days. Faith is harder to come by, and there is an organized effort to push people farther and farther from faith. It wouldn't have such an adverse impact if the result was just that people turned away from religion. But there is no other moral compass strong enough to keep them from becoming selfish and materialistic. The result is undeniably around us now, in every corner of the world. Selfishness has replaced selflessness."

Frank fumbled with the glass in front of him, hardly able to steady it. Chic read his mind and filled the glass.

"Go ahead," Adnan said. "You will need it to calm your nerves. We're just getting started."

Frank looked up at the mirror and watched Claudia in the background as she sat at the table with Kanuik. She noticed him looking at her and smiled. She took off her coat and draped it around her chair. Then she pulled out the chair beside her, tapped her hand on the seat, and looked toward him.

"Come on," Adnan said, and the two walked over to the table

and sat down. Frank took the seat by Claudia, and Adnan sat in the chair against the wall.

"I got her into a rehab center," Dr. Walden said. "That's the most we can hope for. She'll be there for at least ninety days. The description we gave Jennings should help him round up the suspects."

"A successful night," Adnan said. "We will find that most of the men probably have priors. It's no doubt they were weakened prey lacking moral guidance."

"Frank, are you okay?" Claudia said.

"I'm fine." Frank steadied himself and made eye contact with Claudia. Kanuik was still drying his hands and seemed to be examining them as he wiped. "What was that fire you threw?"

"Holy fire," Kanuik said. "A mixture of flammable oils blessed by many faiths. The evil cannot cross the fire." He laid the towel on the table. "But if it's easier for you to believe, it was Indian magic."

"And the canes," Frank said. "More Indian magic?"

"A gift," Kanuik said, "passed down over the generations. The canes are made from wood cut in the Garden of Eden."

Frank looked at Kanuik. Kanuik's face remained serious, and then he smiled, and everyone at the table laughed.

Frank finally took a drink and eased his shoulders back. "I haven't had a late conversation like this for a long time. Probably since before I left the army." He looked at the faces around him and realized they had been having experiences like the one they'd had tonight for a long time. "I've kept myself pretty hidden away in the church I run, listening to a few confessions here and there," Frank said. "I guess I didn't want to believe how bad it is."

"Do not deny yourself," Kanuik said. "What you do is important."

"He's right," Adnan said. "Without your efforts, there would be more people slipping into the world of the shadows."

"What did you see when it touched you?" Kanuik asked.

"It touched you?" Claudia said, leaning forward and putting her hands on the table.

"She has yet to see their true nature," Kanuik said, looking at Claudia. "It may be a blessing."

Claudia looked back at Frank and raised her eyebrows.

"Go ahead and tell her, Frank," Adnan said. "You are among friends here, and we will not judge you. We are the closest support structure you will have from here on out, and you will need to trust us. The evil knows who you are now, and it will come at you when you are at your weakest and tempt you—have no doubt. You must be ready."

"I felt cold, frozen, sick, and nauseated," Frank said. "It paralyzed me for a moment, and a foul stench like burning flesh was all around me. I know because I've smelled this before in Iraq. I wasn't quite conscious for a moment; you know how you feel sometimes right before you go to sleep or wake up. It was like I was just waking up from something."

He looked at Claudia. "I felt a thousand feelings and desires in a moment's time, feelings of a child wanting to be mischievous, of a teenager wanting to rebel and do something bad to get attention, of a man wanting to ..." He broke eye contact. "Not in a good way."

The group was silent. Chic brought over a tray with tall, slender glasses on it, the same type of glass with the same colored liquid that Adnan drank. He put one down in front of each of them. "On the house," he said and walked away.

Frank picked up his drink and held it out. The others raised theirs, and they had a silent toast. As Frank lifted the drink, he noticed the glass was warm. He put it to his lips and took a drink. It was warm tea mixed with something he couldn't quite place, but he thought it might be rum. He glanced at Adnan, who winked at him. *So this is what you've been drinking,* he thought.

"I pushed back," Frank said. "I pushed back hard, and it fled."

"Lead us not into temptation and deliver us from evil," Adnan said. "There are reasons for our prayers."

"Well," Claudia said, pushing her chair from the table, "I've had enough for one night. I need to be in the office tomorrow, and it's almost morning. My first session with David is at ten. Frank, you might want to come by and meet him. Perhaps you can help since he knows you."

"I'll do that," Frank said.

"Does anyone need a ride?" Claudia asked.

"Chic will take us anywhere we need to go," Adnan said loud enough for his voice to travel across the empty bar. Chic leaned on the bar with both arms and nodded.

Kanuik stood. "I will see you to your car."

Frank watched as Kanuik helped Claudia with her jacket and escorted her to the door. He noticed Adnan watching him.

"You reached out and touched the shadow that haunted that girl," Frank said. "Yet you tell me to be careful. How did you manage to drive it away?"

Adnan sat back and looked into the air, as if glancing into the past. His eyes wandered, and he sighed before responding. "I have been fighting these things for more years than I can remember," Adnan said. "I have never doubted my faith that a higher being and energy exists that has good intentions for us. I have seen fear in others so much in my life, in children, women, and grown men, that I knew it was my God-given destiny to drive that fear from the face of this earth."

"Your faith gives you power over them?" Frank asked.

"Yes, but not absolute. Studies show men of faith have the ability to channel pain and handle more of it than those who have no faith. It helps with the physical part, but they attack constantly, and it's personal." Adnan's eyes stared into a past that Frank could tell was still too close.

The dimly lit bar where he, Adnan, and Chic sat was a quiet place, a lonely place, Frank thought.

"Never heard of a prophet or messenger that was not lonely or didn't have to sacrifice a lot, have you?" Adnan said. "Don't worry, Frank. You don't have to completely give up your parish. They are your family more than we are. They will be your support. But they cannot understand the road you are traveling on now, not exactly."

Kanuik walked in and headed to the table. He took a seat and pulled out his pipe, packed it with tobacco, and lit it. No longer worried that Adnan would be alone, Frank decided it was time to go. "I will see you both tomorrow."

As Frank stood and waved to Chic, Adnan grabbed his arm. "There is one more thing I must warn you about. I said I needed your energy. Understand, every time you go to sleep, every time you daydream, you are at risk now. I didn't intend for you to make direct contact, but they will know your face now. If you have any unfinished business that you carry with you, make peace with it as soon as you can so it can't be used against you. What we did tonight was simple work. Starting tomorrow, we are going deeper into darkness."

Kanuik stood, removed the pipe from his mouth, and blew out the smoke directly in Frank's direction. He looked around him as if searching for something. "You are clean."

Frank nodded politely and headed toward the door. He took his coat off the rack and buttoned it up tight, a chill clinging to him as though the touch of the shadow was not completely gone. He stepped out the door. It had grown colder outside, and he shivered as he looked up at the overcast sky. The chill of the encounter with the shadows clung to him like prolonged exposure to the cold. "Now I know why they recommended long underwear and a thicker coat," he said out loud.

"There you are."

Frank was surprised to hear Claudia's voice. She was standing a few feet away with one of the men who had been with the police earlier, the one dressed in a suit.

"Frank, this is Detective Jennings," Claudia said.

"Yes, I saw you earlier tonight," Jennings said, and the two men shook hands.

"Thank you, Detective," Claudia said. "I've promised Father Frank a ride home tonight." Her face pleaded as she walked toward him.

Detective Jennings shot a glance at Frank. The priest nodded back and turned as Claudia swung her arm under his and moved him in the opposite direction, walking with him.

A few steps later, she broke the silence. "Sorry, but I needed an escape." She stopped beside a classic green car.

"I've always had good timing," Frank said. "In helping people, I mean."

Claudia smiled. Detective Jennings was still watching. "You don't mind?"

"It is a bit cold tonight," Frank said. "And we've been up all night. I suppose I could use a ride. Is he still watching?"

She nodded.

"I guess we'll have to go through with it then."

She unlocked the door.

Frank stepped back and looked at the car. He put his arms out. "This is an old AMC Ambassador. I haven't seen any of these around for ages. This is yours?"

"Nineteen seventy-two to be exact," Claudia said.

"That's the year they switched from a V-6 to a V-8 engine," Frank said.

"It's why my father kept it," Claudia said. "It has great power and still handles like a charm. Get in, and I'll show you."

"What happened to the other car you were driving earlier?" Frank said.

"That belongs to the church," Claudia said. "We get into some hairy situations at times, and we go into some neighborhoods that aren't safe for a car like this."

Frank glanced to see Detective Jennings still outside the bar. Although the detective tried to appear like he wasn't watching them as he fumbled with his phone, he occasionally looked in their direction.

"Are you sure it's not a problem?" Frank said.

"It's no problem, really. I drive those two around all of the time," Claudia said, looking toward the Kozy Tavern. "Just not in this car. Besides, I could use some conversation."

"I could too," Frank said. He watched the steam coming from the manhole covers that lined the street. He shivered again as he opened the door and sat down on the cold leather seat. He buckled his seat belt. "I'm used to walking," Frank stated, "but I wouldn't want to pass up a chance to ride in this car."

"You know about cars?"

"My father worked in a factory and used to take us in once in a while to see the production line. I was always amazed at all the machines and the sheer size. He collected old cars—bought them cheap because they didn't work. But he never really got around to fixing any of them. It took time and money, neither of which he had."

"Sounds like our fathers would have liked each other," Claudia said. "Mine did the same thing, but he did manage to get a few of them fixed, including this one."

"How did you get involved with Adnan and the church," Frank said, "if I may ask?"

"Of course you can ask," Claudia said. "Haven't you heard that intense emotional situations bring people together faster? After tonight, I feel like I've known you for years."

"Maybe it's all the research you did on me prior to us meeting," Frank said.

"Sorry about that," Claudia said. "It's just that we are all putting our lives at risk out there. We can't be too careful about who we let in our group."

"I wasn't ready for what happened tonight," Frank said. "It was …"

"Extreme," Claudia said. "It took me some time to adjust, but I'd been around some hard cases before I met Adnan and Kanuik."

"Adnan and Kanuik fit together, but you …"

"I know," Claudia said. "I seem much too classy to be hanging out with them." She smiled. "My father was a psychoanalyst; that's what they called it back then. He's the reason I got started in the field of psychiatry. Prior to that, I had twelve years of Catholic school," Claudia said.

"Your father influenced your career then," Frank said.

"He got me interested," Claudia said. "Part of me wanted to know what made people tick, why they behave the way they do. So I wanted to be a researcher, and that led me into the field of psychiatry."

"A scientist with faith?" Frank said.

"My faith stayed with me but became tempered by the scientific side. Over the years of study, I found things that could not be explained. My peers and elders scoffed at my research, but my results eventually won me the merit I deserved. I am not broadly accepted in my field, but I am left alone to treat my patients."

"How long have you been working with them?"

"Six years now. I contacted the church for help on a case. Adnan showed up, and we've been working together since then."

"Kanuik was with him when you met?" Frank asked.

"The church has a policy that no one can go it alone. Adnan wouldn't allow one of the other clergy members along, but he and Kanuik are inseparable. I'm quite surprised he's letting you in."

"Adnan doesn't seem the type to allow someone else to control his agenda," Frank said. "Kanuik seems to follow him without question, but I can't imagine it started that way."

Claudia laughed. "You sure you're not a psychologist?"

"I deal a lot with counseling and people in difficult situations," Frank stated. "In seminary school, I had a lot of classes on psychology and counseling. Probably not the same type you had, but similar."

"I wanted a challenge, so I deal with hard cases like David," Claudia said.

"Never married?" Frank asked.

Claudia flashed her eyes at him and then returned them to the road.

"Sorry if that was a sore subject."

"No," Claudia said. "It's okay. During the day I run my practice, and you've seen who I spend my evenings with. I have no complaints. I had plenty of opportunities when I was younger." Claudia reached her arm over and opened the glove box. "Sorry," she said.

"Can I help you find something?" Frank said.

"It's not important," Claudia said. "I keep thinking I might have left a pack of cigarettes in this car. Just making sure."

Minutes passed before he thought of something to say. "Car sure rides smooth."

"Yes," Claudia said. "They don't make them like this anymore."

"Detective Jennings seems like an okay fellow."

"He's been a lot of help to the group," Claudia said. "But that's not what you meant, is it?"

"It's none of my business," Frank said.

"It's not?" Claudia raised her eyebrows.

Frank coughed to clear his throat. "Do you have any family here?" Frank asked, attempting to steer the conversation in a new direction.

"Only child," Claudia said. "My mother died when I was eighteen. My father, the psychiatrist, passed away just a few years back."

"I'm sure he would be proud of you."

"We were very close," Claudia said, but she offered no more on the subject.

"What about Kanuik and Adnan? Do either of them have family?" Frank said.

"Kanuik has a wife, but he rarely speaks about her. She's in the same line of work and travels. I don't know how they do it."

"Adnan?"

"The man seems to know everyone, but I've never heard him speak of family. Well, here we are." She pulled over in front of Frank's apartment. "Don't forget to change those bandages on your legs."

"I won't," Frank said. "Thank you for the ride … and the conversation." Frank got out. "I've been up all night, but I'm not sure how I'm going to sleep with all that's going through my head."

"I have some pills," Claudia said, but Frank shook his head. He was about to close the door when she called out, "Hey, do you drive?"

"I know how," Frank said.

"Next time, you can take it for a spin," Claudia said. She winked as he shut the door. The car pulled away.

After the morning incident, Frank opened his door with full knowledge that he had adopted a cat and that something unexpected might be in store. He turned the light on expecting some surprise—a torn-up newspaper, scratches on the couch, turned-over knickknacks, or something of the sort. But his place was in order.

He hung is coat on the rack by the door and looked around. The cat was neither in the living room nor in the kitchen. He went down the hall to the bathroom, washed his face and hands, and brushed his teeth, and still, no sign of the cat. He walked back to the kitchen and checked to make sure the cat had eaten, adding a little food to its dish and giving it some fresh water, but still, it did not appear.

Frank checked his windows to make sure he hadn't accidently left one open. "Where are you?" he called out. *Maybe I should have given it a name*, he thought.

He checked his closets but could not find the animal. Finally, way past tired, he sat down on his couch. He flinched when he caught a reflection in the distance, but it was nothing, a shadow in the single lamp that remained on. He felt chilly and uncomfortable sitting with his back against the door.

"I'm not afraid," Frank said to the empty room. He remembered Adnan's words: *Every time you go to sleep, every time you daydream, you are at risk now.*

He reached out and turned off the lamp, sitting in complete darkness now. Then an idea occurred to him. He went to his bedroom and retrieved his book light from the nightstand. Kneeling on the floor, with the light in hand, he slowly lifted his bedspread and looked underneath the bed. "Aha, there you are," he said, looking at two yellow glowing eyes. "Come here." He patted his hand on the floor to no avail. "Well, okay, if that's where you are going to spend the night ..."

Frank said a prayer, crawled into bed, tuned off the small light, and attempted to sleep. After tossing and turning for what seemed like hours, he reached out and turned on the clock radio, hoping the music would give him something to focus on other than how much his legs were itching. Twenty minutes later, he got up, removed a blanket from his closet, and hung it across the single window in his bedroom to make it darker. His mind raced with thoughts about all that had happened the day before.

He thought of the shadow and how it had approached him. He analyzed his own reaction. His first instinct had been to defend the girl and help. Perhaps Bishop Tafoya and Adnan were right about him; he wasn't afraid of the darkness and was a warrior. Flashes of the moment when he came into contact with the form raced through his mind. "Form, but no form," he whispered. He looked at the clock; the minutes rolled by, and his eyes stayed open, staring at the wall.

He tried fluffing the pillow. He turned on the ceiling fan to make the room cooler. He recited his favorite poem multiple times. But he could not go to sleep. Lying on his side, he watched the minutes pass on the digital alarm clock. His mind raced with too many thoughts. "I've been up too long; that's the problem. I'm past sleep, past exhaustion."

Suddenly, his bed moved a little as he felt something close to his feet. He looked down to see the cat sitting there, looking at him. It walked up beside him while he stay still, lying on his side. He put out his right hand and patted it on the back. The cat raised its head and accepted the grooming. "Oh, you like that, do you?" He stroked it some more.

The cat plopped down on its side and started purring, a loud continuous purr. Frank was amused, and soon, he was asleep.

Chapter 5

The Questor

"Pray for us, Father; pray that all is not lost!"

Frank woke with a start, causing the cat to jump from the bed. He'd dreamed of the old man in the park and his words. He wiped the sweat from his forehead and kicked off the covers, feeling particularly warm. He went to the bathroom and washed his face, and the cool water soothed the tension.

He stumbled to his couch and sat down with the small towel he was using to dry his face still in his hands. The events of the night before seemed distant and almost unreal. His cat sat on the floor looking up at him, its tail flicking side to side. He looked at it and then at the clock. It was after one in the afternoon. He sat back. The cat didn't move but sat with its eyes fixed on him.

"Persistent little thing, aren't you?" he said. Just then, someone knocked on the door. He went to the door and looked through the peephole. "Claudia?" Frank said as he opened the door.

"I'm sorry," Claudia said. "Maybe we weren't very clear on times."

Frank stared blankly as she crossed his path and walked into his apartment.

"You were going to come into the office with me today to visit David. It's my first session with him. I think you would be very valuable." She handed him a sticky note. "This was on your door."

Frank looked at the note. It was from Father Mark. "Came by today to see if you wanted to take a jog. Things at church are fine."

"Give me a minute," Frank said. Then he noticed he'd left the door open. He stuck his head out to see if any of his neighbors were in the hallway. His neighbors might be suspicious of him having a female visitor, and he could only imagine how hard it would be to explain what was going on. "I'm sorry," Frank said. "I didn't sleep well."

"That's all right," Claudia said. "I was late myself this morning, so I changed David's appointment to this afternoon. We were out pretty late last night."

"Please, have a seat," Frank said. He showed Claudia to the couch and went to pour her a cup of coffee, but it wasn't made yet, so he quickly started a pot.

"Here," Frank said as he handed her an empty cup. "It should be ready in a minute." He looked down at his sweat pants and T-shirt. "Pardon me while I get changed." He went to his room to dress, and when he returned to the living room, Claudia was on the couch with the cat sitting in her lap.

"What a friendly cat you have here," Claudia said.

"Yes, I'm just getting used to it."

"Oh, is this a new addition to the family?" Claudia asked.

"I think it was Adnan's idea," Frank said, still unsure who had written the list of items he had to get, but assuming it was Adnan.

"What's her name?"

Frank sat down by Claudia, and the cat moved between them. He raised his eyebrows.

Claudia laughed. "You haven't given her a name? Frank!"

"No, not yet. Just got her this week."

"Well, I think this little patch of black on her head that winds around here"—she used her fingers to trace it—"reminds me of a rose. And she has the prettiest green eyes."

Frank got closer and noticed Claudia was wearing perfume. He inhaled it deeply; it reminded him of something he wanted to remember but couldn't. "I guess she does," he said, making eye contact

90

with Claudia. Inside of him, something stirred he'd never felt. He'd been attracted to women before, but this was different. It wasn't just physical; he enjoyed her presence.

"Name her Rosie," Claudia said.

He looked into Claudia's blue eyes and sensed a caring person behind them, someone who was sincere. He broke eye contact, not wanting it to appear he was staring at her. "That's a wonderful name, Doctor," Frank said. "Thank you for your assistance in that matter. Now, shall we take that trip?"

Before Frank left, he noticed the grocery bag on his counter that had the salts and candles in it. He reached in and pulled out the bath salts and left them on the counter. Then he removed five small candles and a lighter and stuffed them in his coat pocket.

True to her word, Claudia let Frank drive her AMC Ambassador to the psychiatric wing of the hospital. Claudia signed him in as her guest, and he was given a visitor's badge.

"You seem to know your way around here," Claudia said.

"Yes," Frank said as he attached his badge to his shirt so that it was visible. "I've had some experiences with people here—families in crisis whom I've tried to counsel." He looked down the long hallway with its narrow doors. "I never paid attention to how big this wing was. Are there really that many people interned here?"

Claudia nodded. "It's only a small preview of the problem." She walked with Frank down the hall. "The patients here are in the first stages of their ordeal. They will be treated and released, which doesn't always mean freedom. Some will go back into society because although we know they have problems, we don't have the resources to help them, and we don't consider them a threat to anyone. Others will be sent to a center that treats more severe cases. Rehabilitation at these places is less than 3 percent." She opened the door to her office and led Frank inside.

"Uh-oh, she's quoting statistics again," said a familiar voice from inside the office.

Frank entered Claudia's office to see Jimmie there. He still looked as young as the night before and was dressed in a brown sport coat with a faded yellow shirt underneath and tan pants.

"Hello, Frank," Jimmie said, putting his hand out. "Nice to see you again. Man, you don't look much better than last night. Didn't get any sleep, did you?"

"Forgive Jimmie," Claudia said. "He has a habit of being brutally honest and open."

"It's okay," Frank said. "I prefer candid people."

Jimmie sat down on a black leather couch that ran along the left wall of Claudia's office while Claudia went directly to her desk chair. Her desk was in the back, surrounded by bookcases and filing cabinets, but well organized. Frank sat in the only other chair available, across from the couch.

"She's quoting statistics to you," Jimmie said. "Probably told you how low the rehabilitation rate is here, eh?"

Frank nodded.

"Then you can understand why Adnan and Kanuik like this place; it's a playground for the shadow creatures they've been battling. People here are in bad shape—phobias, lack of confidence, identity problems, depression, drug and alcohol abuse, sexual abuse and violence. That's just a start."

"What brings you here?" Frank asked.

"Research," Jimmie said. "Has she told you about the suicides?"

"No," Frank said. "What about suicide?"

"Well," Jimmie said, leaning in, "suicides are like the ultimate prize for the shadows; they, like, feast on them. I have instruments set up all over the place, and any time there's a suicide attempt, the energy reading are just, well, off the charts."

"If what Adnan says is correct," Frank said, "the shadows don't feed on fear; they feed on insecurity, weakness, and doubt. What you are saying confirms that their ultimate goal is the ruination of a person."

"Exactly," Jimmie said. He looked at Claudia, who looked up from her computer screen to give Jimmie a disapproving glance. "I like this guy," said Jimmie. "He catches on quick."

"I'm glad you approve, Jimmie," Claudia said. "Do you want to participate in our session today?"

"Sure," Jimmie said. "This guy has no family that can be reached. I don't have to worry about anyone trying to sue me or the university. Besides, Russ and Mike have a van parked outside of his house, monitoring it, right now."

"A van outside David's house?" Frank asked. "Why?"

"Research," Jimmie said. "Mike's cable van, so no one will suspect. The house is closed off as a crime scene, or we'd be inside. I've been trying to help isolate where the energy originates—you know, the portal we were speaking about yesterday."

"Portal, right," Frank said.

Jimmie gestured with his hands to make a twisting circular motion. "Think of it as a doorway where the energy comes from—you know, the shadows, their energy. The church believes it's an opening to hell, literally, but I'm hoping for a parallel dimension or wormhole to another part of the universe." Jimmie lowered his voice as though someone was listening, and the next thing he was about to say was secret. "Truth is, we don't really know what it is." He then slapped his hands against his knees, which surprised Frank, and raised his voice again. "That's why I'm studying it. I'm trying to find out if it exists around the subject, David, or if it comes from a physical location, his house."

"I'm sorry," Claudia said, looking up from her computer again. "I need to respond to a few messages and update some patient files. Give me about fifteen, and then we'll go see David. Jimmie, would you mind walking Frank down to the vending area? Maybe you can buy him a coffee or something."

Jimmie looked down at his watch. "Okay, but I have an Introduction to Physics class at six. Come on, Father, let's give the doc some space. I wouldn't want to upset the person who's the key to my next publication."

Frank followed Jimmie out into the hall and down to the vending machines. They passed a few nurses, who gave them suspicious looks.

"Make sure you don't lose that badge; you don't want them to think you're a patient here," Jimmie said.

They rounded a corner and entered an empty waiting room area with a coffee machine and several vending machines.

"You know, I usually complain about how much college teachers make," Jimmie said. He looked at Frank before he continued. "But I probably make more than a priest, so this one's on me. What will it be?"

"Don't believe everything you hear," Frank said. "We get to keep 10 percent of the collection, and although church attendance has dwindled in some areas, those who come give generously."

Jimmie looked up from the pocketful of change he was counting. At first Frank kept a straight face, but he couldn't help but smile when confronted by the young college professor's confusion. The two men laughed.

"A priest with a sense of humor," Jimmie said. "That's refreshing."

"I'll just have regular coffee," Frank said.

Jimmie put the change in the machine, and it produced a small paper cup full of coffee that he handed to Frank. After he made his own selection, the two took a seat on a padded bench.

"So why does everyone call you Jimmie instead of Professor Barnes?" Frank asked.

"Trust me—it doesn't happen at the college. I think it's because I seem like a kid to them, compared to everyone else in the group. I mean, once you get to know Adnan and Kanuik and hear all of their experiences and travels, man, they've been everywhere. That kind of life experience makes everyone around you seem naïve. And Claudia, she's a prodigy in her field, way ahead of the others in her treatment methods and techniques, and not a bad body at all. Wouldn't you agree?"

Frank choked on his coffee. "I hadn't noticed," he said. "You said you're working on a paper?"

"Yes," Jimmie said. "I love teaching." He looked around, as if checking to make sure no one else was listening. "The truth is, the research is more exciting than teaching. The things I've seen and discovered—they'd blow your mind. I can't even publish half the stuff I've witnessed. No one would believe me."

Frank didn't say anything but thought about his encounter the night before. He imagined Jimmie had had similar experiences with the group. "What made you get interested in researching this type of stuff?"

"You mean spiritual activity?" Jimmie said.

"Well, if that's what you want to call it," Frank said.

"I guess it's not really the same," Jimmie said. "Paranormal is more like ghosts and hauntings, and this is more good versus evil with religion and demons and stuff like that, but overall, similar." Jimmie sipped the hot coffee, and his eyes narrowed. "I guess it started when I was a young boy, about eleven or twelve. I didn't grow up here. I grew up in Topeka, Kansas, a rural area. There wasn't much to do, and life was not that exciting. I found a set of books at my school library called *The Questor's Adventures*, about a group of boys in similar circumstances to mine who set out on adventures to explore the paranormal. The series piqued my interest in the subject, and I've been chasing adventures since."

"*The Questor's Adventures*," Frank said. "Sounds interesting. Inspired by a book—that's a great story."

"And how about you, Frank?" Jimmie said. "How did you get involved in all of this?"

"Claudia's patient, David, is a member of my parish," Frank said. "I was counseling him and his family before this happened. The church thought I might be of some help."

"Oh," Jimmie said.

"There you are," Claudia said, coming around the corner. "I thought you'd just be a few minutes." She put her hands on her hips.

"We were having a wonderful conversation," Frank said, "the professor and I."

Jimmie lifted his paper cup and tapped Frank's cup in a thankful toast. "Here, here."

"Well, if you two are ready, we'll go see David now," Claudia said.

"Professor?" Frank said.

"Oh, after you," Jimmie smiled as the two men stood.

The three walked down the hallway and past Claudia's office, where Jimmie stopped momentarily to retrieve a bag of equipment.

"If you have any pens, pencils, tweezers, scissors, or other objects in your pockets, you need to get rid of them now," Claudia said. "You can leave them in my office."

Claudia led them down the hallway from her office. They took a right at an intersection, which led them to a set of locked doors; a camera bore down on them from above. Claudia scanned her card, and the lock released.

"David is down this wing," Claudia said. "This is where we keep hard cases. Jimmie held up his camera and smiled. Claudia led them down the empty hallway.

"The patients here are under restraint, locked up and in straitjackets," Claudia said. "Don't let that affect your judgment; they can be highly dangerous still. It's for their own good. David is under evaluation, but he's basically a prisoner of the state at this time until I finish my evaluation and let the state know if he is fit for trial."

"What have you found so far?" Frank asked.

"David doesn't remember what happened. He's admitted to having dreams of killing people. When asked to describe the dream, he describes the same scene as in the video."

"Video?" Frank asked.

"I'm sorry," Claudia said. "I guess no one has told you. The night David killed his family, he videotaped the entire event. When we found him, he was sitting in front of the television, watching the video."

"Psycho with a capital P," Jimmie said. "I'm glad he's restrained."

"David Jenson is his name," Frank said. "I have a nephew the same age as him."

"Sorry," Jimmie said.

"David used to come to church with his family," Frank continued. "He had a younger sister. I'd see her with the parents, but I hadn't seen David for some time. I thought it was just a matter of him going through those teen years of rebellion."

"Oh, he was rebelling all right," Claudia said. "He had cigarettes, joints, and other drug paraphernalia in his room. He went from a 3.5 GPA last year to a 2.0 this year."

"Has anyone been in to see him?" Frank asked.

"Only immediate family would be allowed," Claudia said. "We haven't been able to find any grandparents or aunts or uncles. He appears to be alone."

"The perfect target," Jimmie said. "Adnan did tell you these things attack people when they are weak and insecure. I can't think of a more perfect target than a teen with an identity crisis and poor family structure. If only we had a cure for adolescence."

When they reached the door to David's room, Claudia scanned her badge and opened the thick door. The room was narrow and rectangular, with the bed at the very end fixed to the wall. To the right as they entered was a seat extending out from the wall, and to the left sat a toilet and sink. Frank noticed that even the pillow was built into the bed as a block, with a small covering over it. David sat in the center of the bed, facing the door, with his legs over the side and his feet touching the floor. His head was tucked into his chest, and his arms were restrained.

"We're going in," Jimmie said to his cell phone.

Frank looked at him curiously.

"Sorry. I wanted to let Mike and Russ know we were entering the room … No, I wasn't talking to you," he said into the phone. "I'm talking to someone here with me in the room. Just text me if you see anything on your end." Jimmie took out a piece of equipment from his bag and switched it on. The black metallic object had a dial indicator and an antenna.

"Does he know we're here?" Frank asked, looking at David.

"He is mildly sedated, but aware," Claudia said. She went over to the bed and sat down by David. He didn't respond. Claudia undid the straps behind his back and moved his left arm free. She took a blood pressure monitor out of her bag and ran it around his arm. When she started to pump it to take her reading, David's head lifted, and he stared forward. His eyes were glassy and hollow.

"Hello, David," Frank said, moving in front of David. He bent down so that he was eye to eye with David. "Do you remember me?"

Jimmie's cell phone rang. In the soundproofed room, the ringtone echoed loud enough to startle everyone but David. Claudia and Frank looked at Jimmie.

"Sorry," Jimmie said, scrambling to answer the phone. "I thought I told you to text."

"David," Frank said, turning his attention back to the teen, "I'm Father Frank from St. Joseph's Church. You and your family go to church there. Do you remember me?"

"It's reading *how* high?" Jimmie's voice rose as he talked on the phone. "No, no one's supposed to be in the house ... You see movement on the second floor. Which window? ... That's David's room."

David didn't respond but stared toward the door. Claudia put the blood pressure gauge away and pulled out her flashlight. She shined it in David's eyes, checking for a response. David's arms lay limp on either side of him.

"I didn't think he was this sedated, but he probably doesn't know what is going on," Claudia said. "I asked them to cut back, but he's threatened suicide. Physically, he's fine ... just some withdrawal symptoms." She stroked his cheek with her hand. "I wonder what is going on inside of him after such a traumatic event."

"Hello, Dr. Walden," David said in a whisper, startling Frank.

"David?" Claudia said. She took out her light and checked his eyes again.

"Father Frank," David said. His eyes moved, and he looked right at Frank, who still knelt on one knee before him.

"Yes, David, it's Father Frank." He took David's hand. "Do you know where you are and why you're here? Tell me what you remember."

David slowly looked around the room. "I don't remember anything, Father. I mean, they say it was me that did those things, and they got the video and stuff, but I would never do a thing like that. Never," David said.

"Hold on a minute, Mike," Jimmie said into his phone. He moved forward to stand beside Frank. "May I?"

Frank moved aside.

"David," Jimmie said, "have you ever experienced moments of missing time? Do you ever go to sleep and wake up in a different place, or wake up tired like you haven't really slept?"

David nodded his head. "All of the time! How did you know that?"

"Classic signs," Jimmie said, lowering his voice. "Frank," Jimmie said, pointing to his device, on which several lights were flickering, "one of those things is latched onto him; it's here in the room with us." Jimmie's attention turned back to his phone. "No, tell Russ not to go in the house, not without the others. It may be dangerous."

Frank thought about what he'd seen with Adnan at the bar and what he'd seen in the alley. He remembered that the shadows could disappear within the person they were tormenting. He looked closely at David, who seemed to be paying attention to Jimmie.

"Don't you worry about that," Frank said, patting David's hand. "You just need to do what Dr. Walden here tells you and get better. Would you pray with me?"

David bowed his head and closed his eyes.

"Father, please help your servant David," Frank said. As he started praying for David, he reached out to touch him. When his hands met David's, the boy's skin felt ice cold. Jimmie remained beside him, and suddenly, Frank heard the voice on the other end of Jimmie's cell phone start screaming.

"I told you not to go into the house!" Jimmie said. "Frank, the meter is spiking." Jimmie thrust the machine in front of Frank.

Frank looked at the meter. "What does it mean?"

"It measures energy," Jimmie said. "The energy of the shadows!"

David's head went back, and his eyes glazed over. "The whispering voices told me to tell you it's too late; you've already lost."

Frank removed his hand from David's and placed it on top of

the boy's head. "Don't listen to the voices, David; they are trying to mislead you. Trust in God; trust in your Savior."

"I don't know, Father Frank," David said. "I don't think God is looking out for me. I don't think He cares about me."

"Of course He cares, as do I," Frank said. "I am here to help you, David." Frank began to shiver as the cold he felt on his hands started to work its way up his arms and to his chest. His breath materialized in a white fog.

Claudia stood from the bed and backed away, facing David.

"You should leave now, Father Frank," David said. "I am going to kill again, and I don't want it to be you. I don't want it to be you. I'm going to hell; I don't want it to be you."

Frank removed his hand from David. He retrieved the candles from his pocket and placed them on the floor in front of David and lit them. David remained seated and watched.

"Stay on that side of the candles," Frank said to Jimmie and Claudia. Frank knew he was placing himself in danger by staying inside the circle of candles with David. He remembered what Kanuik had said about the shadows having problem crossing fire and hoped he was doing enough to protect Claudia and Jimmie. He placed his hands on David's head and closed his eyes.

"Help your servant, Lord. Protect him from evil." Frank reached deep inside himself as he uttered the words. He thought he'd be afraid, but instead, confidence built in him and told him to stand strong. David suddenly stood up on the bed. Frank tried to grasp David's hands to keep them contained.

"Get out of the house, *now!*" Jimmie hollered into his phone. "Oh my God, what should I do? Frank, be careful!"

"You're not helping, Jimmie," Claudia said. "Call Adnan. Hang up, quick, and call Adnan."

"I can't stop, Father Frank," David said as he started convulsing. "Father Frank, where am I? Mom, Dad, what are you doing? Why won't you wake up?" David's eyes were still glazed over, and his arms reached out in front of him, searching.

Frank's hands felt like they were burning with cold, and he had to break contact to rub them. He then reached out again and grasped David, shaking him. "David, look at me. Look at me David! Listen to me." He spotted a dark form around David's torso, but when David moved forward, the form stayed in place, as though detached and out of energy.

David's eyes closed, and his body went still. When he opened his eyes, he looked at Frank. "You will die." He collapsed and fell right on Frank, who tried to brace him. As the pair crossed the line of candles, the flames flashed and then went out.

Claudia and Jimmie rushed forward to help Frank keep David from hitting the floor. They put David back onto the bed, and Claudia secured his bonds. She reached into her bag, pulled out her stethoscope, and checked his pulse and breathing. "He's out cold," she said.

Frank leaned over David and looked down at him.

"What the hell was that about?" Jimmie said. "I've never seen readings like that before."

"Quiet," Claudia scolded. She leaned over to take David's pulse, and his eyes snapped open, causing her to jump back. Frank stood beside her and looked down at him.

"Father? Father Frank?" David sounded confused. "When did you get here?"

Frank stepped back, looking first at Claudia and then at David, and stumbled.

"Frank?" Claudia came up beside him.

He felt dizzy, and then, he felt nothing.

✦ ✦ ✦

"Frank?"

He woke in Claudia's office to the sound of her voice. He was lying on the couch. He tried to sit up and grabbed his head.

"Take it easy," Claudia said. She handed him two pills and a glass of water. "Take these."

Frank sat up, took the pills, and drank the water. "Lot of good I did."

"You did fine," said Jimmie, who sat in the chair across from the couch. "I got some good readings. I've never seen them spike so high, only during a suicide attempt."

"David?" Frank asked as he rubbed his temples, trying to reduce the pain in his head.

"He's fine right now," Jimmie said.

"I'm glad it benefited one of us," Frank said, still massaging his temples.

Claudia sat on the couch beside him. "Whatever you did seemed to calm him and bring him back to the present. He started talking. He's even eating. But he's severely depressed. We've still got him on suicide watch."

"Truth is, I don't know what I did," Frank said, putting his hands over his eyes. "I overreacted and got excited and locked my legs. Blood rushed to my head. That's all."

Claudia put her hands on Frank's and pulled them down. She looked at him. "When Adnan fights the shadows, he is often drained like this."

"It's nothing. I'm fine," Frank said. "My head aches, and I feel a little light in the stomach, but I'm okay."

"You've been out for five hours," Claudia said.

"That must be why I'm hungry."

"Why don't we get something to eat?" Jimmie said. "Adnan's going to want to hear about this." He stood and put on his sport coat.

"He'll probably be upset," Frank said. "I'm pretty sure he mentioned in his instructions that I was not to do more than observe."

"And yet you've taken on these things twice in the same week," Jimmie said.

"I guess you really are a warrior," Claudia said. She moved to her desk, shut down her computer, and put on her jacket.

Frank let Jimmie help him off the couch and then stood on his own while Claudia watched carefully.

"I'm fine," Frank said. "Really."

Claudia pinched her lips together tightly. "I'll drive."

Chapter 6

The Last Supper

The boys were throwing rocks at the dog they had trapped between a tall fence and a wall in the alley. The dog cried out from where it sat against the concrete wall. A mean dog would have growled; a wild dog would have charged. This dog, its spirit broken from a number of beatings, cowed as the boys picked on it.

Young Frank Keller turned the corner. He'd heard a whimpering sound from the street where he was walking home from school on a Wednesday afternoon with his older sister Dee Dee, and instinct had told him to investigate.

Dee Dee stood at the entrance to the alley with her hands on her hips. "Frankie, what are you doing? No missions today, please."

When Frank walked a few steps into the alley, he spotted short, stocky Johnny Witherson, whose brown hair was never combed, and tall, lanky Tad Garrison. Finally, the leader of the trio of trouble, Randel Krage, bigger than all the other boys, stood closest to the dog.

"Frankie, it's Randel. Don't go back there," Dee Dee pleaded, but Frank gave a scolding look.

"Don't call me Frankie. I'm twelve years old now." Frank walked out to where he was visible to the other three boys.

"Look," Randel said, "it's the little prayer boy. What do you want, Frankie Keller?" Randel held a large rock in his right hand and waved it menacingly.

"Oh, it's just you guys," Frank said. "I usually don't see you out of school this early. Did they cancel detention today?"

"Very funny, Frankie," Randel said. "Aren't you supposed to be in church or something, little prayer boy?"

"Little prayer boy?" Johnny Witherson said.

"That's what he is," Randel said. "He's always praying at lunch."

"Let's just forget about him," Johnny said. "Besides, his sister is with him, and she can get us into a lot of trouble."

Frank looked upon the white and black boxer sitting against the wall, panting, its face bloodied. Overwhelmed with compassion for the creature, he realized why he felt compelled to turn into the alley.

"Watch this," Randel said. "I bet your praying can't stop this." Randel turned back to the dog and threw the large rock, but it was too big for him to aim, and it missed.

"Stop it!" Frank said as he ran between the dog and the other boys.

Randel backed away and looked at the dog, who lay down as though ready to die. Then he stared at Frank and raised another stone. He tossed it up and down in his hand.

Frank kept his eyes on the boys, all three of them. He was bigger than Johnny and faster than Tad, but Randel was two years older than him. Held back twice, Randel was still in the seventh grade but should have been in high school.

Randel fumbled his toss, and the rock he held fell to the ground. He bent down and picked up another rock, a large one. "There's only one of you and three of us. What you gonna do, Frankie? Go cry to your mommy?"

"No. But I will tell Tad's mom and Johnny's mom when we see them this Sunday ... They go to church too, or didn't they tell you?"

The remark was enough to cause Johnny and Tad to flee, but Randel stood his ground. "You're lucky your sister is here," Randel said, "or you'd be toast."

Frank moved forward quickly and raised his hand, and before Randel could grasp what was happening, Frank had taken the rock from him and stood before him. Randel put his hands in front of him in a defensive posture and backed away. Frank dropped the rock.

"You'll get yours," Randel threatened and ran away.

"Have you gone nuts?" Dee Dee said, walking up beside him. "You could have gotten us both beat up."

"I wasn't afraid," Frank said. He looked at his sister, who raised her eyebrows.

"Come on, Frankie … I mean, Frank," Dee Dee said. "Don't worry about them. Let's get home … What are you doing?"

Frank had turned and moved toward the dog. As he approached, the animal cowered, placing its paw above its head. "Don't worry, boy. I won't hurt you." He lowered himself enough to wrap his arms around the dog.

"Mom's not going to like it."

✦   ✦   ✦

Two weeks later, young Frank Keller stood in the dark outside his house in his backyard, staring at the wooden cross he'd hammered into the ground. Tears fell from his eyes.

"I don't understand. I thought God put me there to save the dog. It still died."

"It's okay," Frank's mom said as she put her arm around him. "He's in a better place now."

"He didn't even live two weeks; it's not fair," Frank said.

"Come, Frankie," his mom said. "You need to get to bed tonight. We have church in the morning, and you need your rest."

Frank turned and looked into his mom's compassionate brown eyes. "All the kids at school tell me I'm going to grow up to be a preacher because I pray so much."

"I would be very proud of you."

"I don't want to be a preacher. I want to fight injustice. I'm going to be a policeman or a soldier."

"That's certainly up to you," his mother said. "Let's get you to bed."

◆　　◆　　◆

Frank sat back in his chair across the table from Adnan. "At least that's how I remember the story." He was at the Kozy Tavern with Adnan, Claudia, Kanuik, and Jimmie. They'd just finished eating a meal of pasta and garlic bread Chic had prepared for them, and Frank had told them the story of when he was a kid and saved a dog from certain peril.

"That's a great story," Claudia said. "A classic bully story that shows the character of who you became. Did you continue to interact with those boys?"

"Randel got hauled away to foster care, and none of us ever saw him again. Johnny moved, and Tad and I became good friends."

"It was not for you to decide the fate of the dog that day, but the fate of your own soul," Adnan said. "This is what I believe. It was on that day that you were put on a path that led you here. If you want some consolation, consider that the dog was about to suffer a cruel death. You stopped that. Although it did not live long, it lived without fear and pain for the last days of its life. And here you are, all these years later, still fighting injustice."

"I suppose so," Frank said.

"Did you give the dog a name?" Claudia asked.

"Jules," Frank said, "after my favorite author, Jules Verne."

"Can I get you anything else?" Chic asked as he approached the table.

Frank pushed his plate forward. "No, thank you. I'm stuffed."

"I really think you missed your calling," Adnan said, nodding at Chic. "You should have been a master chef instead of hiding out in this bar."

"And then who'd be here to take care of you hobos?" Chic said.

"He has a point," Frank said. "That really is some good cooking."

"Why, thank you, Frank," Chic said. "I can trust your opinion."

He grinned at Adnan as he said this, picked up Frank's plate, and walked away.

"Now," Adnan said, "let's talk about what happened this afternoon."

"Frank thinks he just overreacted," Jimmie said. "But the readings were real. The energy was there, and more than that, I confirmed what we've always suspected: there is a source portal. The energy stayed active at David's house when Frank made contact. This could mean that the portal is not always in the same place as the target."

"That's why we have trouble finding it sometimes," Adnan said, nodding to Kanuik, who remained silent.

"The readings at both places went higher than we've ever experienced before," Jimmie said. "And there was movement within David's house."

"Movement?" Adnan said.

"Yes, from his bedroom," Jimmie said. "I wish I had more to go on, but I haven't heard from Mike or Russ since what happened at David's house. They're really freaked out."

"What does this mean?" Frank asked. He turned to Claudia. "Do you know what they are talking about?"

Claudia shrugged her shoulders.

"What this means, Frank," Adnan said, "is that you have not only helped David, but you have also learned to see into their world as it is. You have learned to see what others can't, what is hiding in the shadows. They were probably testing you."

"The shadows were testing me?" Frank said.

"David wasn't in that room, not consciously at the time you first approached him," Adnan said. "That is why he didn't recognize you until later. He was somewhere else with the shadows."

"They were influencing his moments?" Frank said.

"Now you are catching on," Adnan said. "What you did was dangerous. You reached out and touched him without a spiritual partner. Claudia and Jimmie, they don't have the complete faith and tools to fight; they are vulnerable. The shadow could have easily dragged you out of your reality. When that happens, it's hard if not impossible to get back without the intervention of another, which is why the church has rules."

"His power is strong," Kanuik said. "I'm glad you remembered the candles."

"It's what we were told," Adnan said.

"Told about what?" Frank asked.

Adnan glanced at Kanuik, who nodded. "We have allies that claim there are those among us who are touched by divine intervention," Adnan said. "They call it being touched by an angel. The shadows cannot influence these people and are intimidated by them."

"Adnan believes you are one of these people," Kanuik stated. "Are you?"

"I don't know," Frank said.

"The shadows reacted when you went to see David," Kanuik said. "They felt your power."

"If Bishop Tafoya found out what happened, he'd scold all of us," Adnan said.

"But you're not going to tell him?" Frank said.

"We need to pick our moments. Clearly, there was a need for intervention. You helped David come back to the present. I am impressed. It can take years to teach someone what you have mastered in days."

"I don't feel like I did much. What he said worries me," Frank said. "He said I would die."

"The shadows are deceivers, just like you've read in the Bible," Adnan said. "But don't take the warning lightly. They will try to take down anyone that combats them. Just look at the condition of the church."

"Maybe I should have waited," Frank said. "He wasn't a threat to anyone."

"You did fine," Adnan said. "In fact, you did exactly what I needed you to do. You confirmed the shadows have latched onto David. They are still influencing his moments. That's exactly the condition I've been seeking."

"I still don't understand what you are talking about," Frank said. "What condition?"

"You confirmed that we have them in a place," Jimmie said, "a defined place, and we know they are there."

"See," Adnan said, "most of the time we are searching for them, and they show up at random. We can guess the conditions where evil preys, but not always the place. Therefore, our response is always reactive."

"How can they be in a place but not there?" Claudia said.

"That's why it's so hard to conceive," Adnan said. "When they intervene, it's not in a place we can go to. It's not a parallel dimension that exists. It's a conflicting moment in our own time, and as they increase their influence over these moments, they try to gather more, which allows them to establish a foothold in their host's reality."

"Now you've lost me," Claudia said. "I was all with you in the description of energy and the theory of a parallel dimension where they come from to cross over into our time frame, but ..."

"It's a theory," Adnan said. "Imagine you physically exist, but you are in a dreamlike state while your true actions are manipulated by something else. The shadows may be able to expand and contract time just like we can change the flow of water to be faster or slower through a faucet."

Claudia held up her hands, politely stood, and headed toward the restroom without letting him finish.

"We can't go to where they come from?" Frank asked.

"No one has ever made it through," Adnan said.

"But you think we need to change that," Frank said.

"Here, let me demonstrate." Adnan stood and walked to the bar. Jimmie and Frank followed him while Kanuik seemed content at the table.

Adnan reached behind the bar and started pulling out shot glasses until thirteen of them were lined up on the bar.

"Hey," Chic said, raising an eyebrow.

"Sorry," Adnan said. "Please, fill a dozen of these with what you have on tap and one more with tomato juice."

Frank watched as Chic looked around the bar. There was no one there except the four men and Claudia, who had returned from the restroom. He pulled out the hose connected to the beer keg and filled twelve of the glasses with beer and then popped open a can of tomato juice and filled the final glass.

Kanuik and Claudia came over from the table to watch the demonstration.

"Okay," Adnan said. "Imagine each of these glasses represents a moment in time, linear and flowing. But as you can see, only the one is different." He grabbed the one full of tomato juice. "Imagine evil as an army that was once roaming free, upright and among men. At some point, they were banned to only this moment, the thirteenth month. Still, as a physical entity, the evil had form, like this glass of juice. It was cohesive."

Adnan took the last glass and poured it out on the counter, making a stream in front of the other twelve, as Chic shook his head at the mess he was making. "Something happened, as Bishop Tafoya told you. There are many interpretations, from the coming of Christ to other stories not included in the Bible. Whatever took place, evil lost its physical presence and was dispersed, but the energy remained, spread out, less cohesive, less solid. The thirteenth month no longer exists; it's spread out, whereas the others are still intact, you see. The force is still there, but not as powerful. It comes and goes but cannot recapture its original state without something physical to attach itself to."

"That must be why the church has been involved so many times in adjusting the calendar," Jimmie said. "Every time evil gains or loses ground in the time continuum, they have to keep adjusting because time isn't linear with these interventions."

"Exactly," Adnan said. "Thank you, Jimmie. Imagine being part of this intelligent energy, suspended in time. You can see into the plane of the physical world but can't wholly exist."

"Kind of like a purgatory," Frank said.

Adnan smiled and nodded. "Exactly the same concept." He reached over to Chic and grabbed the towel that hung across Chic's shoulder. With the edge of the towel, he slowly went down the counter soaking up all the tomato juice until the towel was saturated, and none was left on the bar. He carefully wrung it out over the empty glass, filling it back up.

"This is the goal of that evil—to become whole again," Adnan said, picking up the glass. "But that's not all. Now it's more dangerous than ever." Adnan took the glass and started pouring a small amount of the tomato juice into each beer. "It's no longer confined to a single month; it's contaminating the other months and increasing its presence—to dominate."

Frank watched as the red slowly permeated the liquid in each glass, spreading out, changing the appearance. "Why now?"

"They've never stopped trying," Adnan said. "It's just that the time is right. Complacency is at an all-time high, as is apathy. There is war on religion," Adnan said. "Even if you don't believe in the world's religions, most of them have a strong moral code. Without such a code, humanity lacks direction."

"You think the shadows are gaining ground?" Frank said.

"The proof is all around us," Adnan said.

"How do you stop it?" Chic asked.

Adnan looked at each of them and stopped at Frank. He picked up the glass of tomato juice and drank what remained, causing Chic to shake his head. Chic started removing the other glasses from the counter and pouring the contents down the drain.

Adnan put the glass down on the bar. "We can keep doing what we are doing and watch as humankind slips further into darkness. Or we can go after it at the source," he said.

As Chick picked up the last two glasses, Frank noticed that they were now discolored.

Adnan stood. "If you'll pardon me." He headed to the bathroom. Kanuik and Claudia went back to the table.

Jimmie tapped on the bar. Chic poured him a shot, and he drank it down. "That's some deep philosophical sh"—he stopped short and looked at Frank—"shtuff." Jimmie put a twenty-dollar bill on the bar and headed toward the bathroom too, leaving Frank by himself at the bar.

Frank looked in the mirror. In the background he watched as Claudia and Kanuik sat at their usual table. Kanuik had lit his pipe again. Adnan joined them. They didn't talk but seemed content just to sit as a group.

"Chic," Frank said, "what was that drink you brought us the other night, the warm one?"

"It was a mixture of hot tea, honey, and rum," Chic said.

"Please bring me four," Frank said. He headed to the table, where the group sat in silence. He knew everything they'd done had led up to this moment. He suspected they had recruited him for reasons beyond the ones they'd already given him, and it was time to find out why. He sat down at the table. Kanuik nodded, and Claudia smiled. Adnan sat with his eyes closed.

"Why are you working with the church, Adnan?" he asked. "You don't seem like someone who appreciates being held back by protocol."

"There is no protocol in this. We win, or we lose," Adnan said. He opened his eyes and looked at Frank.

"Is it really that simple?" Frank said.

"I needed the resources," Adnan said. "I've been fighting this battle for a long time. They provide funding and soldiers. You have just started, but I think we both recognize that things are not going well. We are losing ground."

"What's your plan?" Frank said. "I want in."

"I imagined so," Adnan said. "There's only one problem. Bishop Tafoya does not agree with the method. He and the church authorities want us to keep waiting."

"Waiting for what?" Frank asked.

"An intervention from God," Adnan said, pointing a finger to the ceiling of the tavern.

"But you don't believe it's coming," Frank said.

Frank caught the exchange of glances between Adnan, Kanuik, and Claudia. He didn't know what to make of it, but he felt there was something they weren't telling him.

"I think if God were going to intervene, He would have done so already," Adnan said. "I believe that He is waiting for us to make the right decisions."

Frank recognized his own philosophy in Adnan's words and started to understand why the group had picked him.

"We have no room for insecurity or doubt," Adnan said. "I need to know that you are in and that you will support us without hesitation."

Jimmie came out of the bathroom and walked over to the table just as Adnan finished his sentence. He stood between Claudia and Frank's chairs.

"Where do we start?"

"We meet at the hospital tomorrow," Adnan said.

◆　　　◆　　　◆

"Thank you for the ride," Frank said as Claudia pulled into a parking space in front of his apartment building.

"It's the least I can do," Claudia said, "after dragging you around all day. Besides, I haven't had anyone to open up to in a long time other than Adnan and Kanuik. It's nice having a fresh perspective."

"I didn't know I was such a great conversationalist," Frank said.

"Well, compared to the first night we met, you sure seem to be more comfortable," Claudia said.

"I guess I am," Frank said. "I suppose it's because I've wanted to help more for so long. That's why I've pushed myself so hard in everything I've done."

"That's why your parish is so successful," Claudia said.

"I suppose so," Frank said. "I think the people around here have had it so bad that they are just looking for something to believe in, a source of inspiration. Me too." He smiled at Claudia.

"The way Adnan speaks, I really feel what we are doing can make a difference."

"I certainly hope so," Claudia said.

Frank reached for the door handle and turned to say good-bye, but Claudia was getting out of the car.

"Hold on, I have something for you," she said.

Frank waited.

Claudia pulled out two gift bags from her backseat and brought them around to the passenger side. As Frank opened his door, she said, "Come on, I'll walk you up to your apartment."

Frank tried to make as little noise as possible as he opened the outside door to his apartment building. Then he quietly went up the stairs to the second floor and down the hall, with Claudia following behind. He had just started to open the door when his neighbor's door opened, and Ms. Able's head peeked out.

Ms. Able glanced back and forth from Frank to Claudia and then back to Frank. "Father Frank," she said. "I was wondering where you've been. I haven't seen you in the morning lately."

"Yes," Frank said, clearing his throat. "I've had a new assignment. This is Dr. Claudia Walden. She is a psychiatrist, and we are working together with troubled youth."

With her body only half out of her own doorway, Ms. Able didn't move when Claudia held out her hand to greet her.

"Well, I hope to see you back in church soon," Ms. Able said. She continued watching until Claudia and Frank were inside.

Claudia went in and sat on the couch and put the gift bags on the coffee table.

Frank closed the door behind him and looked around for his cat but couldn't see her. He hung up his jacket and went to the couch. "That could have gone better," he said.

"I thought you gave an excellent explanation," Claudia said. "Here, this one's for you," she said, handing him one of the bags as he sat down. "And this one is for your father."

"My father?"

"Why, yes," Claudia said. "I know how hard it must be for him to be in that place. This is a little something to add some ambience to his room."

Frank held the bag for his father as she reached into it and pulled out a decorative wind chime with angels on it.

"Wind chimes? Why wind chimes? Is it because of the list?"

Claudia looked at him, puzzled.

"You know, the list?" Frank said again.

"I don't know what you are talking about," Claudia said. "I just saw these in the hospital gift shop, and they were really nice compared to some of the other gifts. I'm sorry. Is there something wrong with them?"

"Absolutely not," Frank said as she lowered them back into the bag. "I think they're wonderful, and he'll enjoy them. Now what's this other one for me?" He peeked in the bag and laughed as he spotted a small bag of catnip.

"Well," Claudia said, "it's not exactly for you. Now, where is Rosie? You didn't get rid of her already?"

"No," Frank said. "But if she's not out on the couch, she's probably hiding under the bed. I think she doesn't know who has come through the door, so she waits until it quiets down before she comes out."

"Oh," Claudia said. "Now what is this about a list?"

Frank went to his kitchen and pulled the list Bishop Tafoya had given him from a drawer. As he walked back to the living room, he said, "When I was told of this mission by the bishop, he gave me this list." He unfolded the paper and handed it to her. "Wind chimes are one of the items on the list."

Claudia studied the list. "Now that makes me wonder," she said. "Kanuik gave me a set of wind chimes, two sets, actually, one for my office and one for my house. He said they were blessed by a Native American holy man, and he wanted me to have them as a gift."

"I'm sure it was to protect you," Frank said.

"Does this also answer the question of why Adnan and Kanuik keep giving me Dead Sea salts for every holiday? I just thought they were kind of strange," she said, laughing.

"Adnan explained why I needed most of the items on the list," Frank said. "The sea salts are used to purify the body. I've heard before that salt repels evil spirits, but the church has no credible information on this. My real curiosity has been about where the list came from."

"I thought you said Bishop Tafoya gave it to you," Claudia said.

"Yes, he did," Frank said. "But that is not his handwriting, or his assistant's."

"And it's not Adnan's," Claudia said. "A mystery."

"I'm not going to make too much of it," Frank said. "Adnan said there were other groups out there fighting the same fight, so perhaps the list is something passed around between the groups."

"Well," Claudia said, "I really should get going; it's been a long day for both of us. Do you need a ride to the hospital tomorrow?"

"No," Frank said. "I want to check in with Father Mark tomorrow. I'll meet you at the hospital. Let me walk you to your car."

"You sure you want to do that?" Claudia said.

"Why not?"

"I saw the look on your face when Ms. Able peeked out. A priest with a beautiful woman coming to his apartment ..." She smiled. "Don't worry," she said, patting her purse where she kept her pistol. "I can take care of myself. See you tomorrow."

Right after Claudia left, Rosie came out meowing. Frank fed her, watched her roll around in the catnip, and was pleased when she rolled up on the side of the bed and purred him to sleep again.

◆　　◆　　◆

The next morning, he woke to a knock on his door. He went to open it and found Father Mark there.

"Didn't you get my message?" Father Mark asked. "I tried to call you all night." Father Mark looked around the apartment, as if expecting to find something amiss.

"I assure you everything is fine. I'm sorry. I didn't get your message." Frank walked over to his coat, where he'd left his cell phone, and pulled it out of the pocket. It was completely dead. "Hmm, that's funny." He held it up to his nose, and it smelled burned. "That's odd. It's not even that old." Then he remembered his watch and how it had stopped working after the incident in the alley. "Energy," he said as he walked over and placed it on his kitchen counter.

"What's that?" Father Mark asked.

"Nothing," Frank said. "It appears my cell phone is dead. Now what is it you were trying to call me about?"

"The Jensons," Father Mark said. "The funeral is today. I thought you might want to do it."

"Oh my," Frank said. "Yes, give me a minute to get dressed." He ran into his bathroom and looked in the mirror. He hadn't showered or shaved for several days and looked the worse for it. "How long do we have?" he called out to Father Mark.

"A couple of hours. Go ahead," Mark said as though reading his mind. "I can't take you there looking like you do anyway."

After he showered, Frank let Mark drive him to the church, and he went into the back room to prepare while Mark took on the task of greeting everyone as they were seated. When Frank was ready, he went to the door and looked out at the small group of people waiting. Mark walked over to him.

"No contact from the family?" Frank asked.

"No one contacted the funeral home or the church," Mark said. "It seems Mr. Jenson was an only child. His wife … well, she might have family somewhere, but we didn't know how to get in touch with anyone."

As Frank reflected on this, he looked out at the faces before him: probably some coworkers, school friends, and neighbors, as well as members of the church who knew the family. But the front row, where immediately family usually sat, was empty on both sides. Even David was not able to attend.

"How did it come to this?" Frank asked.

"What's that?" Mark asked.

"Nothing," Frank said. "Let's get started." Frank walked out and began the ceremony, trying to pay homage to the Jensons, who were once members of his parish. He gave the eulogy that he'd written out moments before the service. Much of it was the standard wording the church taught, words about the triumph of good and how the deceased would be in a better place, and how no one could explain why such a tragedy had taken place, but they needn't lose hope. That was where he felt himself slipping because he knew the truth.

There was an explanation for David's actions. He suddenly felt the need to warn his sister; he felt the need to warn the congregation of people before him. But what would he tell them? Could he really tell them about the shadows? About how the decisions they made rippled through time, and not just the current moments? How the ripples affected future moments too? That one negative action, one negative feeling or thought, could impact many and open the doorway to an evil force they couldn't see? Instead, Frank turned to his scripture and read several passages before ending the service.

After the service and a small reception, Frank went to the hospital so that he could see David. He waited at the security desk for Claudia. He spotted her coming down the hall toward him, a serious look on her face. She signed him in, and the security guard gave him a badge.

"I'm glad you finally made it; the others have been here for hours," Claudia said.

"I'm sorry," Frank said. "David's family's funeral was today, and I forgot about it. With all that has been going on, I haven't been keeping track of the days. I thought it best that I do the ceremony instead of Father Mark."

"Of course," Claudia said. "It's only right since you were the one they reached out to for help. You should have been the one to lay them to rest."

"Yes, they reached out to me," Frank said. "Did I fail them?"

"You didn't know what you were up against," Claudia said. "We can all blame ourselves for what is wrong if we know and don't take action to correct it. But that is not you, Frank." Claudia stopped in the hallway. "I'm sorry. Are you sure you want to go through with this today?"

"I am sure of it, Claudia," Frank said. "More than I'd care to be. It's time for something to change."

"Then let's go. The others are waiting in my office."

Frank walked into Claudia's office to find Adnan and Jimmie seated on the couch and Kanuik standing against the wall to the left of them. Claudia went to her desk.

"Frank had the funeral today for David's family," Claudia said before sitting down.

Frank knew she was trying to cover for his being late. He knew that what they were about to do was important, and they were all on edge about it. His being late only made it worse.

"Sorry to hear," Jimmie said. He reached out his hand to Frank.

"Thank you," Frank said.

"If you need some time …" Adnan said.

Frank shook his head. "No, we need to stick with the plan." He sat in the chair across from the couch. "If anything, what I did today only solidified the need for what we are about to do. We need a win."

"Yes, well," Adnan said, "now that we are all together, I think it's important we cover the details of what we are going to do here tonight. Jimmie, I'll let you start."

Jimmie nodded. "Although Adnan and I disagree on the origin and purpose of these entities, we do agree there is an opening they come through to cause their chaos, a portal if you will," Jimmie said. "We know there is one at the house, and with what happened the other day with Frank, we think there is one by David."

"This is the portal or doorway that you've said is the reason the church won't let anyone work alone?" Frank said.

"Yes," Adnan said. "Our problem up to this point has been identifying it in a timely manner and using it to our advantage. We've known it has to be close to the event that is happening, but we also know the shadows can latch onto people, and a portal is not always present. They might be able to open a portal through some means we don't understand. It may be caused by behavior in the individual they latch onto. Something triggers the opening."

"With the readings I've been taking," Jimmie continued, "I believe I can pinpoint its location during an episode—measure its size and diameter so we know what can fit through it."

"And do what then?" Frank said.

Jimmie looked at Adnan and then back at Frank. "No one has told you what we were planning?"

Adnan shifted forward in his seat and gestured with his hands. "Imagine this as a doorway where they come in, from wherever it is they come from. All around the world, there are thousands of occurrences just like it. Shutting one door would do us no good; the energy would just enter somewhere else, in another location, another time where we are not ready."

Jimmie nodded in agreement.

"Consider what would happen if you had a sealed structure." Adnan made a ball with his hands. "You could get out, but no one could get in, unless someone used your own exit as a way to penetrate."

Frank said nothing.

"I am going to send an energy wave through that portal," Jimmie said. "You see, these creatures, whatever they are, are not solid like we are, and they seem to be able to get through a small opening. We are going to send a surge at it and make it wider."

"Wider for what?" Frank asked.

Claudia sat back in her chair and folded her arms. Kanuik, who'd started pacing across the small room, stopped and looked at Adnan.

"Then we send in a bomb," Adnan said. "Well, not a bomb in the literal sense."

"Tell him," Kanuik said.

Frank looked up at Kanuik and then at Adnan. "Tell me what?"

"Remember the glasses at the bar?" Adnan said.

Frank nodded.

"I'm going to reverse the effect. Instead of allowing the evil to flow through, I'm going to send a force of good to the other side. I'm going through the portal."

"You intend to reverse the effect and contaminate their world?" Frank asked.

"Yes," Adnan said. "I was worried you wouldn't understand."

"Uh," Jimmie said, "this is all great science stuff and all, but even if you make it through, how would you make it back?"

"I don't plan on coming back."

Adnan's revelation was met with silence.

◆　　◆　　◆

Frank met Chic at the security desk of the psychiatric ward of the hospital. Chic had several sacks with him.

"Is everything okay?" Chic said. "You look a little pale."

"Yes," Frank said. "It's just that we are working late here tonight, and Adnan insisted on having your ravioli. Sorry you had to travel here."

"It's not the first time," Chic said.

Frank took out his wallet and pulled out some cash.

"Put that away, Frank," Chic said. "It's on the house."

Frank looked at Chic as he handed him the bags. "Chic, I don't understand. How do you keep your place open? There's hardly ever anyone in there, and then you do stuff like this."

Chic smiled and shifted the unlit cigar in his mouth. "Do you know how long the lottery has been going on in this state?"

"Can't say that I do," Frank said.

"But you do know that not every winner comes forward in the public eye." Chic's eyes lit up. "God provides for those in need. Now I give back. I only run the Kozy Tavern because I enjoy it. It's my life. Oh, but please do return the silverware."

Jimmie came to help Frank take the food back to Claudia's office, and they said good night to Chic. When they returned to the office, Claudia was by herself.

"Adnan and Kanuik went to get drinks from the waiting area," Claudia said. "Here," she continued, moving stuff off her desk, "set Adnan's plate here."

A solemn feeling came over Frank as he set out the trays of food and laid out the forks and paper plates. He couldn't help feeling he was about to see Adnan eat his last meal. As he set the silverware out, Claudia touched his arm.

"You need to talk to him. This plan is foolish," Claudia said. "He's getting old. He sees that his time to contribute is about over, and this is his final strike, but it could kill him."

Frank moved her hand away from his arm so that he could keep setting up. Finally, he looked up at Claudia. "Even if I wanted to, I don't think I could stop him." He knew these words weren't what she wanted to hear, but the past week had led him to trust Adnan. He realized it was more than that too; he thought about his sister and his nephew Connor, and he drew parallels to David. Adnan was right: the current method they were using to fight the evil was obsolete; they needed a new strategy to win the war.

"You think he's right," Claudia said, "don't you?"

"I think our options are becoming limited," Frank said. "This might be the only way."

Claudia touched his hand, holding it still next to the plate he was fixing. "I sense there's something else you're not telling me," she said.

Feeling the warmth on his skin, Frank didn't move her hand away this time. His skin had been cold, and her touch felt good.

"You can't be serious."

"What are you talking about?" Frank said.

"You're thinking of going with him," Claudia said.

"The thought had occurred to me that he might need some help," Frank said. He remembered the conversation at the tavern about people who were touched by angels. If he was one such person, then he would have the ability to fight.

"It's just the emotion talking," Claudia said. "You're upset because

122

of the funeral today. You are lacking rest, and you are not thinking rationally. Please, tell me you won't do anything rash."

"Don't worry. I'll be fine," Frank said. "I don't have the experience I need to fight them yet."

The door to the office opened, and Adnan and Kanuik came in with several cans of soda. "We weren't sure what you'd like," Kanuik said as he put eight cans on Claudia's desk.

The group gathered around Claudia's desk in a circle and held hands. "Frank," Adnan said, "would you lead us in a blessing?"

Frank closed his eyes, focused his attention on the moment before him, and prayed. "Dear Father, we ask for your blessing on this day. Guide those who follow your path of righteousness in this fight against injustice. Bless this food to nourish and strengthen us, and bless the hands from which it came." He felt Claudia squeeze his hand. Adnan held the other hand; his grasp was not as strong, and Frank sensed he was troubled.

After grace, they sat and ate, and Frank kept a close eye on Adnan.

"This is really good food," Jimmie said.

Other than some brief remarks in agreement with Jimmie's point, the conversation was kept to a minimum. There was none of the dispensing of wisdom or humor that Frank had come to love from the group. No stories or history from any of the members. No philosophical discussions or disagreements. Only quiet chewing. He wished they were at the Kozy Tavern.

When he was finished eating, Jimmie left the room to go set up his equipment and came back a few minutes later. "The room is ready."

Adnan pushed his paper plate forward. "Thank you, Claudia, for allowing us the privilege of dining in your office. If everyone is quite through, I think it's time for us to get on with our business."

"I'll make sure there are no other doctors in the area," Claudia said. "It's late enough that there shouldn't be. I'll meet you at David's room."

"I better go with her," Jimmie said.

Adnan stood with effort and walked toward the door, the use of his cane more pronounced than before, Frank thought as he watched him.

"Is there something you want to say, Frank?" asked Adnan.

"I was just admiring your cane," Frank said, trying to disguise his observation that Adnan seemed weak.

"Yes," Adnan said, handing the cane to Frank, who took it and examined it. "A handcrafted treasure."

"I can see that," Frank said. He handed the cane back to Adnan.

"That's not what you wanted to talk about," Adnan said.

"I've seen it," Frank said. "The shadow that is somehow trapped within you."

"Kanuik did not tell you the entire story of our time overseas," Adnan said. "We've known the shadows emerge from a doorway between their world and ours for some time now. Jimmie is helping us better understand that. If the portal they come from closes, either they are trapped in the host, or they can be dissipated. We don't know if they truly die.

"The last time we attempted to cross through to their world, my partner died in the attempt, but the portal closed when he died, leaving this thing I now have with me outside the portal, on our side. I decided I could use it to help me and captured it. You see, it's attracted to its kind, so it acts as a way for me to find them."

"How do you control it?" Frank said.

"I am stronger than it is," Adnan said. "I let it feed enough off of our experiences to keep it around, but tame. I am hoping to hitch a ride with it back to where it came from when the time is right."

"Seems like a dangerous relationship," Frank said.

He followed Adnan out of Dr. Walden's office, and with Kanuik coming last, the three men made their way to David's room.

Claudia was waiting by the door. "We've stopped sedating David, just like you requested."

Frank looked at Adnan, who smiled as he entered the room. Kanuik didn't speak as he entered, maintaining his usual stern look.

Frank put his hand out to let Claudia proceed in front of him and then checked in both directions to see whether anyone had noticed them before he entered and closed the door.

Inside, David sat on his bed watching the doorway as the group shuffled into his room. Jimmie was there, adjusting his equipment. He had two tripods with electronic monitors and antennae on either side of the room, facing David's bed.

David's face lit up when he saw Frank. "Hi, Father Frank," he said. "What are all these people doing here?"

"Don't worry, David," Claudia said. She took out her blood pressure monitor and her stethoscope. "These are some friends of ours, and they are here to help you."

"I don't want to think about what happened," David said. He started moving around on his bed. "I don't want to remember."

"Take it easy, David," Frank said, approaching him. He looked at Jimmie, who was watching the monitors attached to his equipment.

Jimmie shook his head. "It's clear," he said. "I have no reading from David."

There were no chairs in the room where David was being kept, only a small bench attached to the wall to the right of the door. Jimmie had set up there, leaving the rest of the group with no choice but to stand.

"These people are just here to help you," Frank said. As he approached David, memories from their last encounter flashed before him. He hesitated to reach out to David, worried that whatever force had caused him to black out might still be there.

Frank looked at Adnan, who nodded and gestured with his hand toward David. "Go ahead, Frank," Adnan said. "I need you to engage our young friend here."

"Do you mind if I talk to you, David?" Frank said, still being cautious as he approached.

David fidgeted in his restraints. "Can you get the doctor here to loosen these?" David asked, putting his chin down and scratching it. "I promise I won't try to hurt myself. I just want to move my arms."

125

"Claudia?" Frank looked at her.

"I don't think that's a good idea," Claudia said.

"Please, Doctor," Adnan said. "We need all the help we can get here." He gave Jimmie a questioning look.

"I've got nothing, not even a blip," Jimmie said.

Claudia undid David's straps as Frank got closer and put himself in a position to restrain David if he lashed out in any way.

"Is that better?" Frank asked as David moved his left hand and rubbed his right arm. The teen nodded.

Claudia stepped back as Frank moved closer to David. David moved over and made enough room for Frank to sit on the bed.

Frank sat and asked, "David, do you remember what we spoke about the other day and what happened? Do you remember what you said to me?"

"I don't want to eat, Father Frank," David said. "They keep trying to make me eat. But I know it doesn't matter whether or not I do. They think I'm a killer. My life is over. I'm going to jail. No one believes me. But I didn't do it."

"Why do you think you are going to jail, David?" Frank said. "Why won't you eat?"

"I don't want to think about it," David said. "I don't want to eat. I just want to die. Why won't they let me die?" David started crying. He looked around the room.

"We aren't getting a thing," Adnan said. "You need to press him, Frank. We need to make some progress."

"David," Frank said, getting David to look at him instead of Adnan. "We had the service today for your family, David. I'm sure they are resting in a better place."

David didn't respond but started humming and closed his eyes.

"He's trying to put himself somewhere else," Claudia said. "He's done this a few times since he's been here."

"Father Frank," David said, stopping his humming and looking up at him. "I didn't do anything with my family this past summer. Not one thing. I didn't want to because they all started criticizing me.

But I would do something with them now." David began rocking back and forth, tears streaming down his face.

Adnan started pacing back and forth between Jimmie's equipment and David's bedside. "Why isn't this working? Could we have been wrong?" he said.

"I don't know," Jimmie said. "I just don't know. The readings the other day were off the chart."

"David," Adnan said loudly, causing both David and Frank to jump. "Look at me, David. Do you remember me?" Adnan walked all the way up to the bed and placed himself directly in front of David.

Frank spotted the shadow emerging from Adnan's midsection again, just like at the bar and in the alley. This time, the dark fabric it was composed of seemed smaller, and it moved slower, as if weakened. Still, it was clearly visible to Frank. He looked around to the others to see whether anyone else had taken notice, but no one reacted.

"I was there the night it all happened, David," Adnan said.

David shook his head, and his eyes met Frank's, pleading for help. Adnan's stern tone caused David to flinch.

"I'm the one who found you there on the couch. Do you remember?" Adnan looked back to Jimmie, who'd put on a headset and was adjusting some knobs, but Jimmie only shook his head again.

"David, do you remember what happened that night?" Adnan said, continuing to press him. "Do you remember the video? Do you remember your family, David?"

David resumed rocking back and forth on the bed. He clasped his hands close together, as though they were bound again by the straitjacket. Frank could see the shadow from Adnan pulsing toward David, but nothing appeared from David as it had before.

"David," Adnan said. "David, look at me. Look at me and tell me why you killed your family."

"Adnan!" Claudia scolded from across the room.

He didn't turn around but reached out and grabbed David. "David, are you listening to me?" Adnan said.

"No! No! No! No!" David thrashed himself away from Adnan's grip. He looked up at him, his eyes full of tears.

David turned to Frank. "I didn't mean it!" David exclaimed as he started crying profusely. "I didn't mean it."

"It's okay, David," Claudia said as she came to him to settle him down. She redid his restraints and stroked his forehead until he calmed down.

Adnan turned to face Frank, and the shadow immediately went back into him, causing Adnan to shudder slightly. Adnan raised his left eyebrow and looked at Frank and then walked to Jimmie.

Frank joined Adnan and Jimmie, who was looking at a screen on a laptop. "No reading," Jimmie said. "Not from David, that is."

"Frank may have driven them completely away from him," Kanuik said.

"Yes," Adnan said. "Even I can feel they are not in this room with us tonight."

"Could it be they mean for us to torture this young man while they do nothing but watch us destroy him?" Frank said.

"Let's take a break," Adnan said. Using his cane, he walked out of the room. Kanuik and Claudia followed.

Frank remained while Jimmie made adjustments to his equipment. "You said there were no readings from *David*," Frank said. "Does that mean you had other readings?"

Jimmie glanced at Frank but tightened his lips.

"I know about Adnan," Frank said.

"How?" Jimmie said. "Can you see it?"

"So you do know," Frank said.

"I know I get the same reading from Adnan at times that I do from the people we are trying to help. It is stronger at times, but it always recedes, like he's controlling it."

"Yes," Frank said. "I can see them."

"I knew it!" Jimmie said.

"Don't worry; you're better off not seeing them." Frank stopped talking when the door opened.

"Thank you for comforting him," Claudia said as she reentered the room. She administered a shot to David. "His soul, it's so tortured now."

"Adnan is waiting for us back at your office," Kanuik said, peeking through the door. Claudia led the way back to her office with Jimmie and Frank following.

"It's not working here," Adnan said as the group entered the office. "We need to take him back to the house where the whole thing happened."

"David is currently under my custody for treatment," Claudia said. "I can request a leave if we get an escort. Jennings would probably help us."

"It's that easy?" Frank said.

"No," Claudia said. "It will take some doing, but there is a precedent for taking a patient back to the site of a traumatic incident to draw out memories. The results are mixed as to whether or not it really helps."

"Can we do it by tomorrow night?" Adnan said.

"I'll try my best," Claudia said.

"I know you will," Adnan said. "I suggest we all take the rest of the night off and get some rest. We will need our strength tomorrow."

Adnan left the office, as did everyone with the exception of Frank.

"Is there something you needed, Frank?" Claudia asked.

"I was just wondering," Frank said. "What will happen to David?"

"He is being charged with murder. The police are investigating. I will provide them an assessment of David's mental state that will show he is unfit for trial. He will likely end up in the custody of the state hospital under psychiatric care."

"We've lost him either way," Frank stated. "Even if we stop the shadows from haunting him, they have still won. David will never be free from his actions."

"It's unlikely that he will ever return to a functional state and be allowed to be on his own," Claudia said.

"Thank you, Claudia. Good night." Frank headed to the exit feeling more determined in his quest to help the group.

When Frank stepped out of the hospital, Adnan was there waiting for him.

"You proved it to me tonight," Adnan said.

"Proved what?" Frank asked.

"That you have been touched somehow. I know you saw it. When you came close to David and me, the shadow I was using reacted to you. It backed away."

"Is that a good thing?" Frank asked.

"It is," Adnan said. "It means you are ready to fight the shadows. Let's hope it's not too late."

"You think it's too late for David?" Frank asked.

"It may be too late for all of us," Adnan said. "I feel we need to turn the tide soon, or those things will win. Now let's go home and get some rest."

But Frank would not rest that night. The new world that had been revealed to him, a world of shadows, kept him awake most of the night. When he did sleep, it was out of pure exhaustion.

Chapter 7

Scene of the Crime

Frank opened the door to David's house and entered with Adnan and Jimmie. Jimmie unpacked several electronic devices and a camera and hung the camera over his neck. "I had Mike and Russ set up the equipment at the house earlier with Detective Jennings," Jimmie said. "They don't mind hunting ghosts, but this fighting-evil stuff is too scary for them. It'll be just me with you tonight." He looked at Frank. "The energy or portal in the house is still very much open. We just need to find it."

"You don't think David is the key?" Adnan asked.

"He is," Jimmie said. "These shadows, as you call them, are using David somehow. But he is not their method for coming across from wherever they're from."

"The scientist has his theory," Adnan said. "Let's hope you can provide us with some answers, young man."

There was a knock at the door, and Frank opened it to see Claudia, Kanuik, and Jennings with David.

"Can we remove the restraints?" Adnan said.

"I would rather he be restrained," Detective Jennings said.

"It will be harder for us to reach our goal if the patient feels uncomfortable," Adnan said.

Jennings scanned the street. "At least it's late enough that no one will notice us." He removed David's handcuffs. "I really hope this can help your patient," Jennings said, holding the door open while Claudia, David, and Kanuik entered the house. "We're taking an awful risk."

"All the more reason for you to remain out there," Adnan said. "Let us treat the patient."

"At least keep these close," Jennings said, handing Frank his handcuffs.

Frank went to take the handcuffs, but Jennings did not release his grip. Instead his eyes went to Claudia and then back to Frank.

"I know you might think David looks like a scrawny, confused teenager, but he killed his family in an outburst of homicidal rage. Don't underestimate him."

Frank nodded. He understood that Jennings's intent was to protect Claudia.

"I'll be right outside the door," Jennings said, and Frank closed the door.

The hallway split in two directions. One path went forward to a living room, and the other went to a stairway that led upstairs. Kanuik and Jimmie were at the bottom of the stairs.

"Adnan and Claudia already took David into the living room," Jimmie said. "That's where Adnan said they found him on the night of the murders." Jimmie turned his notebook computer toward Frank so that he could see the screen. "We have cameras in the living room, the stairway, and David's bedroom. I can monitor it all from this."

Frank looked at the monitor, where he could see Adnan and Claudia in the living room. David was sitting on the couch. "What are these?" he asked, pointing to three independent windows on the screen that were filling with numbers and lines like a voice recorder.

"Those are energy trackers," Jimmie said. "We're taking data on temperature, magnetic field levels, and energy fluctuations, and our cameras can also sense infrared, although for the cost, they've never picked up anything."

"That one is really active," Frank said, pointing to one of the lines as it fluctuated.

"Yes," Jimmie said. "That's David's room." He looked up the stairway. "Hate to seem like a know-it-all, but I thought his room would be a hotspot."

Kanuik's left foot was already on the first step as he looked at Frank. "Tell Adnan I went to the boy's room. Please go and help him."

Frank nodded and watched as Kanuik and Jimmie went up the stairs. He headed to the living room, where he found Claudia in the hallway right before the entrance, staring down at a spot on the floor. She didn't seem to notice him as he approached.

"Did you drop something?" Frank asked when he reached Claudia.

She flinched at his words and looked at him and then back down at the floor. "I don't see it," Claudia said. "It was here, but I don't see it."

"Are you okay? Claudia?" Frank looked toward the living room, where he spotted Adnan sitting with David on the leather couch, their backs turned toward him. A single three-bulb lamp lit the room. Where the hallway ended, it opened to a kitchen on the left of where he stood and a living room to the right.

"Sorry," Claudia said. "I forget you weren't here the first time. There was blood all over the place, and I stepped in some right here." She looked back down to the floor. "They must have cleaned it well; I don't see a trace."

Just as Frank started to worry about Claudia's unusual behavior, he had a sudden spell of nausea, and his body felt heavy, like someone was pulling him toward the ground but from inside. His legs were starting to go numb. He stepped closer to Claudia and put his hands on her shoulder so that he could look at her directly. "Why don't we go into the living room?" Frank said.

"It ruined a perfectly good set of shoes," Claudia said. "It does smell a little like sanitizers and carpet cleaner in here."

Frank smiled at her comment. "That's more like it," he said, glad that she'd regained her sense of humor. "Detective Jennings left me these handcuffs," Frank said as he walked around to the front of the couch to face Adnan and David. As soon as he did, the light from the lamp surged. Adnan's eyes were closed, just like in the bar when he meditated. David's eyes were glazed over, and he sat upright and stared forward. Frank waved his hand in front of David's face, but he did not move or seem to register Frank's presence.

Claudia had not moved from the hallway. She had changed her position but still seemed to be obsessing over the area of the floor where she she'd stepped in blood.

Adnan and David were quiet, so Frank went back to help Claudia. As soon as he stepped across the carpeted living room to the tile hallway, the place changed. He was no longer at the house, but just inside the entrance of the Kozy Tavern.

"What?" Frank said, but no one was near him. The door closed behind him, and he stood just inside the bar.

A man was sitting on one of the bar stools with his back to the door. He and Chic were engaged in a conversation. Frank headed over to the bar. He noticed a lady at the table where Adnan and Kanuik usually sat; she looked familiar, but he couldn't quite place her. As he got closer to the man at the bar, he realized who it was.

"Dad? What are you doing here?" Frank asked.

"What do you mean? I come here all of the time," his dad responded, turning to face him. Chic raised his eyebrows and walked away.

"The center knows you left?"

"Sure," he said, slamming a shot. "They don't care as long as no one finds out. They're just trying to make money off of people like you who don't care enough to take care of their parents."

Frank looked around to see who else had heard his father's comments, but other than Chic and the lady at the table, he was the only other person in the bar. "How much have you had to drink?" Frank said.

"Oh, you think it's the booze talking, is that it?" his father said. "You know, you always were too busy for me. I tried to get you to like what I did, to earn an honest living. I showed you the assembly line, where men work hard to earn their living. You were a star football player, a damn good one. What do you do with it all? You turn soft. You go and preach." He slammed another drink.

Frank sat on the stool next to his dad. "I thought we'd had this conversation before. I had a calling. You know that's how I feel."

"What has God done for you? He took your mother, took my job. What good has He done? Your sister, always in my ear about the decisions you made. Blah blah blah, always in my ear about you and how you didn't marry her friend. I'm so sick of hearing it. You know that's why I lost my memory. After your mom, I had no one to help me keep track of things. You were too busy. Your God let this happen to me." He slammed another shot and threw the glass, cracking one of the mirrors behind the bar.

Frank worried that Chic would get upset, but he had his back turned, his towel hung over his shoulder, oblivious to the entire event. He needed to get his father to calm down, and he reached to take the alcohol away from him, but there weren't any drinks on the bar. He struggled with the words he was going to say next. His thoughts were interrupted when the door to the bar slammed open behind him, causing him to whirl around.

"There you are," Frank's sister said as she entered the Kozy Tavern. She walked toward him, arms flailing, with a purse around her left forearm spinning as she moved. Barely keeping balance on her high heels, she stormed across the room, waving her hands in the air and speaking in an elevated voice. "What are you doing, bringing Dad into a place like this? He's not supposed to be drinking! Not with the medication he's on. I knew I shouldn't have gone away to California. Bill and I are getting a divorce because I can't trust you to take care of Dad, and he says I'm always too worried. He said if I'm so worried about Dad and you, I should move back. Well, I'm here, aren't I? I thought you were praying for me. I thought you were supposed to be this popular priest that was making a difference. Look around—a lot of good that did."

"Oh, leave him alone," his father said as he slammed another drink.

Frank put his hands out in front of him and tried to speak, but the words didn't come out. In the background, the lady at the table stood, and for some reason, he was drawn to her. She had on a tight, revealing red top and a short jean miniskirt that revealed her bare inner thighs. She began walking in his direction, and he struggled to keep his eyes on her face; the way she moved accentuated her body with each step of her three-inch red high heels. She wet her lips with her tongue, and her long eyelashes framed deep blue eyes. As she got closer, he realized why she looked familiar; it was Claudia. Her hair was not tied up but flowed about her shoulders.

"That's what I'm talking about," Frank heard his dad say. "What are you waiting for, son? You weren't always a priest. She's been coming on to you since you two met. What's holding you back?"

Frank heard Adnan's voice in the background but couldn't see him in the bar or make out his words. His sister grabbed him and shook him. "Is that why you didn't marry Valerie? You were fooling around with some other woman?" his sister said.

Frank heard his father and his sister arguing, and he heard Adnan's voice in the background, but he couldn't take his eyes off Claudia as she turned in front of him, cocked her head, and went to the door. She opened the door, revealing that it was daytime, and stood there with the light revealing every curve as she moved her hand through her hair. Frank continued to watch her, but something inside of him objected. He knew he wasn't supposed to desire her; his stomach turned, and his head felt light. He looked down at his feet but couldn't focus on the floor. He looked back to the door. Claudia stood there but did not move naturally or look like herself. In the light that shone through, Frank saw a dark, shadowy figure.

"Stop!" he said to his sister and father, who were still fighting about him. "Stop!"

His body convulsed, and the bar around him went out of focus. He heard Adnan's voice, this time louder. He tried to focus on what Adnan was saying to him.

"Frank," Adnan's voice said, making it through. "Come back to me. Come on, Frank."

He closed his eyes and fell to his knees and prayed. When he opened his eyes, he was at David's house in the living room, and Adnan was standing over him.

"Very good," Adnan said. "You found your way back. Now please go help Claudia."

A scream rang out from the hallway, and Frank turned to see Claudia sitting on the floor in the same spot as before, frantically running her hands down her arms. She had taken her shoes off, and her eyes were wide as she screamed again.

"I can't get it off of me!" Claudia said as Frank approached her.

He tried to calm his nerves, but as he reached out to touch her, he noticed his hands shaking. He concentrated as he'd done at the hospital when David was in trouble. He felt the icy chill as he touched her skin and immediately knew what was happening. *The shadows are attacking us*, he thought.

"Claudia, listen to me," Frank said. "Follow my voice. Look at me."

Just as he made contact with Claudia, Jimmie came running down the hallway. He had blood dripping from his left arm, which he grasped with his right hand. "It's a trap, it's a trap! Tell Adnan it's a trap!"

Frank pulled Claudia up with him and put his hands on her face. "Claudia! Wake up! Come back to us!"

Claudia blinked. "Frank, what is it?" Claudia shook her head.

Jimmie was now beside Frank. "It's a trap; the shadows were waiting for us."

The front door slammed open, and Frank spotted Detective Jennings coming down the hall. "I've been banging on that door for ten minutes. Didn't you hear me?"

"No," Frank said. "The door wasn't locked."

"Someone locked it," Jennings said. "I heard screaming, and the lights were going on and off."

Frank shook his head and again noticed the blood on Jimmie's hands and left arm. He was using his right hand to cover a cut, but the blood ran from underneath. "Kanuik?" Frank asked.

"He's fine," Jimmie said. "I did this to myself on my equipment. They got to me. We've got to warn Adnan. The portal's in David's room, and more of those things got through before Kanuik could stop them."

"They?" Jennings said. He pulled his gun from its holster and moved closer to them. "Where's David?"

It appeared to Frank that being outside of the house, Jennings had not been affected by the shadows. "He's in the living room," Frank said.

Jimmie moved his hand to try to stop the flow of blood, but some of it dropped to the floor and splattered on Claudia's shoes. She spotted the blood, and her face went blank.

Frank reached out to brace her but didn't move quickly enough. Jennings arrived in time to catch Claudia before she hit the ground. He knelt down and guided her to a soft landing, still looking for an attacker or the source of the threat.

Adnan's voice rang out from the living room. "Frank!"

Frank turned back to see Adnan waving his cane around him as multiple shadows swarmed him. The shadow that came from Adnan was larger than before, and it seemed to be pulling away from him; its dark form extended enough that it was touching David.

David laughed as he stood and moved behind Adnan. He jumped onto Adnan, grabbing him, and a ghastly gurgle sounded from deep within him as he fell with Adnan, and the two struck the floor. At that moment, Frank watched the dark form flow from Adnan completely and enter David through his chest.

David's eyebrows lowered to where his eyes were nearly closed. He ground his teeth and rolled his eyes. Jennings ran by Frank and took the handcuffs from him. He jumped on David and flipped him over, putting the handcuffs on him.

Frank was stunned. Jimmie stood by him, his arm still bleeding. Frank ran to the kitchen and went through several drawers before he found one with a towel and wrapped it around Jimmie's arm to stop the bleeding. He escorted Jimmie into the kitchen and set him down in a chair. Then he went to Claudia. She stirred on the floor and looked up at him.

"What am I doing down here?" Claudia asked as Frank helped her to her feet.

"I need an ambulance and backup immediately," Frank heard Detective Jennings say from the living room. Frank rounded the corner to see David facedown on the floor, with Detective Jennings sitting on him, his knee in David's back, securing him to the ground.

Claudia put her hand in Frank's to brace herself as she walked around to the front of the couch and crouched down to where Adnan lay on the floor. Frank braced her until she had her knee down. She put her hand out and felt Adnan's neck.

Claudia looked up at Frank. "There's no pulse. He's gone. Adnan's gone." She pulled on Frank's arm as he helped her up, and then she sat on the couch.

Frank scanned the living room and kitchen for any of the shadows before following Jennings to the front door. They were gone. *How could this have happened?* he thought. He opened the door as vehicles with flashing lights began arriving. Soon, the entire neighborhood was lit up.

Kanuik came down the stairs. He did not have his cane, and his clothes looked singed, with patches of burned skin beneath. His hair was frazzled, and his face was stained with blood and black marks, but his eyes remained solid.

"Do you need help?" Frank asked.

Kanuik shook his head. "We have survived a great battle, Father Frank. We are about to be put in a tough position. The less you say, the better."

Frank didn't know what to tell Kanuik. He didn't know how to break the news about Adnan or their complete failure.

"Adnan will rest now," Kanuik said.

"How …" Frank started to ask, but Kanuik stopped him with a hand on his shoulder.

"Never mind that. We must keep trying. Adnan leaves us to carry on the fight."

As the police arrived, Kanuik followed Claudia's previous advice and stayed visible. Frank didn't tell anyone about his episode or about Claudia's behavior.

Frank, Claudia, Jimmie, and Kanuik sat in the kitchen as the medics dressed Jimmie's wounds and treated Kanuik's burns. Adnan's body was photographed and then taken out on a stretcher. David was led out in handcuffs.

"I think we're done here," Detective Jennings said, "since none of you will tell me what really went on."

"I told you," Jimmie said. "Some of my equipment caught on fire upstairs. That's all."

"When I entered, you said 'they' got to you. Who were you talking about?"

No one answered Jennings.

"I know you thought bringing that boy back to his home could help him," Jennings said. "But it was a mistake to let him out in the first place. Exactly what were you doing? And don't give me any crap about therapy. I know something else was going on with the professor and his equipment and a priest."

"You are right," Frank said. "There was more going on here. We were fighting evil."

His words quieted Jennings. "I'll let you know if I need any information," Jennings said after a moment. "It was Adnan's idea, and he paid the price." He went over to Claudia. "Can I give you a ride home?"

"Thank you, Detective," Claudia said. "I have my car outside."

Jennings started to walk away, and Claudia stood and grabbed his arm. "Thank you, really."

Detective Jennings looked at the group gathered in the kitchen. "The press is out there. I would advise you to ignore them and remain silent. All we told them is that you were helping with a police investigation into the murders that happened here."

"What about Adnan?" Frank said. "They saw his body being carted out of here."

"He had a heart attack," Jennings said. "That's what the paramedics say. He had a heart attack during the investigation, and that's all we know."

Kanuik stood, followed by Jimmie, and they walked outside.

Frank looked at Claudia. "I don't think you should drive."

She pulled her keys out and handed them to Frank. "I don't think I can drive."

Frank took the keys and walked out of the house with Claudia, shielding his eyes from the cameras. True to what Jennings had warned them about, a reporter thrust a microphone into his face. "Father, can I have a word with you? Is it true that members of the church were here tonight performing an exorcism?" the reporter asked. "Can you tell me what happened here?"

Frank kept a steady pace and headed right for Claudia's car, opening the passenger door for her. But by the time he moved around to the other side, she had gotten out of the car. She headed for the ambulance where they'd taken Adnan.

A stream of reporters followed her, but Kanuik stepped between them and the ambulance. His presence was enough to ward them off. Frank went with Claudia.

"It's okay," Jennings said as they approached and stepped inside the ambulance. "Get those people back."

Adnan's body was on a gurney. They had tried unsuccessfully to resuscitate him and had a sheet over him. Claudia leaned over his body, and tears streamed down her face as she kissed him on the cheek. "Good-bye," she whispered and wiped her eyes. She turned to Frank. "Please get me out of here."

Frank took Claudia to her car, opening the door again; this time Kanuik followed them to keep the reporters back. Frank started the engine, backed out of the drive, pushed the pedal to the floor, and sped down the road. He drove for several minutes before he spoke. "I don't know where you live."

Claudia did not reply right away but turned her head to face Frank. "I don't think I can be alone tonight."

Frank drove to his place and took Claudia up to his apartment. "I'll take the couch," he said as they entered.

He sat down for a moment, and flashbacks to the episode at David's house appeared each time he tried to close his eyes. He needed some comfort. The images of Claudia that his mind had created came back to him, but he knew he could not give into the temptation. Perhaps it was a test of his strength.

"I just need to clean up a little," Claudia said. She went into his bathroom while he headed to his bedroom to straighten up the room and pull the covers back on the bed for her. He turned the lights off except for a small bedside lamp. When Claudia came out, she was wrapped in a towel.

"I don't suppose you have a shirt I can borrow," Claudia said.

"Sorry," Frank said as he stared at her bare shoulders and noticed her toned arms. He turned his head away and went toward the closet, where he pulled out a shirt and took some sweatpants out of a drawer. He handed them to her, and she went back into the bathroom. He was leaving the bedroom for the living room when he heard her voice.

"Don't leave," Claudia said. She came out from the bathroom, went to his bed, lay down, and pulled the covers over herself. "Here, I didn't mean to embarrass you. Is that better?"

Frank didn't know how to respond at first. He clasped his hands in front of him. "I'm not used to having a woman in my bedroom."

"Yes," Claudia said. "I understand. I am a psychiatrist, and one might take my actions as being too forward. We've both been through a terrible tragedy and might be vulnerable."

Please give me strength, Frank prayed silently. "You are correct," Frank said. "I cannot be with you. Please understand."

"Can we just talk?" Claudia said.

"Hold on," Frank said. He stepped out of the room and brought in a chair from the kitchen. He positioned in by the bed and sat down.

Claudia put out her hand, and he grasped it, still repenting in his mind about the temptation he had been feeling and now felt toward Claudia. He understood that the loss of Adnan was affecting his judgment, and he proceeded with caution.

"Thank you," Claudia said. "David was so weak, so hurt. How could he do this? I don't understand."

"I don't think any of us do. We just need to get some rest," he said.

"When I first started working with Adnan and Kanuik, it was mainly a consulting role," Claudia said. "Strictly in the office. Later on, I started going out in the field with them. I've seen some stuff I can't explain, even watched and heard them speak about the shadows, but I've never been attacked by them, until now."

"You're safe now," Frank said.

"I told you my mother died when I was eighteen. What I didn't tell you is my father committed suicide," Claudia said. "A risk of my profession. I wasn't there when he did it and didn't know the specifics, but when I went into the house, there were still traces of his blood. I stepped in some of it. The image still haunts me to this day."

That's why she had problems in the hallway, Frank thought. He was starting to understand what Adnan had been telling him: the creatures, or shadows as Adnan referred to them, were able to probe their minds, find their weaknesses, and somehow exploit them.

"They used that against me," Claudia said, "didn't they? They somehow knew. They showed me images of my father slashing his wrists. I was there but couldn't reach him in time."

"It wasn't real," Frank said. "The force of evil has been known to deceive, to lie. Its purpose is to weaken its foe. We can resist this attack; be strong."

Claudia smiled. He had encouraged her. But privately, he was worried about his own courage. What would Bishop Tafoya do when he found out what had happened? Frank was worried the shadows would attack him again; he was worried that he would lose everything—his parish, his faith—and then what would he be left with? He would have nothing.

"Maybe that's what they want," Frank said out loud.

"Sorry?" Claudia said.

"Nothing," Frank said. "I was just thinking to myself. I'm sure tomorrow we will figure out a way to put the pieces back together and move on."

In a few minutes, Claudia fell asleep. Frank grabbed a blanket from his closet, took his shoes off, and headed for the couch. Thoughts of the night's events rapidly ran through his mind, and he felt another sleepless night was before him. He laid his head on the throw pillow and stared into the darkness. He was pleasantly surprised when Rosie jumped up beside him and purred. He stroked her back and let the sound sooth him. Soon, the exhaustion overtook him, and he fell asleep.

Chapter 8

Lead Us Not into Temptation

When Frank woke the next morning, Rosie was no longer by his side. He stretched out, feeling depressed and beaten from the events of the day before. His couch was not a comfortable place to sleep. He looked into his bedroom. Claudia remained sleeping, and Rosie was curled up at the foot of the bed.

"Good cat," Frank said. "She needs your protection more than I do right now." He went back to the kitchen and started the coffee. He put his elbows on the counter and placed his hands on his aching head. He felt lost and unsure about what steps to take next.

He heard footsteps in the bedroom and then heard the shower turn on as he considered making something for breakfast.

The shower stopped at the same time there was a knock at the door. Frank went to the door, looked through the small peephole, and opened the door.

"Father Uwriyer," Frank said, using his formal name. "Please come in. I was just getting ready to make breakfast."

Mark entered the apartment and went to the counter that split the living room and kitchen and sat down. "Sorry I didn't come by last night," Mark said. "The bishop had me rather busy after he was briefed on what happened yesterday. I was worried about you. He told me one of the members of your group had a heart attack?"

Frank didn't offer any information on the subject but instead fixed Mark a cup of coffee and put it in front of him. He wasn't sure how much he could tell Mark. "Yes, it was quite an event last night, but I'm okay. Who briefed Tafoya?"

"He has friends in the press and on the police force," Mark said. "But he wants to see you today."

Inside, Frank didn't know whether he was feeling better or not. He thought about making pancakes and ham. They sounded good, but his stomach was upset. Why? *Adnan, of course!* he thought. *Yes, he was killed last night. But it wasn't a heart attack. Those things got to him somehow. So what the hell am I doing thinking about pancakes like nothing happened? Is this my way of coping?*

"Thank you," Mark said, raising his cup to take a drink of his coffee. His voice pulled Frank back into the present moment.

"Hello, Father Uwriyer," Claudia said, walking into the living room. She was dressed in the clothes she had worn the night before minus her shoes, and she had a towel wrapped around her hair.

The cup of coffee headed for Mark's mouth halted midway and went back to the counter. His eyes flashed to Claudia and then to Frank.

"Mark," Frank said, "This is Dr. Claudia Walden. She is a psychiatrist I've been working with. She was very close to the person who died last night and was upset. I let her stay here last night. I slept on the couch."

"I'm sure everything here is appropriate," Mark said as he stood up from his chair. "You'll forgive me, Dr. Walden," he said. "I'm late for a meeting."

Frank headed to the door to catch up with Mark. "Wait. There's no reason to hurry off."

"I know you are going through something very traumatic," Mark said, "and I am here to help you in any way I can. I trust your judgment, but you can't afford any more bad press right now."

"What do you mean?" Frank said.

"Your neighbor, Ms. Able, went by the church offices asking if you'd quit and asked about you. Said you'd had a lady visitor and have been keeping very late hours. She even mentioned that you smelled like alcohol one night."

"We're working together," Frank said. "That is all."

"I came here to check on you per the bishop's request," Mark said. "I won't tell him anything about this, but if he asks specifically …"

"I understand," Frank said.

"He told me he wanted to see you in his office at one." With that, Mark exited the apartment.

Frank considered what Mark had said. He knew the young priest to be a man of great faith and integrity, but Mark did not understand what they were up against or what was really going on. Frank realized it was the machine at work, just like in any bureaucracy: leaders not truly in touch with what was happening were making decisions they felt were better for everyone. He knew his next move would require caution.

The breakfast of pancakes and ham that Frank and Claudia shared was quiet after Mark left. Neither one ate well, and soon they were both in their own thoughts. Frank picked up the dishes and put them in the sink. He noticed the cat's empty dish and took the time to fill it.

"I'll need to go check in at the hospital," Claudia said. "Do you need a ride to Bishop Tafoya's office?"

"No," Frank said. "I have a car at St. Joseph's that I need to return to him anyway." He didn't want to tell her that he was worried what Bishop Tafoya and Mark might think of him being seen with Claudia so much. Would they really doubt his faith? His commitment? Now was not the time for him to risk it.

Claudia left, and Frank looked around his apartment. It seemed quiet and empty. He took a long, hot shower, changed clothes, and shaved before he headed to his church. When he arrived, the place was empty. He searched for a seat that seemed appropriate and started to pray.

"Yes, it's me," he said to the cross hanging above the altar. "I'm usually the one up front giving everyone else something to think about, trying to inspire hope, but I am in need of it now. I thought Adnan was someone I could learn from, who could teach me how to put meaning into this fight against the evil in this world. I thought you sent him into my life to give me direction. I was making a difference before, reaching out to the youth and helping people with problems. That was real!" he said, raising his voice. "That seems so trivial now in the scheme of things. Why did you send this man into my life if all he was going to do was fail? How can I help David now? I don't understand. Please, guide me." Frank put the kneeler pad down and moved to a kneeling position. He stayed there until it was uncomfortable. He then took the keys from Pat's desk and drove himself to Tafoya's office.

The back door to the church housing Bishop Tafoya's office was locked. Frank rang the bell, and Madeline opened the door for him. She smiled. "The others are already inside waiting," Madeline said as she escorted Frank down the hall. He spotted Kanuik, Claudia, and Jimmie standing in the hallway outside the bishop's office. Jimmie waved a hand as Frank approached.

"Can I get you anything to drink while you're waiting?" Madeline asked.

"No," Frank said. She walked away, and he turned to Claudia, Kanuik, and Jimmie. "I didn't expect to see you here."

"Of course we are here," Claudia said. "We're in this together."

Kanuik, who had been leaning against the wall, stepped forward and faced Frank directly. "Adnan was my friend and a great warrior, and now, he has passed on to the world of the spirits. I stand with you because you are a fellow warrior. I tell you, the battle is not over. You must decide where you will stand and what role you will take from here."

Frank looked into the solid eyes and sensed strength emanating from them. He wished he could be as solid and determined as Kanuik in the quest before him. But he wasn't. He didn't know whether he would be able to continue with the group, or whether Bishop Tafoya would let him. He had tangled with the shadows a few times now and had not come out on top. Complicating his situation was his knowledge of the truth. Now that he knew of the shadows, he also didn't know whether he could go back to being a simple priest leading his congregation.

He tried to think of something to say to Kanuik. He wanted to convey the same confidence back; after all, Kanuik had just lost his friend and companion. But both men's attention went to the door of Bishop Tafoya's office as the voices beyond became louder.

"Yes, sir," said a voice from behind the door. "I understand."

The voices in the room were familiar; Frank recognized them as Bishop Tafoya's and Father Uwriyer's. When Mark spoke, Frank and Claudia looked at each other at the same time, the morning incident still fresh in their minds. Frank wondered what Mark had said.

They had just a moment to greet him when the door to Bishop Tafoya's office came open. Mark exited without a word and headed down the hall toward the church.

"Please, come in," Bishop Tafoya said to the group.

Claudia entered with Kanuik and Frank. Jimmie followed but remained standing toward the back of the office with Kanuik, leaving the seats open for Frank and Claudia, who sat, uncomfortably.

"Thank you for coming," said the bishop. "After the events last night, it is important for you to know the direction we are heading. Please understand that I report to others, and although I've asked for patience while we sort this out, they believe this is a fiasco that brings attention to the church that we do not want. The press was on the scene last night, and they are already having a field day with the event. I've been asked to suspend support at this time. With what happened to Adnan, I might even say the group's mission is over."

Frank searched the faces of the people in the room, looking for a reaction. No one made direct eye contact; each person was in her or her own personal hell, dealing with the previous night's incident. Frank reflected on Claudia's story from the night before. If the shadows had attacked him and her, they had attacked everyone in the group. He wondered what issues each of them was trying to cope with today.

"I'm sorry," Bishop Tafoya said. "I apologize for my tone. You have been through a lot." He sat back in his chair. "Can someone tell me what exactly happened that it came to this?"

Jimmie opened his mouth as if to speak, but his eyes went to the floor, and he remained silent.

"Was it Adnan who recommended taking David back to his house?" Bishop Tafoya asked.

"I did not take orders from him," Kanuik said. "He knew what he was doing. So did I."

"It was his plan," Frank said. "But it was the correct plan, and we were all there of our own accord." The others nodded in agreement.

Bishop Tafoya moved forward in his chair and put his arms on his desk, hands folded. "What was this plan, Father Frank? Can you explain?"

"Adnan thought, and Jimmie confirmed, that the shadows use some type of doorway to get through, a portal if you will," Frank said.

"I am familiar with this concept," Bishop Tafoya said.

"Adnan thought he could cross through the portal," Frank said. "He thought if he could cross over and introduce some good into their world, we could turn the tide in this battle and fight these things on their own ground."

"Those things knew we were coming," Jimmie said. "They ambushed us."

"Adnan wasn't strong enough to fend them off this time," Frank said. "They attacked him and David. They used David to overwhelm and kill Adnan."

"Kill him?" Bishop Tafoya raised his left eyebrow. "I was told Adnan had a heart attack."

"Adnan was somehow attached to one of the creatures," Frank said. "He kept it subdued, but it's how he knew where to find them."

"I knew it," Jimmie said.

"Combined with the one he was fighting internally, he couldn't handle the onslaught. Those things used David to overwhelm him and kill him."

"My goodness," Bishop Tafoya said. "Is it possible?"

"Frank speaks the truth," Kanuik said. "Adnan was merged with a shadow and was hoping to use it to go through the portal into their world."

"You knew of this plan going in?"

Frank nodded.

"And you approved?"

Frank stood and stepped closer to the bishop's desk. "I didn't at first. But everything has happened so fast, and with all that's going on … well, you've seen it out there." He pointed toward the window. "We are losing this fight. What Adnan proposed was a game changer."

"Please, Father Frank, be seated," Bishop Tafoya said.

"Yes, of course," Frank said.

"You should have known better," Bishop Tafoya said, looking at Kanuik. "This is not the first time someone has tried to breach the portal, and every time, it's failed."

"My readings indicated we had a chance," Jimmie said. "We just underestimated them. They were already through when we got there. We thought we could contain them in the bedroom, and they were already in the living room. Our plan to contain them only drew more of them out."

"You put your patient at risk, Claudia," Bishop Tafoya said, ignoring Jimmie's comments. "The administration at the hospital might not look favorably on what you've done."

"My patient is already beyond rehabilitation and will spend his life behind bars," Claudia said. "There is nothing I can do to help him. You are right; the administration is looking at suspending my privileges."

"I can't tell you what do, but I cannot support you any further," Bishop Tafoya said.

"I guess that's it then," Claudia said. "Adnan's gone, and we throw in the towel. I believed in what the group was doing. Adnan was a great man. I thought—we all thought—he could succeed, and that's all that matters." She stood and walked out of the room.

"If you don't need me anymore, I'll just show myself to the door," Jimmie said.

Frank watched as Jimmie left. In his haste, he did not close the door all the way. Kanuik leaned against the wall near the door but remained silent. Bishop Tafoya went to the door and closed it. He returned to his desk and sat on it, facing Frank, with one leg up underneath him on the desk and the other dangling off.

"Father Frank," Bishop Tafoya said, "you must understand, I am merely trying to piece together what happened. If what you are saying is correct, and David is the one who killed Adnan, then I cannot understand how that boy could be capable of such a thing."

"He didn't kill Adnan," Frank said. "The shadows did."

"But I thought you said they took control of David, that they possessed him," Bishop Tafoya said.

"It's not like that. He was susceptible to influence. The shadows used him—caused him to panic and lash out. We could probably go to the hospital where he is right now and have a lucid conversation with him. He might not even remember what happened."

"I've known Adnan for a long time," Bishop Tafoya said. "I can't believe he'd be so careless."

"From what I've learned in the short time I've been with the group," Frank said, "these things have an intelligence of their own. I believe they knew what Adnan was planning. They knew, and they plotted an ambush, and it worked."

Bishop Tafoya raised his hand to his face as someone does when deep in thought, stroking down from his cheek to his chin. He returned to his chair and pulled out a file and a pen and started writing. He did not look up when he began speaking. "For the time being, I recommend you keep your distance from the group. No need to give anyone a reason to snoop around. This thing is already messy enough. The press is fickle. They'll move on to the next story quickly if we don't give them any reason to stick around."

"What is it you expect of me?" Frank said.

"I don't think it would be right to put you back at your parish, not right away," Bishop Tafoya said. "You are vulnerable. Take some time off, Father Frank. You deserve it. Father Uwriyer has everything well in hand."

Frank stood and leaned forward, putting his hands on the bishop's desk. "Time off from what? We failed. I was brought into the group to contribute, and I've done nothing," Frank said. "Why did you pick me for this mission if you weren't going to give me time to succeed?"

Bishop Tafoya stopped writing and looked up. "I didn't pick you. Adnan did," he said, raising his voice. "He knew your history and felt that God had intervened on your behalf, that you were protected, chosen. He saw a reason in that."

"And you don't?" Frank said.

"I see a great man before me," Bishop Tafoya said. "But no one can accomplish what Adnan wanted. These things come from a place beyond us, perhaps hell itself. Wherever it is, men were not meant to go there."

"And you had no idea of his plan?"

"Adnan picked the mission," Bishop Tafoya said. "I didn't know he would try the same thing again. He knew I didn't support it. He tried it before in Somalia. He attempted to cross over with an entire group of holy warriors, men he'd trained to be the solid and faithful. It failed, and all of them were killed. All but one." His eyes went to the back of the room. "Adnan was the only survivor."

Kanuik hadn't moved. Frank stepped back from the desk and sank down in the chair.

"It's out of my hands," Bishop Tafoya said.

Frank looked at the bishop, who had resumed writing. Kanuik's hand tapped him on the shoulder. "Come, let's go," Kanuik said.

Frank rose from his chair as Kanuik opened the door, and they walked into the hallway. He expected Claudia would be waiting, but she was nowhere to be seen.

"What now?" Frank said.

"We say good-bye to our friend and search for a way to go on," Kanuik said. "I know you will find a way to continue. If I am not at the tavern, Chic will know how to reach me." Kanuik went to the exit.

Frank turned in the car keys to Madeline and walked back to his church. It was late enough, and there would be no services. He sat in the sanctuary until the sky grew dark outside the windows. Then he started his walk home alone. He did not end up at his apartment, but at the Kozy Tavern. He stood outside, watching the door.

Scenes from the previous night replayed in his head. He wasn't sure he could bear going into the tavern. He worried about seeing his father there as in his dream. This was the first time he would walk in without Adnan there. He wondered whether the others were there—Kanuik, Jimmie, and Claudia. He checked the street for Claudia's car but didn't see it. She had driven a different car the first night they had gone out with Adnan, but he didn't remember what it looked like.

His stomach growled. When he entered the Kozy Tavern, Chic was standing at the table where the group always sat. To his relief, Kanuik, Jimmie, and Claudia were there. He noticed Mike and Russ up at the bar as they waved at him, but there were no other customers besides them. As he walked up to the table, Chic had just delivered fresh bowls of soup. Chic had an extra place set and pulled back the chair for Frank.

"You're late," Chic said.

Frank sat down and looked around the table. No one had started eating. He understood the message and bowed his head. "Dear Lord, we ask for you blessing in this time of need. We look to you for guidance and strength. Let us share this meal together in remembrance of our friend, Adnan. Amen."

As the others said "Amen," Frank noticed Adnan's chair was empty, but his hat sat on the seat, and his cane was hanging on the back of it. When Chic brought drinks at the end of the meal, he put Adnan's favorite drink on the table in front of his chair.

"To our friend and a great warrior," Chic said. The group toasted Adnan.

The door opened, and Detective Jennings entered the bar. Not wanting to give up Adnan's seat, Chic pulled up another chair.

"Thank you," Jennings said as he sat down, "but I won't be staying long."

Chic collected the empty glasses and headed back to the bar.

"I just stopped by to tell you that I was successful in talking the assistant DA out of pressing any charges," Jennings said. "He was upset that I wasn't in the house with you and put me on suspension."

"Suspended," Jimmie said. "I never thought I'd use that term again once I was out of school."

"The hospital is debating whether or not to revoke my license to practice there," Claudia said.

"Bad news all around," Frank said. The others looked at him when he said this. It felt to him like they were longing for him to say something more, something of purpose. Or maybe it was his own feeling of loss that was overtaking him.

"The autopsy on Adnan was rushed through today," Jennings said. "Someone high up from the church requested it not be done. I've never seen such pressure, but the fact that his death happened under suspicious circumstances made it the state's right to conduct one. Still, the coroner, a friend of mine, stopped midway through the damn thing." Jennings looked around the table. "Do you mind?" he said, noticing Jimmie had a drink in front of him.

"Go ahead," Jimmie said, offering up his drink.

Jennings drank the dark liquid and looked surprised.

"Sorry," Jimmie said. "It's a Roy Rogers. I don't like to drink and drive."

Jennings laughed. "It's okay. I appreciate people like you. Now get this," he said, leaning in. "My coroner friend thinks your friend was well over a hundred years old."

Frank turned to Kanuik, who didn't seem surprised one bit by the revelation.

"He also said that parts of his organs were so damaged, he shouldn't have been alive. The coroner was so freaked out, he called the assistant DA. The whole thing is so strange that they are afraid to make anything of it. That's probably why they aren't considering any charges."

Frank turned his attention to the empty chair where Adnan usually sat. All that Jennings had said deepened Adnan's mystery.

"I thought you should know," Jennings said. He looked down at his watch and moved his chair back from the table.

"I'll walk you out," Claudia said, and the two left the tavern.

"I guess I'll be going too," Jimmie said. "I have some papers to grade."

Frank sat there in silence with Kanuik. He thought about the events the night before, about how everything was going wrong. This was definitely evil's plan, if it had one.

"When I asked how you and Adnan met, you told me the story, but not all of it," Frank said. "Why didn't you tell me the entire story? Why didn't you tell me that Adnan had failed before?"

Kanuik took out first his pipe and then a small pack of tobacco from his pocket and put them both on the table. "Doubt and deceit are the weapon of our enemy. We needed you to believe in our plan." He packed the pipe with some tobacco and put it to his mouth. "The leadership of your church does not believe we are losing as Adnan did. You must decide your path now."

"How can I decide?" Frank said. "Bishop Tafoya told me I'm not working with the group anymore. I've been put on leave. I don't even know if I'll be able to go back to my church."

Frank had never seen Kanuik so much as flinch, but for a moment, he thought he caught such a movement as they locked eyes. Kanuik failed to light his pipe. He examined it.

"Something wrong?" Frank asked.

"I believe," Kanuik said, "that we all knew the risks we were taking, including Adnan, but we still thought it was the right thing to do. Once Adnan discovered we had been trapped, he fought the battle for us. His fight weakened him too much. In the end, he was ready to go. But we must not grieve in a way that brings sorrow to the fight, or else the influence of evil will have won its way. Instead, we must search for the truth in what he did, his sacrifice. Look into it and find an answer. I know it is there."

"I didn't mean any disrespect to Adnan," Frank said.

Kanuik nodded.

"I've got a busy schedule tomorrow," Frank said. "Good night." He waved to Chic and headed for the door, glancing back at Kanuik, who continued to watch him; he still had the pipe in his mouth but couldn't get it to light.

When he exited the bar, Claudia was leaning against the wall. "Can I give you a ride?"

"You driving?" Frank asked. "I didn't see your car earlier."

"You were looking for it?"

"Sure," Frank said. "I wanted to know who was here before I entered."

"I'm in my car tonight, not the one my father left me," Claudia said as she headed to a black sedan with Frank at her side. "The other one reminds me too much of my father, and after last night ..."

"I understand," Frank said. "Claudia, I think that we ..."

Claudia put her fingers up to her lips. "I'm a doctor and a psychiatrist. I know we've both been through a lot and are very vulnerable. My feelings are just confused now. My experience and education tell me what we are going through is natural; to desire comfort or some means of escaping the stressful situation we find ourselves in. I cannot rationalize it."

Frank reached inside of himself for something to say, some words of wisdom, some encouragement, anything he could say. But he felt empty. He was struggling himself with all that had taken place.

"Just a ride home then," Claudia said.

The empty, quiet streets matched the atmosphere in the car as Claudia drove Frank to his place. A few glances and brief smiles were all that the two shared.

"Will you be going back to your church soon?" Claudia asked, breaking the silence.

"I don't know," Frank said. He didn't want to tell her what Bishop Tafoya had said to him. "I believe I have some time off coming to me."

Claudia didn't ask any more questions. Frank considered several things to say but decided to enjoy the company without conversation until the car stopped in front of his apartment complex.

"Thank you," Frank said, getting out of the car.

"See you tomorrow?" Claudia asked.

"Not sure," Frank said. "But if you need anything, you know where to find me."

He went up the stairs to his apartment. He opened the door, and the smell of pancakes still lingered in the air. He made sure Rosie had food and water and then sat down on the couch. "Rosie," he called out, but she didn't come. His hands remained in his coat pockets, and his shoes remained on as he stared down at them. He wasn't sure how long he stared, but soon, he fell asleep.

◆   ◆   ◆

Frank woke up the next morning still on his couch in the same position, noticing as his eyes focused that his shoes were still on. He stood and looked around for Rosie, but she wasn't there. He walked to his bedroom and looked under the bed.

"There you are, you silly cat. Why don't you come out here?"

Rosie didn't move. "Suit yourself," he said. He took a shower, got dressed, and decided he needed to go see his dad. He took the bus across town to the nursing home and entered through the front office. A nurse he recognized greeted him.

"Hello, Frank," the nurse said.

"Hello, Judy," Frank said.

"I haven't seen you here for a couple of weeks."

"Yes, Judy, I've been away on church business," Frank said. "I'm sorry. I should have called."

"Your father isn't here today," Judy said. "We had to take him to

South General for some tests. He left this morning and won't be back until this evening. We tried to call."

Frank instinctively went for his cell phone and then remembered it had been burned out after the incident with David at the hospital.

"Yes, well, my phone's been on the blink, and I haven't had time to get a new one," Frank said. "Looks like I'll have time to get that done today now." He laughed nervously. "If I don't make it back tonight, please tell my father I was here and that I'll see him soon."

The nurse nodded. He knew that even if she relayed the message, his father's condition made it unlikely he'd know when Frank had visited him last.

He boarded the bus back to his apartment. He thought about going to the Kozy Tavern to see whether the others were there. He thought about going to his church and checking in with some of his friends there. But he was tired, and his head throbbed. He went up to his apartment and lay down on the couch.

"Must be all that staying up I've been doing lately," he said to himself. "I just need to adjust back to being up during the day, that's all."

He awoke to darkness and looked at the clock across the room in the kitchen: two in the morning. Without changing into his pajamas, he went to bed and awoke the next morning to someone knocking at his door.

Frank looked through the peephole to see Claudia there, all dressed in black. He opened the door. "Claudia," he said, "what brings you here?"

"Oh my," Claudia said, "are you all right?" In her typical fashion, she entered his apartment and walked right by him.

"I'm fine," Frank said as he closed the door and followed her.

"You look like you've been up all night drinking," Claudia said.

"No," Frank said. "Nothing of the sort." He walked back to his kitchen, where he poured a glass of water and drank it, refilled and drank a second glass, and then changed out Rosie's water. He noticed the food dish was still full. "I assure you, I am not one to drink."

Claudia went to the kitchen counter and put her hand out, gesturing at his appearance. "Surely you're not going like that?"

"Going? Going where?" Frank said.

"Adnan's service. It's in"—Claudia looked down at her watch—"just over an hour. I tried to call you, but your phone isn't working."

Frank filled his glass with water again and drank. His stomach felt empty. "It's Saturday?"

"Yes," Claudia said. Her eyes floated about the apartment.

"If you're looking for an empty bottle, you won't find one," Frank said. "I went to see my father yesterday … well, maybe Thursday … and got back late. That's all."

Claudia walked to where he was standing. "I'm sorry," she said. "I didn't mean to be rude. Are you ill?" She put her hand to his head.

Frank closed his eyes for a moment and envisioned a different life as Claudia touched his head, and he surrendered to her gentle warmth and reassurance. He considered that he would have liked to have been a father and that if he'd met Claudia before he'd become a priest, he might have chosen a different path. But he searched inside of himself, and the answer that returned told him that was not his path. He had a mission to stand up to the evil confronting him. She removed her hand, and he stepped back into reality.

"Well, I don't feel a fever," Claudia said. "In fact, you feel a little cold."

"It's nothing," Frank said. "Give me a moment, and I'll get ready." He raced into his bedroom and put out some clean clothes before he went to the bathroom to wash up. When he saw himself in the mirror, he understood why Claudia was concerned. His eyes had dark circles under them, his hair was disheveled, and he hadn't shaved for two days. Soap and hot water did him good as he shaved and combed his hair, but the dark circles remained under his eyes.

"Ready," Frank said as he exited his bedroom. Claudia sat on the couch with Rosie by her side. "Hmm, I'm glad you came over. She's been under the bed for two days."

"I can understand that with the way you were looking," Claudia said and laughed. "Come on, I'll drive. And I brought the car you like."

They arrived at the front of the church where Bishop Tafoya presided. Claudia parked and got out. Frank exited but stayed back as she started walking. She turned around.

"I think it might be best if we don't enter together," Frank said. He didn't know what Mark had told the bishop about the morning he'd seen Claudia at his apartment and didn't want to give the bishop any reason to doubt him.

"Don't be too long," Claudia said, and she turned back and went into the church.

Frank entered the sanctuary through the front door. He wasn't used to doing so because he'd always entered from Bishop Tafoya's office, which was down the hall behind the sanctuary. From his position, he spotted Kanuik, Chic, and Claudia in the front row. Jimmie and Detective Jennings were also present, but each sat a few rows back by himself. Adnan's body lay in the open casket. The funeral was a closed service, and no paper had carried the obituary.

Frank walked to the front row and took a seat by Claudia. He looked at Kanuik, who nodded back at him. He noticed Kanuik held Adnan's cane and hat. "Any luck contacting his family?" Frank whispered.

"No," Claudia said. "He had none that we know about. I think Kanuik was the closest thing he had to family."

"It's times like these we realize we didn't really know the person he was," Frank said. "I don't even know where he lived."

"He had a room at the Kozy Tavern," Claudia said. "We are going there later to see if we can find any information on a relative or someone to contact. You're welcome to join us."

Frank heard a door open and close behind the main altar and turned his attention to the front of the church. Bishop Tafoya came out in full dress for the funeral and ran the service.

Frank listened to the sermon and the reading from scripture; most of it was a standard generic service. He knew because he'd performed dozens of them for people who were alone or estranged from their family. There was no mention of who Adnan really was or what he'd accomplished in his life. Just a kind farewell.

His thoughts strayed from the funeral. He wondered about Adnan's room at the Kozy Tavern; he hadn't even known there was a room at the tavern. That explained why Adnan was always there. What a lonely life he had led. Suddenly, Frank imagined his own ending being much like Adnan's if he continued with the group. At his church, he had been in the forefront and was very popular with his fellowship and would surely be missed. His current mission took him behind the scenes, with no one really noticing him or who he was; it meant living a life of obscurity with only a few friends to his name.

He looked around at the mostly empty church. It was quiet. The bishop had stopped talking and had taken his seat on the presider's chair.

Claudia and Kanuik went to the casket. Her pale face stuck out from underneath the large-rimmed black hat she wore. Frank went to her side. She reached out her hand and grasped Frank's. Her hand trembled as the tears began to fall. She squeezed once and then let go of his hand. "I'll see you outside," she said.

Kanuik stood over the body, looking down at Adnan's face. He closed his eyes for a moment and then looked back at Frank. "He was a great warrior."

Frank nodded.

Kanuik took Adnan's homburg hat and placed it in the coffin. "It seems right that he should have it. He was fond of it." Kanuik turned to face Frank. He held up the cane. "This is for you. The wood is blessed and is very powerful. He would have wanted you to have it, as a fellow warrior."

Frank took the cane from Kanuik, who joined Claudia and walked down the aisle and out of the church. Detective Jennings followed them. Jimmie stood and nodded at Frank, turned, and walked out. Bishop Tafoya sat in the chair, his eyes closed.

Frank closed his eyes and started praying. Images came forth.

Conversations that he'd had with Adnan echoed in his head. One scene in particular took form: the evening Adnan had demonstrated to him what he thought was the shadows' plan, using the glasses with tomato juice. But this time, in Frank's mind, all the glasses were full, and the contents looked like blood. Frank blinked, trying to focus, and they began to spill. Frank stepped back to get out of the way, but the liquid splashed and spilled on Adnan as he lay in his coffin. Frank reached forward to close the coffin, but it wouldn't shut. Adnan's nice suit became saturated in the red color as it spilled on him and started to fill up the casket. Frank looked around for help. He was no longer at the church but was at the bar. *Where is everyone?* he thought in a panic.

Something grabbed him from behind, and Frank reacted instinctually, parrying and raising his hand to guard himself as he faced his attacker.

"Father Frank?" Bishop Tafoya stood beside him, a bewildered look on his face.

Frank looked around him and saw that he was still at the church, still standing over Adnan's casket, which was now closed but showed no signs of being flooded with the red juice.

"Father Frank, are you all right?" Bishop Tafoya asked.

Frank thought before he responded. He wasn't okay. He was lost in his current mission and searching for an answer as to what he needed to do next. The man who might have had that answer lay in the coffin before him and was more a mystery now than when he was alive. *Why me? What am I supposed to do?* These were the questions in Frank's mind, but he was not ready to share them with Bishop Tafoya.

"Yes," Frank replied. "I just need some air." With that he turned and left the church.

Claudia was waiting for him outside. "Would you like me to give you a ride back to your apartment?" she asked.

"You said you were going to Adnan's room to see if you could find out more about him," Frank said. "I think I would like to go and see if there is anything I can help with." Not used to carrying the cane Adnan had left him, he put it in the backseat of Claudia's car.

They arrived at the Kozy Tavern and asked Chic to take them to Adnan's room. Kanuik was not there, and Frank wondered where he stayed when he was not at the tavern. He realized how little he actually knew about the group of people he'd been spending so much time with.

"Just let me close the door for a minute," Chic said, and he walked to the front door and locked it. Then he motioned Frank and Claudia to come back behind the bar and led them through a doorway that went into the kitchen. From there, they entered a stairway and went down into a lower level of the building. The stairs opened to a storage room where food and supplies were kept for the bar. Chic continued to the end of the room and opened yet another door that led into a room full of tables and chairs.

"This used to be a meeting room for those who shared our causes," Chic said, "years ago. It's hardly used these days."

As they entered the room, Frank couldn't help but notice the smell of tobacco, the same smell that came from Kanuik's pipe.

"The furniture looks antique," Claudia said, stopping briefly to admire the chairs and tables.

Chic nodded. "Yes, well, the pub has been around for some years now. It hasn't always been the place you see currently."

The room ended at another doorway. Chic opened that door and then stepped aside to let Claudia and Frank enter. "Adnan's room," he said.

Frank expected to walk into a small room with a bed and maybe a dresser and nightstand complete with books and maybe a journal or two. Instead, the room that opened up before him was larger than his apartment and was full of books, weapons, paintings, suits of armor, and hundreds of crosses and religious artifacts. Among them was the mirror Adnan had let Frank use to see the shadows.

"Adnan was a collector," Chic said.

"I never would have imagined," Claudia said as she entered the room and went to a suit of armor that was displayed upright. "It's Adnan's size."

Frank remembered what Detective Jennings had said about the coroner's report on Adnan. Could he really have been over a hundred years old? Walking around among them, fighting evil?

"Look at this," Claudia said, pointing to a painting that hung near a large bed. The bed frame looked hand-carved, as did the frame of the picture.

The picture, a portrait of a man and a young lady, hung on the wall across from the foot of the bed. Frank imagined it was positioned so that the person in the bed could glance upon it before going to bed and upon waking.

"The woman is beautiful," Claudia said. "That dress looks seventeenth-century. The armor the man is wearing is the same as the set over there."

Frank looked upon the painting, glanced around the room, and turned to Chic, who remained in the doorway. "Did you know all of this was down here?"

"Of course," Chic said. "It's my place. Now you know: the man you had a chance to meet was no ordinary man. He dedicated his life to God, to the cause of good. He was a true warrior."

Frank walked to a table that was full of crosses, some metal, others of wood, some gold with many jewels adorning them. A particular wooden one drew his attention, but when he reached out to grasp it, he suddenly felt faint and stumbled. Chic hurried across the room and caught him before he fell to the floor. Claudia pulled a chair out from the table, and he sat.

"The air down here isn't the best," Chic said. "Perhaps we should go."

"Yes," Frank agreed as he stood with both Claudia and Chic at his side. "I'm fine," he said. He looked at the room one more time before leaving.

✦   ✦   ✦

Frank and Claudia left the tavern in Claudia's car, and he had her drop him off at his church. "I have some stuff to finish here," Frank said.

"We're all meeting at the tavern later. I'm sure everyone would like it if you came," Claudia said. He didn't respond as he exited the car, and she drove away.

It was Saturday evening, and there were no cars parked outside except Pat's. He walked in and spotted Pat at her desk. "What are you doing here so late?" Frank said.

She slightly jumped, surprised by the voice behind her. Then her face lit up, and she smiled. "We miss you, Father Frank," Pat said. "We miss your sermons, and the youth group is missing you too. Not that Mark is doing anything wrong. It's just, well, he doesn't have your composure."

Frank smiled. "Thank you, Patricia. I hope to be back soon." Then he had an idea. *That's it!* he thought. *That's what I need. I need to get up and do a sermon; that's where I've felt the most confident.*

He went to the back room where he kept his garments, took a set out, and brushed them off. He left them out so that they would be ready for him in the morning. He walked back to his apartment at an accelerated pace and straight to his counter, where he pulled out some paper and began writing his sermon.

Chapter 9

Out of the Embers of Sorrow

The Lord tests the righteous,
but the wicked and the one who loves violence His soul hates.
⁶Upon the wicked He will rain coals;
fire and brimstone and a burning wind
shall be the portion of their cup.
⁷For the Lord is righteous,
He loves righteousness;
His countenance beholds the upright.
—Psalm 11

Frank woke with a start and shot into an upright position. He'd slept in longer than he liked. He hummed in the shower and while he was shaving afterward. Looking in the mirror, he put his fingers up to his face and felt the puffy sacks that had formed under his eyes. His hair needed a trim, but it lay down fine, and shaving improved his appearance, but the dark circles under his eyes had not disappeared.

"Hmm," he said to the mirror as he poked at the puffiness. "Must be all those late nights with the group."

He ate a small breakfast of toast and reviewed his notes on his sermon. He made sure there was food and water in Rosie's dish before he left.

When he entered the church through the side door, Mark was there. It was ten minutes before morning mass. "Good morning, Frank," Mark said. "I thought you might come by today, but I wasn't expecting to see you here this early."

Frank didn't know what to say. The garments he'd put out the night before were still hanging on the closet door. He removed his jacket and opened the closet and hung it. Then he put on his robe. He looked at Mark.

"Mark, I've been down for days, praying and looking for guidance. I stopped by here last night and felt inspired. Let me go out there with you today. I need to do this."

Mark did not say anything but dressed and prepared for mass. Although it was uncommon for two priests to lead a mass, they did on occasion. The organ sounded, and the choir began to sing. Mark opened the door and let Frank lead.

Frank led the mass without so much as a thought. The words and responses flowed as though he'd been doing it his entire life. He didn't miss a single cue. When it came time for the reading and the sermon, he got a jump start to the pulpit, leaving Mark seated.

"It is good to see everyone this morning," Frank said. As he looked around to the faces, he saw two people come in late and make their way to the front. He recognized Kanuik right away. Kanuik stopped at the end of the third row from the front, and people scooted in to the center, making room for him and Claudia to sit. Frank was surprised to see them and wondered how they had known he would be giving the mass.

"I have been away on an important mission but thought it was time to come back for a visit and to make sure Mark was keeping all of you on the straight and narrow." The audience chuckled. He was happy to see his attendance was still holding; all three hundred seats were filled, and folding chairs lined the sides and back of the church.

"I know you have been studying the story of Peter," Frank said. "But I would like to talk to you about something else and take a moment to reflect on it. For this, I would like to turn to Galatians, chapter 6, verses seven and eight: 'Be not deceived; God is not mocked: for whatsoever a man soweth, that shall he also reap. For he that soweth to his flesh shall of the flesh reap corruption; but he that soweth to the Spirit shall of the Spirit reap life everlasting.'

"When we hear these words, some of us might think they refer to the labors of our lives as an example of how hard work will return reward, where being lazy will get you nowhere. But we can point to many examples in our world where that is not so, where the savvy, the liars, those that cheat can prosper. But our promise is that they will get theirs, and that we are not to give into this temptation put in front of us.

"The conflict of temptation is born within us as we hunger for things, as we struggle to control our cravings, our desires, all things we don't quite understand. Today as I read this passage, I think of the conflict, the conflict of good versus evil that today we speak very little of. When I talk about this conflict, some of us may envision one of the paintings that so easily find their way into books or our movie screens, with angels holding swords, with demons that have physical form. But the fight has become spiritual now.

"Some of us have the ability to see the fight in ourselves, in our efforts to escape drug addiction, abuse, gambling, or some other form of sin that we know is harmful. These are the more difficult battles to deal with for they are in our minds and our hearts." He moved from behind the pulpit, taking the microphone with him. He gestured with his left hand as he spoke. "It would be easy if evil would take a form and stand in front of us so we could know it is there, put a face on it, strike at it, have something solid to blame and overcome.

"But the truth is, the battle is not in front of us anymore, not directly. The battle is internal, in our actions, our thoughts. Apathy, complacency—these are the weapons of our enemy. Our failure to act when we see actions we know are wrong is a victory for evil every time.

"We don't always comprehend the results of our actions or of the example we are setting, its impact on the world around us. But those actions are the seeds of what we are sowing: our selfish intents, our quests for popularity or power. Our actions set in motion energy that radiates through every living thing around us. When our actions are negative or hurtful, so is this energy. When they are righteous or just, so is this energy. That is what is meant by sowing corruption.

"If we do not take responsibility and hold ourselves accountable, who does? God? Jesus? We are told we are being held accountable in the eyes of heaven. But what about those who don't believe in heaven? Do they have the right to be free to act as they want because we are going to turn away and say it is not our problem? We should pray for guidance. That prayer is not the ending. It is not for us to lose ourselves in prayer as an excuse for our lack of action; we are God's sword. We are His image, and we are here to act out His will. When we don't, and we ignore injustice, we destroy a part of the world, a part of goodness, a part of innocence, of compassion. And as this part dies, there will be less and less until we are out of tolerance, out of patience, out of love. This, then, will be the root of what suffering is, the plant we have grown."

The silence before Frank was deafening. He could hear his heart racing and felt sweat upon his forehead. His legs were tingling, and his stomach felt empty as he continued.

"Our actions do not just affect ourselves, but start a ripple that continues in the world around us, in the world we leave behind that others will inherit. And it is our right to demand this action of others, to tell them it is not okay to turn away and let darkness exist. It is not okay to let injustice exist. Whether they believe in God or not, they are not alone in the world and must act as responsible parties to a larger agreement: that we all share this place. And each of our decisions has an impact that can last well beyond our time into the everlasting, which is the legacy we leave for those that come after us."

He paused. The congregants before him were silent. He had given many powerful sermons from the spot where he stood, and his congregation loved him for his words of hope and inspiration. But he didn't see hope or inspiration in their faces and knew he wasn't finished. He'd broken them down, given them something to think about. Now it was time for the call to action. But something was wrong. His feet were not cooperating, and he felt numb. He moved a few steps back and toward the pulpit. His head felt dizzy, and his vision blurred. He switched the microphone to his left hand and reached out to grab the pulpit with his right to steady himself.

Mark walked over to him. Frank spotted Claudia looking up at him, a concerned look on her face. He smiled.

"Sorry," he said. "I guess I was adding too much dramatic effect." His statement produced mixed laughter.

"So what do we do now that we realize the impact our decisions have not only on us but also on this energy that surrounds us? How do we sow a better garden? I am not asking you to wield a sword and promote violence, but to promote goodness. We shed light and inspiration, turn from the darkness in everything we do. Resist the temptation to do things for selfish reasons." He looked at Claudia as sweat poured down from his forehead. He stepped around and gripped the pulpit firmly with both hands. Both his legs were numb. A glass of water sat on the shelf in front of him. It was protocol for the altar boys to set it there in case he needed a drink during his sermon. But he couldn't bring himself to reach for it. He hesitated. Sweat dripped into his eye and burned, but he couldn't let go of the pulpit for fear he would fall. The room was spinning.

"It's our responsibility to celebrate the death of our Savior in this way," Frank said, pushing on. "There are many who think they honor Him by bowing down, by living in the past. But He was a figure of inspiration, and more than bowing to him, he would want us to honor him through our actions."

He hadn't been up in front of his congregation for weeks. He looked out and couldn't recognize some of the faces. His collar felt too tight, and the sweat from his forehead continued to irritate his eyes. He looked for a friendly face. He looked at the row where Kanuik and Claudia sat. Kanuik had his eyes open and looked right at him and nodded. He nodded as if he agreed with him. *I got it right!* Frank thought. He smiled and felt good about it as he collapsed.

◆　　◆　　◆

Frank awoke at his apartment. He was lying on his couch. Kanuik looked down at him and gave him a start as he sat up. Kanuik blew smoke in his face, causing him to cough.

"Thank you," Frank grumbled.

"You *should* thank him," Claudia said from across the room. "He carried you out of the church, to the car, and all the way up the steps to get you here." She brought him a glass of water.

Frank drank the water and watched Kanuik as he went on puffing on his pipe, blowing the smoke around the apartment.

"The leaves I smoke have been blessed by holy men from many nations," Kanuik said. "It will cleanse your surroundings. You did not follow the instructions as Adnan said. I thought I saw something that night at the tavern, but I was not sure. Now it is clear: the shadows from that night did not leave you. Where is your cat?"

"She's been hiding under the bed," Frank said. He put his hands to his head, which ached terribly.

"Rosie," Claudia called, heading into the bedroom.

"That is the feeling of the shadows weakening you," Kanuik said. "The one Adnan had with him attacked him constantly. That is why he was close to no one. If you are going to do battle, they will be near you always, and anyone you are around will be in danger."

"I thought I was supposed to be able to drive them away," Frank said.

"If you weren't as strong as you are," Kanuik said, "you might have joined Adnan that night, and we'd be burying both of you."

"Here she is," Claudia said, emerging from the bedroom holding Rosie. She sat down beside Frank. He put his hand out, and Rosie let him pet her, but as soon as Claudia let go of her, she jumped off the couch. She didn't run to the bedroom but ran to her food dish.

"You must cleanse yourself further and rest," Kanuik said. "Do you still have the salts from the list?"

"Yes," Frank said. "What do I need to do?"

"You need to bathe in them," Kanuik said. "But that is not all." He went into the kitchen, used a paper towel to empty his pipe, put the towel in the trash, and put the pipe back in his pocket. He sat down beside Frank on the couch, causing the cushions to sink down.

Frank adjusted his position to allow some space between them. Claudia grinned.

"This is something Adnan meant to tell you, and perhaps he did, and you don't remember. The shadows have no power to exist in our lives or in our world without us inviting them to do so. They are not responsible for the actions we take; they merely influence those actions, and the weaker you are, the stronger they are."

"We did speak of this," Frank said.

"Yes," Kanuik said. "That is good. Then he must have told you that once you have interacted with the shadows, they are with you, and you must be constantly vigilant. I see you have not hung your wind chime. Had you, you would have known that they were here in this apartment with you. They are not here now, but they are attracted to something." He reached over and tapped Frank on the chest. "Something you are carrying in your heart. You must not allow them to find this weakness."

"You said bath salts were on your list, right?" Claudia asked. Frank nodded. "Then I'm going to run you a bath."

Frank watched as Claudia stood and went into the bathroom. Soon, he heard water running. He noticed Kanuik watching him intently.

"I see now," Kanuik said. He got up from the couch. "Of course they would use this to get to you; you have not always been a priest. If you cannot stay true to your vows, how does that affect your faith?"

"I would be excommunicated," Frank said.

"You desire her?"

"Yes," Frank said. "I do. It's not just physical; it's a deeper need."

"You are experiencing only what is meant to be experienced," Kanuik said. "There is balance in this world and a reason for male and female."

"My vows forbid any union except with God," Frank said.

"She is hurt and vulnerable; you may be mistaking her loneliness and need," Kanuik said.

When Frank considered what Kanuik was saying, he realized his friend was right. He knew he needed to continue fighting the temptation and focus on his mission.

"You have the heart of a warrior, stronger than any I've known," Kanuik said. "That is why Adnan picked you. You have the power to overcome this. You have the ability to continue the fight and make a difference. Only you can make that decision."

The sound of running water stopped. Both men looked to the bedroom entrance expecting Claudia to come through the door as the bathroom was through the bedroom. Claudia did not emerge.

"I will be at the tavern when you have decided," Kanuik said.

"Decided what?" Frank asked.

"Whether or not you will continue this fight."

Frank nodded and watched Kanuik leave. He locked the door behind him and was standing there with his hand still on the doorknob when Claudia walked into the room.

"I've poured you a bath and put the salts in," Claudia said. "I also took out some clean clothes and laid them on your bed. I hope you don't mind."

Frank turned from the door and looked at Claudia. "Thank you."

"If you have a laundry bag, I can take your clothes and have them done tonight."

Frank walked over to Claudia, reached out, and grasped her hands. He closed his eyes as he held them. They were soft and firm and warm—comforting. He reminded himself of his mission and commitment to follow through. "You've done so much."

"It's a pleasure," Claudia said.

"You've done enough," Frank said, opening his eyes.

She leaned in.

"I can't," Frank said. "If I have a mission here, it's not to recede into my own insecurities or want the pleasures of a normal life, no matter how desirable it may be."

"I just wanted you to know ..." Rosie jumped on the top of the couch, interrupting Claudia and startling both of them. She looked at them and flicked her tail back and forth.

"If you need anything," Claudia said.

"I'll let you know," Frank said.

Claudia left.

Frank bathed in the hot, salty water. When he got out, he ate a good meal of potato soup and crackers. He lit the candles Adnan had given him, hung the wind chimes, read, and prayed, and when he went to his bed, Rosie was there to greet him. She purred, and he looked forward to a night of peaceful sleep.

He rose the next morning, put on his jogging clothes, and left for a run. The weather was warm and sunny, almost hot for October. Birds sang, and the air was fresh as he ran with energy he hadn't felt for days.

"I just needed a good night of sleep, that's all," Frank said as he went along the road and into the park. He wasn't sure how long he'd been running, but soon he found himself outside of the city limits and on a path leading up a mountain trail. His thoughts were on his sermon and how he would need to come up with a new one within the next week. As he considered whether to go in and hear confessions, he failed to notice the landscape changing in front of him until something inside of him told him to look.

Suddenly, the ground shook, and the trail before him gave way, splitting apart the hill. The path he was on ended at a cliff. He could see where the path continued on the other side of the gap, a good distance away. Frank slowed and walked the last few steps to the end of the trail. There, he looked down, only to see that there was no ending to how far the ground had given way; only darkness greeted him. He heard a voice from the other side of the crevice and was stunned to see Adnan standing across from him, on the other side of the trail. Adnan had his cane in hand, but he wore only a white robe and sandals. His eyes were closed, and he was praying out loud, loud enough for Frank to hear.

"Adnan!" Frank yelled across the distance, but Adnan didn't stir.

"Don't move," Bishop Tafoya's voice yelled out from behind him. Frank felt a hand on his shoulder as Bishop Tafoya came beside him and looked down.

"How did you get here?" Frank said.

"That could lead straight to hell," Bishop Tafoya said, looking at the crevice. "It's a good thing I caught up with you and kept you from doing something you might regret."

Frank noticed that Adnan had opened his eyes and was looking at him. Adnan turned and started walking away.

"Adnan, wait!" Frank yelled, and this time Adnan stopped for a moment but then started walking again.

"Father Frank, don't," Bishop Tafoya said.

Frank backed up to give himself more room and then started running. When he reached the edge, he jumped across the opening, which, though deep, didn't appear to be very wide. His body soared, and he felt the cool air rush through his hair and the sweat on his skin chill. It felt good at first but then turned colder. He continued across, but something was wrong; he knew it shouldn't take so long to jump the distance. He started falling. Both the ridge on the other side and Adnan disappeared as he fell into the darkness. "Nooo!" he cried.

He heard another voice as he entered the darkness; it was Kanuik chanting.

He woke in the darkness of his room. Sitting up in his bed, he realized he could not simply go back to his church and the life he'd had before. He needed to continue the fight. He needed to complete Adnan's mission.

Chapter 10

Desperate Measures

Frank woke the next morning and calmly removed the covers. The dream the night before had disturbed him but had also served as a revelation. He knew it was time to face the darkness head on.

"Frank?" Mark called out.

"In here," Frank called from his bedroom. He had just finished shaving and was putting on his shoes. Rosie sat on the bed beside him.

Mark stepped into his room.

"What? You look surprised," Frank said as he finished tying his shoe and stood.

"It's a good thing you gave me a key," he said, approaching Frank. "My next step was to have the fire department break the door down. Didn't you hear me come by last night? I knocked."

"Sorry, I kind of had a rough night. Is something wrong that you needed me for?"

"I received an urgent call from your sister, who says she can't get a hold of you," Mark said.

"Yes, she's probably worried because we haven't spoken for over a week," Frank said. Frank patted Rosie on the head and went into the living room. Mark followed.

"I'm concerned about you as well," Mark said. "I've come a long way to work with you and hope to continue."

Frank poured himself a cup of coffee. He measured what Mark

was saying. The part about his coming a long way to work with him surprised Frank. As far as he knew, Mark had been assigned as a visiting priest and hadn't known who he'd been working with. He didn't know how much to share with Mark. He worried that anything he told him about what he'd been doing with the group might make the situation worse. Mark might think he was crazy or report his actions to Bishop Tafoya. At the same time, he thought he could use another ally.

"I've been removed from the assignment and put on leave for the time being," Frank said. "Would you like a cup?"

"No, I'm fine," Mark said. "When will you be coming back to the church?"

"I'm not sure right now. I haven't been myself lately," Frank said. He took a drink of coffee and made a face. He'd forgotten to put any sweetener in, and it tasted bitter. "I need some time to rest and collect my thoughts. The last month has been stressful." He leaned over and put his arms on the counter.

Mark sat down on one of the stools across from him.

"I thought I knew a lot," Frank said. "About my faith, about who I wanted to be, and who I was." He took another drink; the bitter taste bothered him less. "I met a man during this mission, a great man who was a teacher. I started to realize he had much to offer. Just when I thought I was learning from him, our time was cut short."

"The man the funeral was for? Adnan?" Mark said.

Frank nodded.

"And now you feel guilty?" Mark said.

"I feel like there was something more that I should have learned; the lesson was not complete."

"That's understandable," Mark said. "You have every right to mourn."

"Now I feel like I am regaining my composure, but ..." Frank reached over and turned the coffee pot off and set his cup in the sink. "I feel like there is more to do, but I don't know what."

"Is there anything I can do for you?"

"Are you driving the car the bishop loaned me?"

Mark nodded.

"You can come with me to see my father," Frank said.

"Sure, and then we can get some lunch," Mark said, patting his stomach.

The two men drove to Sacred Hills nursing home in the car Bishop Tafoya had loaned Frank. On the way, Frank borrowed Mark's cell phone to call his sister, but she did not answer.

"You can come with me," Frank said as Mark parked the car. "I'm sure my father would enjoy seeing you again."

They entered the nursing home, and Frank stopped at the front, glad to see Nurse Judy there since she was always helpful to him.

"Hello, Frank," Judy said. "You're in luck today. Your father isn't out for any appointments, and I just saw him in his room."

Frank signed himself in. "Judy, you remember Father Mark Uwriyer."

"Of course." The short, dark-skinned, voluptuous woman with long black hair came out from behind the desk, dressed in scrubs. "I'll walk with you to your father's room," she said.

"Is everything okay?" Frank said.

"Your father has been more confused lately," Nurse Judy said. "It's worse when nobody visits him for long periods of time because he gets his days mixed up, and then he loses track of time. His physician changed his medication, but we took him in for some tests because he wasn't responding to it."

"Yes," Frank said. "That was the day I came, but he wasn't here."

Judy nodded as she led them down a corridor and past a cafeteria. "This morning, he woke up as lucid as ever. He called me by name, had a smile on his face, and just went on and on about you."

"He did?" Frank said.

"Yes," Judy said. "I thought he was fine, but when I left the room, he was holding a conversation with himself. He said you were going to visit him today. Did you call him or something?"

"No," Frank said. "My phone's been out. Should I be worried?"

"I don't think it's anything serious," Judy said. "He's just getting old. Aren't we all?"

They finally came to the room where Frank's dad stayed and stopped outside the door.

Frank hesitated. "Thank you for taking care of him," he said to Judy. He then turned to Mark. "Would you give me a minute before you come in?"

"We have some folks who would love it if you went and prayed with them, Father Uwriyer," Judy said.

Mark and Judy continued down the hall while Frank stepped inside the room. "Dad?"

Frank's father was sitting in a large, red leather recliner, looking out his window to a garden that lay beyond. He was dressed, what was left of his gray hair was combed, and his eyes were wide open.

"Hello, son," he said, a smile on his face. He continued looking forward.

"You always did love that chair," Frank said.

"I think it's the only furniture I have left from the house."

"Sorry I haven't been coming to see you as much, Dad," Frank said as he walked up to his father and placed his right hand on his father's left arm. "I've been busy with something at work, and well, things haven't gone as planned."

"It's okay, son," Frank's father said. "You're a busy man. You have important things to do. Your friend stopped by and told me what you've been doing. I'm very proud of you."

"My friend?" Frank said.

"The Middle Eastern man with the hat and cane," his father said. "He was a pleasant man. He just went on and on about you and all the good things you've been doing."

Frank looked about the room for some sign of the visitor. "Did he tell you his name?"

"He might have, but you know this mind of mine." He twirled his right hand over his head. "It's not what it used to be, and I forget a lot of stuff.

"But he did leave you a message—he said he didn't want you to give up on his plan. He still thinks it is the best way forward for you and said the group would support you. He also said to thank Kanu, Kanak, something of the sort, for remembering his hat. He liked his hat." His father looked closely at him and smiled. "I'm proud of you, son." Then he closed his eyes and sat back in his seat. Soon, his deep, steady breathing indicated he was fast asleep.

Frank sat in the quiet room pondering what his father had told him. He felt a strength building inside of him, a strength he'd felt before, when he decided to leave the army and join the priesthood. It was confidence that he knew the path he'd chosen was right for him—not easy, but right.

"The battle is real," he said quietly. "Evil is real, and it's among us. Adnan picked me because he knew I would keep going."

Frank sat and prayed for his father. Then he went over to his father's bed and picked up the phone that sat on the nightstand. He dialed his sister's number. No one answered, and voice mail picked up.

"Dee Dee," Frank said, carefully choosing the last words his sister might hear from him, "this is your brother. I'm sorry I haven't called sooner, but my phone has been broken. I am here with Dad, and he is fine. I'm going to need you to check on him and take care of him because I'm going away. I appreciate what you've done, paying for the home, and I'm sorry to ask you to do more, but there's something I have to do. It might help you with Connor. My friend Father Uwriyer will be at my church and can help you with Dad." He paused and then added, "I'm not sure when I will be back. You've been a great sister, and I wish you all the happiness in the world."

Frank hung up the phone and whispered, "Tell your son Connor help is on the way." He went to his dad and kissed him on the forehead. He stepped out to the hallway, where Mark had just returned from the other rooms.

"Well, you look like you had a good visit," Mark said. "In fact, you have that confident look that I haven't seen for a while."

"Yes, I had a good visit," Frank said. "My father is sleeping now. You said you were hungry for lunch. Let's go."

The two men headed out to the parking lot. "It's real," Frank stated.

"What's that?" Mark said.

"I'm sorry," Frank said. "Just thinking out loud." The man his father had described was Adnan; Frank had no doubt. Adnan had reached out from beyond the grave and communicated to him through his father. "Are you hungry for Italian?" Frank asked as they reached the car.

"Sure," Mark said.

"I'll drive."

Frank drove them to the Kozy Tavern. "Trust me," Frank said when they arrived. "The bartender in here should be a master chef. Besides, there's something I need to do in here."

Mark didn't move from the passenger seat.

"Look," Frank said, "you told me back at the nursing home that you saw confidence back in my face. That's because I know what I must do, and it includes the people in there. You can trust them."

The two men entered the Kozy Tavern. Frank spotted Kanuik at the usual table, but he was by himself.

"You are feeling better, I see," Kanuik said as they approached.

"Yes," Frank said. "Thank you for your help and your advice. You know Father Uwriyer?"

Kanuik nodded, extended his right hand, and gestured for the men to sit down. Chic walked over to the table right away, and the men ordered lunch.

Until and after lunch arrived, Frank led the conversation, telling stories from his childhood and recalling how he'd been at the Kozy Tavern many times to meet his grandfather and father after work.

"You were right," Mark said as he finished his lunch. "This food is great." He pushed his plate forward. "Forgive me, but I must use the washroom."

After Mark walked away, Kanuik leaned in to Father Frank. "That man works for the bishop," he said.

"Yes, he is the one covering my services," Frank said. "Are Claudia and Jimmie coming here tonight?"

"I do not know," Kanuik said.

"I had something I wanted to talk to you, all of you, about," Frank said.

"You have a plan. Perhaps I am ready to listen," Kanuik said. "But I do not know this man you have brought, and he may tell Bishop Tafoya. We cannot take that chance."

"He won't be able to stay that late," Frank said. "Then we can talk."

Kanuik pulled out his cell phone.

"What are you doing?"

"Claudia and Jimmie should be here any minute. I will tell them to wait outside until Mark leaves."

"You lied?"

Kanuik winked. "I told you, we need to be cautious."

Mark returned but didn't sit down. "Well, that was a nice lunch, and I'll sure be coming back. Are you ready?"

"I'm going to stay a while if you don't mind," Frank said. He handed Mark the keys to the car. "Reminisce a little more."

"It would be good for you to take it easy," Mark said. "You want me to come by in the morning? Maybe we could go for a jog, get back on track."

Flashes of his dream passed through his mind, and Frank held up his hand. "I think I'll pass for the time being. If you don't need the car, please park it at the church and leave the keys with Pat."

Mark left, and within a few minutes, Claudia and Jimmie walked in together and came to the table. Although Jimmie was in his usual attire, a sport coat and slacks, Claudia was in dress jeans and a long-sleeved shirt.

"It is good to see you are doing better," Claudia said.

"Yes, thank you," Frank said. "You look nice." Frank thought she'd look good in anything but was happy to see her looking less formal. "I'm not used to seeing you in jeans."

Claudia looked down at her clothes. "Well, I took a casual day today. Besides, it's starting to turn colder. The hospital has not told me if they are taking any action yet regarding the incident with David. I still have my own practice, and the most they can do is ask me to leave their facility. It's time for a change anyway. I've already made preparations to leave."

"And what are you thinking of doing?" Frank asked.

"I'm thinking it's time to take some time off," Claudia said as Chic walked up.

"Time off? I hope you aren't planning on going anywhere," Chic said. He glanced around the bar. "I won't have anyone to talk to if you stop hanging out here."

"I think Kanuik will be here to keep you company," Claudia said.

"Heck," Chic said, "he was the first one of you to tell me he'd be leaving in a few weeks."

The rest of the group turned to look at Kanuik.

"Now, can I get you two anything?" Chic asked.

"Bring us a round of Adnan's honey tea," Claudia stated.

Chic nodded and left the table.

"Where are you going?" Claudia said to Kanuik.

"I must go where I am needed," Kanuik said. "I do not feel that this is the place any longer, unless someone has a need for me." He looked to Frank.

The table was silent as Chic brought a round of drinks. "To Adnan," Chic said, toasting with them. After the toast he went back to the bar.

"How is David?" Frank said.

"He has been on suicide watch since we brought him back. He tried to kill himself twice," Claudia said.

"Suicides always make the portal spike—you know, get larger," Jimmie said. "It's like those things feed off of them."

"I suspect," Frank said, "that after that night, the shadows didn't leave."

"Yes, we know," Kanuik said. "But now that you have cleansed yourself, you should be fine."

"No, that's not what I'm getting at," Frank said. "They didn't leave David either. In fact, I think the one that that was with Adnan transferred to David the moment before David jumped on him. I saw it leave Adnan but never leave David. If I'm right, they're still feeding off of him."

Claudia and Jimmie looked down at the table. Kanuik was the only one making eye contact.

"Don't you see? It's like Adnan said," Frank continued. "Their whole purpose is to wreck a family. They've done that. They wrecked the support structure and took them out. Then they took out Adnan. Their final blow is the ruination of a soul, David's soul."

"His suicide," Jimmie said.

"No," Frank said. "In his current state, he's much more valuable as a host for them."

"If they are with him, that means they must be crossing over somehow," Jimmie said.

"From his house?" Frank said.

"No," Jimmie said. "Kanuik sealed that one with his fire. If they are with him as you suspect, I should be able to get a reading, and maybe we can locate the source."

"What does it matter?" Claudia said. "It's too late."

"No, it's not," Frank said. "It means we have another chance."

"Another chance for what?" Jimmie asked.

"For Adnan's plan," Kanuik said.

No one else responded. Claudia took another drink, and Jimmie stood and went to the bar.

"Are you okay with this?" Frank said.

"I am a warrior; this is what I do," Kanuik said.

"Claudia?"

"Are you sure this is what you want to do?" Claudia said.

"Yes," Frank said. "More than ever. I know what is out there, and it's time to stop it. Can you get us in?"

"As David's priest, you have visitation rights. I'll do what I can to get Kanuik through, but Jimmie ..." Claudia said.

"I'm going to bring Father Uwriyer with me," Frank stated. "I'll tell him we are going there to counsel David."

Kanuik shifted in his seat.

"We need a witness," Frank said, "someone who can tell the bishop what happened. Besides, Mark's been kept in the dark long enough. It's time he knew the truth."

Frank left the table and went to sit by Jimmie at the bar.

Jimmie immediately started talking. "That night, at the house …" Jimmie took a drink, his eyes closed, and coughed.

"You said to make it a double," Chic said.

Jimmie took a deep breath and started again. "I never quite believed in evil. I knew we were dealing with something. I was hoping for extraterrestrials, parallel dimensions, something more science fiction genre and less, well, horror."

"I understand if you don't want any part of this," Frank said.

"That's not it," Jimmie said. "I mean, you're sorta right—part of me wants nothing to do with them again, a part that's afraid to expose myself and take the chance that they'll get back inside my head."

Frank watched Jimmie as he gazed forward into a moment of personal agony. Frank looked around, half-expecting to see his father at the bar talking with Chic.

"You remember that story you told us that night about saving the dog and standing up to bullies and all?" Jimmie said. "I mean, of course you do; it was your life. Well, when I was a kid, I had a similar thing happen.

"I grew tall early on. I wasn't big, but I was tall. That was enough to keep anyone from picking on me. But my best friend in sixth grade wasn't so lucky. Todd was short and an easy target. The eighth graders picked on him regularly. There was one in particular, Kent Bradley McComb. He was a big kid, not afraid of anyone. He was picking on Todd one day at recess." Jimmie laughed. "How is it the teachers are never around in these situations? I wasn't with Todd at the time, and he got beat up good. Later that day, while waiting for the buses to pull up, I saw Kent. I saw Kent Bradley McComb standing there.

And I looked, and there was a teacher in the area, and I knew that if I did anything, I'd get in trouble. I also knew that he was bigger than me. But something came over me, something that said, 'It ain't right what he did.'"

Jimmie turned back around and put his empty glass on the bar. Chic got the signal and filled it up, putting in two ice cubes. Jimmie picked up the drink and moved the glass so that the ice cubes circled around and chased each other.

"What happened?" Frank asked.

"I went straight up to Kent Bradley McComb and told him if he ever picked on my friend again, I would kick his ass. He looked at me, and I thought nothing would happen. Then he smiled and laughed." Jimmie took a drink and laughed again.

"Something about that arrogant laugh set me off. I kicked him in the nuts so hard that his face couldn't change from that stupid smirk fast enough. He looked like he rather enjoyed it, so I kicked him again. This time I connected good, and he bent over and fell to the ground and threw up. All the kids saw what I did, and so did the teacher."

"Did you get in trouble?" Frank asked.

"Detention for two weeks," Jimmie said. "They should have suspended me, but Kent had a reputation, and I figure they must've decided he had it coming. He never came around Todd or me again."

Frank nodded. It was a good story, he thought.

"Those things at David's house," Jimmie said, "the shadows. What they did to me ... they took control of my mind and warped it. I never want that to happen again."

"I understand," Frank said.

"No," Jimmie said. "I don't think you do." His eyes went cold, and he put down his drink. "I still have equipment at the hospital. I can round some stuff up, and we can open that portal. I'll help you anyway I can to rid this world of that vile, evil crap. In fact, I'll do one better."

"What are you thinking?" Frank asked.

"I analyzed the data from the last readings. I can open up the portal large enough for a man to get through, but before we do that, I'm going to send a shockwave through it."

"I'm not sure what you mean," Frank said.

"Well," Jimmie said, "Adnan and Kanuik were worried because the shadows always have some of their own guarding the portal. Keep in mind, these things are energy." Jimmie put his right arm out straight. "I believe I can shoot a pulse of electricity through that will fry those dark SOBs in the portal, leaving a clean entranceway. It should also disrupt their ability to alter time and change our perception of reality."

Frank raised an eyebrow.

"Sorry for the colorful language," Jimmie said. "But it's time for some payback. All we have to do is get them to come to us this time, without them knowing we are expecting them, and I'll send them straight back to …" He paused. "To wherever they came from. We just need some way to bait them."

"Leave that to me," Frank said.

Chapter 11

End Game

Frank approached the security desk with confidence. Mark was beside him. "We are here to see David Jensen. We're counselors from St. Joseph's Church," he said.

"Yes," the security guard said, "I see your names on the visitors' log. Please sign in here, and I'll get your badges."

While the priests signed in, the security guard paged Dr. Claudia Walden. "He's on suicide watch, and you'll need her permission to see him," the security guard explained.

The guard supplied them with badges, and a nurse arrived a minute later and escorted them to Claudia's office.

"Come inside, please," Claudia said as she opened the door. She was wearing her white lab coat and had her hair tied back, revealing small blue sapphire earrings. "The others are already here."

Kanuik and Jimmie were inside. Kanuik got up from the couch to greet Frank while Jimmie, wearing a cable guy's uniform, was busy in the middle of the room assembling his gear.

"What's with the outfit?" Frank asked.

"It's my disguise," Jimmie said. "The patients here have better cable than I do at home. I had to borrow this from Mike to have a reason for the equipment I was bringing in. By the way, you were right: I scanned David, and he is definitely active again."

Frank nodded. "I suspected. Well, I'm glad to see you have all made it. I know what this means to all of us and how risky it is, but I thank you for participating."

"I'm sorry," Mark said, "but am I missing something? I thought we were here to counsel David."

"We are doing more than that," Frank said. He turned to Mark and put his hands on his shoulders. "I need you to trust me, and I need you to be a witness to the events that are taking place."

Mark nodded.

"I also need this," Frank said as he pulled on the chain to Mark's cross.

Mark took off the cross and handed it to Frank, who held it tightly in his hand.

"There," Jimmie said, mounting what looked like a laser gun onto a tripod. Electrical cords ran out of the device and to an outlet. He turned to his computer, and after some typing and a few mouse clicks, he stopped. "It's ready. But we might want to grab a fire extinguisher or something like that on the way in to David's room."

"Kanuik?" Frank said.

"I'll get one," Kanuik said.

"David is in his room," Claudia said. "I was able to get all of you in without causing too much suspicion, but I could lose my whole practice if this thing blows up. So David doesn't leave his room, understood?"

Kanuik and Frank shot her a look, and Claudia raised her eyebrows. "What?" she said.

"Let's not use that term, 'blow up,'" Jimmie said.

"We need to wait an hour," Claudia said as she sat down at her desk and put reading glasses on. "We can do this during the dinner shift change. There will be minimal staff out on the floor." She began typing at her computer.

Frank sat on the couch and looked at Claudia and then at Mark. Kanuik waited by the door, peeking out the window.

Mark looked as if he was ready to leave any moment, but he surprised Frank by taking a seat on the couch beside him.

"When we go into David's room, you are to stay by the door," Frank said. "No matter what happens, do not interfere, or you could put the lives of everyone here in jeopardy. I brought you here to witness the events and show you what it is I've been doing."

"I understand," Mark said.

"All this paperwork," Claudia said, "it just drives me to the point of wanting to give up." Her blue eyes began to tear up. "If we fail again, if all of this is for nothing, I don't know if I can do this anymore." She started looking through her desk and pulled out a pack of cigarettes and a lighter, but the pack was empty. She threw the lighter at the trash can beside her desk. It slammed against the metal with force, and the sound echoed through the room.

Kanuik stepped away from the door. Frank thought Kanuik might comfort Claudia, who had returned her attention to her computer, but instead, he sat down on the floor, folded his legs, and put his hands together. He closed his eyes as though meditating. Frank searched for some words to change the sullen mood in the room.

"I needed Adnan to be right," Frank said out loud. Claudia stopped typing, and Jimmie looked at him. "I needed to know that we are able to ward this evil off and win. It's so easy to get down with the way things are these days; you can lose yourself in the madness of it all. It's too easy to lose hope. I needed him to be right, so I wouldn't lose mine."

"We all needed him to be right," Kanuik said, opening his eyes. "We just sent our great warrior into battle, and he was ambushed by our enemy. There has been great loss. We must mourn, not by weakness, but through action." His eyes fixed on Frank. "Especially you."

"Me?" Frank said.

"Adnan knew he was getting too old to fight," Kanuik said. "He knew he might fail. He mentored you to be a stronger warrior. He knew conventional methods were failing and that we needed a nuclear weapon. You are that weapon. I wish there was more time. I have seen your power and your belief. Take his cane with you on your journey so that you won't forget."

Frank sat in silence and watched the minutes tick by. Kanuik meditated while Jimmie dozed off. Claudia typed, but the number of times she hit the backspace key told Frank she could not concentrate. Mark sat on the couch and waited with him. When he saw that it was past six, he started to give his instructions.

"There will be four of us in his room. Jimmie ..."

Jimmie shook his head as if to wake himself up and sat up in his seat.

"Jimmie," Frank continued, "you will be in the back by your equipment. Kanuik, keep Jimmie and Mark safe. I want to make sure we are prepared to contain the shadows when they emerge and are not taken by surprise. I want a scan of the room when we get in."

Frank stopped for a moment. He was addressing people who had been working with Adnan for years and knew each other better than he knew them. Yet in just a short time, with Adnan gone, they had turned to him to lead.

"When we find it, don't block the portal," Frank said. "We want to draw them out. Mark, you will stand by the door and make sure no one comes in the room. If I am correct, the shadows are still with David, and it will not take much to get them to show themselves. I will confront David with what he's done, wear him down until the shadows come."

"Then?" Jimmie said.

"You do your stuff with the equipment and open up the portal so I can slip through."

"That easy?" Claudia said from behind her desk.

Frank didn't respond.

"There's no guarantee I can lock on the portal and open it enough for you to get through," Jimmie said.

"Leave that to me," Frank said. He grasped Mark's cross and stood. Claudia got up from her desk and opened the door, and the group cautiously started toward David's room.

"I don't understand," Mark said to Frank as they walked down the hall. "What's with all the equipment?"

"We are going to fight evil," Frank said. "You will understand once you see it. I trust you will have the strength to see it through."

"I guess I will just have to have faith," Mark said.

"Yes," Frank said.

Claudia scanned her card to open the door to David's room. The light that would indicate access had been granted did not come on. She scanned the card a second time with the same result. "They must have revoked my access to him," Claudia said.

"Here, hold this," Jimmie said as he handed his contraption to Mark. "I thought we might need this." He pulled out what looked like a Taser from his jacket pocket and put it up to the door lock. A blue spark shot out, and the magnetic lock to the door released. Jimmie looked toward the ceiling and cocked his head. "Ha, did it without triggering the alarm," he said in a moment of personal triumph.

Claudia shook her head.

"What?" Jimmie said. "This is the first time I've ever done something like this. I wasn't sure that was even going to work. After you."

"David is on heavy medication," Claudia said. "He might be unresponsive."

Frank looked in the room as Kanuik and Jimmie entered in front of him. David sat at the edge of his bed, fully awake and facing them as they entered.

"It seems we may have lost the element of surprise again," Frank said.

Mark entered the room, leaving Frank and Claudia outside by themselves.

"Claudia," Frank said, "you can wait out here."

Claudia reached out and grabbed his arm before he could move into David's room. "Don't forget this," she said, handing him Adnan's cane. "You left it in the backseat of my car."

"Thank you," Frank said, taking the cane.

"Don't go," Claudia said. "Just walk away."

Frank pulled her close, knowing it would be the last time they embraced. He felt her warmth and wished the circumstances were different. If he stayed, he imagined leaving the priesthood to be with her. "I can't," he said, "not with what I know and what I've been shown. There's no other way." He released his hold.

Tears streamed from Claudia's eyes. "It's okay," she said. "I guess we'll never know if there was more to this than just an attraction based on an emotionally intense situation."

Frank smiled. "Take care of Rosie for me," he said and turned to enter the room. Frank closed the door behind him and stepped toward David.

"The equipment is online," Jimmie said. He stood behind the device and pivoted it on the tripod, stopping to aim it at various spots throughout the room. "Range is good, and the room is hot. I'm ready." He nodded.

"You are an observer here," Frank said, stepping up to Mark. "I want you to watch and take note on what happens so you can report back to Bishop Tafoya. Pray for David and talk to him."

"I'm not sure I understand what you want," Mark said.

"I am going to fight evil," Frank said. "You may or may not see the forces in this room, but they are there, and you must not try to help me. It's very important that you listen to me now. No matter what happens, you must keep praying, and do not interfere with what I do. Do you understand?"

"Yes," Mark stated.

"Here," Frank said, handing Mark a stopwatch. "The alarm is set at fifteen minutes. Once the alarm stops, reset it so that it will go off again. Whatever you do, don't forget to reset it."

Mark nodded. "Got it."

Frank embraced Mark. "You are ready to lead your own congregation. I will always be in your debt." Stepping back, he looked back and forth between Mark and Jimmie. "Don't either of you step over the line of fire." He turned around, made eye contact with Kanuik, and nodded.

Kanuik reached up and wrapped the fire suppression system's

sprinkler with a plastic bag. Then he put his hand into his pocket, and when he brought it back out, he threw balls of fire in a protective semicircle around where Jimmie and Mark stood. Then he nodded to Frank.

David did not move as Frank approached him. Frank took the cross that Mark had given him and pushed on the top, causing the knife blade to extend from the bottom.

Kanuik went over to David, undid the straitjacket, and stepped back from him. David did not try to move.

"Get ready, Jimmie," Frank said. "Mark, start the watch." He moved closer to David's bed. "David, are you listening to me now?" Frank said.

"Yes," David said.

"Do you know where you are?"

"Yes."

"Do you remember what happened at your house?"

"Yes."

"You killed your family, David," Frank said. "Then we took you back there to help you. Do you remember this?"

David's eyes narrowed, and he turned his head from side to side, as though searching for a way out of the room. He looked up at Kanuik, who hulked over the small-framed teenager.

"The person who was with you," Frank said, noticing his breath materialize as the temperature in the room turned cold, "his name was Adnan. He was going to help you."

Frank shivered and looked around the room, suddenly drawn to an area by the sink. There he spotted the creatures appearing. He could see them clearly now: dark, with form but not quite solid. The eyes were empty, but sometimes he saw a hint of gray as though they were looking around. They approached David from the opposite side of where Kanuik stood. One appeared slightly behind Frank; Frank wondered whether it recognized Mark's presence in the room and was intentionally placing itself between them. Frank hesitated, worried that he'd put Mark in jeopardy. The young priest made no indication that he could see the creature, and true to his nature and his promise, he was praying.

"Father, be with your young servant David, and guide him through these troubled times," Mark said. "Walk beside him and give him strength, for you are the spring of life from which all renewal flows."

The shadow moved away from Mark and stalked Frank. It did not walk but floated like an apparition, upright, but tilted, unbound by solid form. Unlike the first time he'd seen them, Frank was not disturbed or afraid. His heart was angry at them, but he accepted that he could resist the thing in front of him. He looked over to where the shadows had emerged and spotted the opening.

"Jimmie?" Frank said.

"I've got it, but it's not big enough yet," Jimmie said. "I warned you this might happen. I need a bigger target."

Frank looked at David's bed, but instead of David, it was his father looking at him. "Son, your friend came by to see me again—you know, the one with the cane. He told me to tell you he was wrong in what he did. It was foolishness and could get you killed."

Frank closed his eyes and opened them again. His sister was standing over the bed, which was no longer a bed but had turned into a casket. His father lay inside. "I suppose you will want to do the funeral," his sister said. "Didn't you know he needed more tests? And after this funeral, you can do mine and Connor's 'cause he's going to kill us because you failed."

Again, Frank closed his eyes and prayed. He knew what he was seeing was not real, and he tried to fight it. He concentrated and soon heard the beeping sound he'd been waiting for. The sound of the alarm brought him back to David's room, back to reality.

"Thank you, Mark," Frank said as he looked around the room. The others were there, but they were staring, not even blinking. They looked like mannequins in a storefront, frozen. Frank looked down at his hands and moved them. They moved so fast, they blurred. He stepped toward Kanuik, whose eyes were closed tightly. He reached out and put his hands on him. Kanuik opened his eyes.

"I am here with you," Kanuik said. "Use your power; you have been touched by angels. Take the cane to herd the shadows. Use it and remember who you are."

Frank looked down, but Adnan's cane was not in his hand.

"It is there," Kanuik said. "Feel it."

Frank closed his eyes. He heard the voices of his father and sister calling but did not open his eyes. Instead, he concentrated on his right hand where he held the cane and his left hand where he held Mark's knife. He felt someone touch him; the touch was warm, and the hands were soft. He opened his eyes.

"I am here for you," Claudia said, standing in front of him. Her hair was down, and her blouse was unbuttoned, showing her cleavage. She tried to pull Frank closer, but he resisted. She moved toward him, and he felt the heat of her body and her lips as she went to kiss him.

"No," Frank said. He started to push her away.

Somewhere he heard the alarm sound again; the beeping seemed very distant, but he focused on the sound. Again he imagined feeling the cane and cross in his hands, and soon, he did feel them. He opened his eyes and saw the cane in his right hand and Mark's cross in his left hand.

"Very good," Kanuik said to him.

"Get ready," Frank said. He nodded to Kanuik as he changed position to get closer to the opening. "God, forgive me for what I am about to do," he quietly prayed.

Kanuik moved closer to David but did not get directly in front of him.

Frank found himself in David's house. David sat on the couch alone. On the floor in front of him lay a body covered in a bloodstained sheet. David was crying. Frank knew he was now in David's delusion where the shadows had taken him. He was somehow sharing what David was seeing. Frank closed his eyes and concentrated. He knew he could not lose himself in the false world the shadows presented. When he opened his eyes, he was back in the hospital room.

"David," Frank said. He moved the cross to his right hand so that it was closer to David and shifted the cane to his left, closer to the portal. He held the knife so that the sharp end was clearly visible to David. "You are a weak boy, given to temptations. You have failed to fight the weakness that surrounds you. You are responsible for this."

Frank heard Mark stop his praying. "What's he doing?" Mark said.

"Suicides!" Jimmie said. "The shadows are attracted more to suicides. He's trying to get them to swarm and open a bigger portal."

"Do not be distracted by what is going on!" Frank yelled. "Mark, keep praying like I instructed. You must keep praying."

He turned back to David and stepped between him and the portal, keeping the knife within David's reach. *Take the knife!* he thought.

"It's starting to spike," Jimmie said. "Just a little bit more."

"David," Frank said, stepping closer. "Do you remember what you did to your family, what you did to Adnan? You are a troubled boy."

"I didn't mean it," David pleaded.

"But you did," Frank said.

"Yes, I hated them because they didn't let me do what I wanted," David said. "But I didn't mean to kill them."

"It's too late, David. They're gone," Frank said.

"Forgive me, Father."

The shadows moved in, and the forms touched David. Frank heard the whispers this time. They were closer than before. He could not make out what they said, but one word came through. "Kill," the voice said.

"Help me, Father Frank," David said.

Frank watched as David's face contorted and his body convulsed. His eyes showed pain, and he choked, coughing. Then blood flowed like tears from his eyes.

"The opening is moving toward you," Jimmie said.

Frank tried to spot the opening without taking his eyes off the knife. One false move, and he could end up dead like Adnan. He knew he had to be quick. He could see the outline of the portal, pulsing in the air like a mirage. David stood from his bed, facing Frank.

"Get ready," Frank said.

Kanuik stood beside David, who stopped convulsing and focused his attention on Frank. In his peripheral vision, Frank could see a dark mass coming through the portal, much larger than the shadows already in the room.

Kanuik started chanting in his native language. Frank did not understand what Kanuik said, but he'd heard it before. He was preparing to move when David stepped forward quickly and was suddenly in front of him. Frank felt the cross leave his hands as David grabbed it with surprising speed. Fear gripped him as he waited for the end, but David stepped back.

"Forgive me," David said. He rotated the cross and went to stab the sharp end into his own chest, but Kanuik reached in, grabbed the boy's hand, and stopped him. The two fell back on the bed. Kanuik grabbed at him and prevented the knife from going in.

"No!" Mark cried out and ran across the room toward David but stopped at the edge of the flames as they roared up in a wall, preventing him from crossing to where David was on the bed.

"Now!" Jimmie yelled. He released the pulse from his machine, and a flash went across the room. Ashes filled the air. The fire system was triggered, and an alarm went off. The bag over the sprinkler reached its bursting point, and water began raining down on the men.

Frank looked at David. The dark form had surrounded him. Kanuik moved back and forth, struggling as one of the forms wrapped itself around his neck. "Go now," Kanuik said through clenched teeth.

Frank could see the portal in front of him, but instead of going in, he reached out toward David and Kanuik, and as Adnan had done, he grabbed the darkness. He felt for it and found the energy. It burned his skin, but he clutched it and pulled. He pulled it away from David and Kanuik and took it with him as he stepped into the void.

Claudia pounded on the door. Jimmie opened it. She looked around the room. Kanuik and Mark were securing David's straitjacket.

"They're evacuating this section," Claudia said. "We need to get out."

"It will work to our advantage," Jimmie said. "Maybe they won't notice us in the confusion." He grabbed his equipment, handed some of it to Mark, and headed down the hall.

Kanuik helped get David to the door. Claudia stepped aside to let them pass and kept looking around the room.

"He's gone, Doctor," Kanuik said. "Father Frank is gone. It worked."

Chapter 12

Amen

Claudia parked her AMC Ambassador in an open space in front of the conference center. Removing the letter from the envelope, she read it again and checked the address; this was the right place. She'd driven ten hours straight to get to the location. It was the contents of the letter that attracted her. She looked in the rearview mirror and checked her appearance before exiting the car.

She reached into the backseat and grabbed her bag full of books, bookmarks, flyers, and other marketing material. With the bag over her shoulder, she headed into the conference center, which was teaming with people, and went to an information desk.

"Can you help me?" Claudia said.

The receptionist's eyes lit up. "It's you!" Her excitement attracted the attention of several other people in the lobby.

Claudia moved her right hand across her head to smooth out her hair.

"I'm sorry," the receptionist said. "It's just I've seen you on all the talk shows and stuff. Would you mind?" She reached down, pulled a book out of her purse, and set it on the counter in front of her.

"Not at all," Claudia said. She took out a pen and signed inside the front cover.

The receptionist smiled and looked at the autograph in a daze. "I really love the way you take your cat, Rosie, on all the tours with you and on the talk shows," she said.

"Yes," Claudia said. "She's a very special cat. Can you help ..." Before she could finish, someone touched her on the shoulder, and she turned around to see Father Mark Uwriyer standing behind her. He was dressed in black pants and shirt and still looked like the priest she'd met two years ago.

"I wasn't sure you'd get my letter," Mark said, "or if you'd come. You're quite a celebrity these days. This is Dr. Claudia Walden," he said to the receptionist.

"Yes, I know," the receptionist said with a smile, holding up her autographed book.

"This way," Mark said. He led Claudia through a set of double doors and down a hallway to an office. He let her in and then stepped inside and closed the door behind him. "Please." He pulled out a chair from a small circular table.

Claudia placed her bag on the table to and took a seat. Mark sat next to her.

"It was very nice of you to dedicate your book to the memory of Father Frank Keller," Mark said. "I'm sure he would have been grateful."

Claudia smiled and tapped her fingernails on the table. She wanted to dispense with the formalities and get right to the point.

"You do remember me?" Mark asked.

"Of course," Claudia said. "How could I forget? It's been more than a year since I've seen you."

"Yes," Mark said, "at the funeral for Father Frank."

Claudia broke eye contact and looked down.

"Sorry," Mark said. "I know you and Frank were close. I'm sorry it took the church so long to give him a service. It took them a while to quit looking for him and lay him to rest."

"It's okay," Claudia said. "We went through a lot together."

"Yes," Mark said. "I know he considered you a close friend."

"When people go through traumatic events, it makes everything more intense, including memories," Claudia said.

"I have been on a new assignment," Mark said.

Claudia nodded. "I was surprised to hear from you. Once you left St. Joseph's, I thought I'd never see you again. I haven't seen anyone for so long. Jimmie disappeared doing his research. He drops a line here and there, but I haven't heard from him in months. Kanuik left to go work with his wife, but I haven't heard from him since."

"I'm sorry to hear that," Mark said. "I had hoped you wouldn't be left alone after what happened. It's important to have support."

"I don't have time to feel lonely, Father," Claudia said. She unzipped her bag, took out a hardback copy of her book, laid it on the table, and pushed it toward him. "Besides, I'm a former psychiatrist and know a lot about grief counseling. I found a way to move on."

"Thank you," Mark said, accepting the book. "I am glad it has helped you find meaning and continue the cause." He held the book in his hands and examined the cover. "*Reaching Out: Time to Make a Positive Change in the World*. Great title, might I add. I'm glad to see you've continued the cause in a less dangerous manner than before."

"Yes," Claudia said. "It includes Frank's last sermon and much of his advice." She clenched her hands tight. "Now can you please tell me about the letter?"

"Yes," Mark said. "I apologize. That's probably where we should have started, and I know it's why you came. It's just, well, complicated."

"You said you had news about him," Claudia said.

"Yes," Mark said. He stood from the table and put his right hand to his mouth. His eyes narrowed. "I'm not sure how to tell you this," he said. "When we met, you knew me as just a colleague to Frank. The truth is that I was sent to work with him by a group much like the one Adnan ran. We were the ones who gave Adnan the intelligence on Father Frank, the insight that he was gifted or touched by an intervention. I was sent to observe."

"I don't understand why you are telling me this now," Claudia said.

Suddenly, there was a knock on the door, and another priest stepped into the room. "They're about to begin," the man said.

"We'll be right there," Mark said. He turned back to Claudia as the priest left and closed the door again. "I'm sorry. It seems we've run out of time. I do want to answer all your questions, and if you follow me, I think you'll understand. You can leave your stuff here."

Mark held out his hand, and Claudia took it as he helped her stand from her chair and opened the door for her. They joined a line of people heading toward a set of windowed doors. As Claudia approached, she could see into the large auditorium, where hundreds of people were seated around a center stage.

"I'm sorry to invite you on such short notice," Mark said. "I'm sure you have a lot of questions. You will find your answers in here."

"Are you leaving?" Claudia said.

"I'll be close by," Mark said, and they entered the huge auditorium. There were people sitting in the seats facing the stage, and a large group sitting on the stage, behind rectangular tables that formed a semicircle. As Claudia climbed the stairs to the stage, she noticed that each table had four of five people sitting at it, and signs in front of them gave the names of countries, tribal names, or religious designations. A man stood in the middle of the tables and was speaking, but Claudia was too busy adjusting to her surroundings to hear what he was saying.

As Claudia looked around, she read the signs: Jewish, Orthodox, Indian, Muslim, Christian, Hindu, even a delegation from Tibet. Her eyes caught a familiar face smiling back at her. At one of the tables, sitting among others from his tribe, was Kanuik. He stood as Claudia walked over to him, and they hugged.

"Please," Mark said, reappearing at her side, "have a seat here." He pointed to a chair close to Kanuik's table. Then Mark went to the podium and took the microphone.

"Thank you for coming," Mark said. "I am happy to see such a large turnout at what I hope will be the first of many more conferences and the start of a new era of hope and inspiration. It has been the goal and desire of many generations, the sweat and toil of many hardworking men and women, to bring us here.

"We must never forget the sacrifice of those who have asked us to put aside our differences and come together now, to come together and consider one mission and one mission alone; it is time for us to work together and realize the foundation of all of our religions has one purpose: to rid the world of evil and end suffering. Such is the goal of this conference. If we are to consider ourselves leaders, we can no longer afford to compete with each other; that is how we will lose the battle. Instead, we must open our eyes to a new way of cooperation, peace, and understanding without compromise to governments or politicians and their political whims. I am here before you today as a witness. The battle is real. Evil is among us, and it wants to take more. It is up to us to come together and stop the suffering, to turn the tide."

The room erupted in applause as both those at the tables and those in the packed seats below stood. Claudia stood as well. Mark smiled back at her and then led introductions for the next speakers.

Claudia sat and listened for the next two hours to testimonies from many different people around the world. They spoke about times when they felt they were under attack by evil or tempted to do evil. A dozen or more described a man who came to their aid—a tall man who was dressed as a priest and carried a wooden cane. When they mentioned him, nods and chatter came from the audience, leading Claudia to believe others had shared the same experience.

After the presentations, the bulk of the audience left, but the people at the tables on the stage remained and shuffled about. Claudia remained seated. Kanuik poured her a glass of water from a pitcher on the table.

"Thank you," Claudia said. "It's so good to see you." She stood and hugged him again. She noticed a lady seated next to him watching her.

"This is my wife," Kanuik said. "She is the head of the tribal council represented here. Over fifty native tribes have all come to join in the fight. Among them, Father Frank is a hero."

Claudia shook the woman's hand and turned to Kanuik. "Do they think this man they are describing in their testimonies is Frank?"

"Yes," Kanuik said. "That is what we believe and what we are trying to convince the council of today."

"Claudia," Mark said, coming up behind her. "The group would like to ask you a few questions. Are you ready?"

"I've been presenting in front of audiences all across the country. I think I can handle a room full of holy men," she said with a smile.

She stood in front of the group as everyone sat back at their tables. The auditorium was not as crowded as before, but a few people had remained behind.

"Is it true that you knew Father Frank Keller?" asked someone from a table where several men sat dressed in religious clothing that she recognized as Catholic. The man who addressed her was dressed like a bishop.

"Yes," Claudia said. "We worked together for a short period of time."

"I am Bishop Denaro. We," he gestured to the table where the other men sat, "have spoken to two of the witnesses who were present, Kanuik here and Father Uwriyer," Bishop Denaro said. "We have been told what happened to Father Frank Keller, and as you have heard, witnesses have testified to seeing a man fitting his description."

Claudia remained silent, waiting for him to continue.

"Are you of the opinion that Father Frank Keller somehow disappeared into thin air and is now fighting evil in some plane of time?" the bishop said.

Claudia rubbed her hands together. She felt the long road trip catching up to her. "Father Frank was a great man. I knew him for only a short time but could tell he was the type of man I would want beside me: confident, strong, and morally guided toward what was just. I believe—"

"I understand you weren't in the room at the exact moment the incident took place," the bishop said, interrupting her.

"Incident?" Claudia said.

"Yes," the bishop said, "where he supposedly crossed through the portal to where the shadows come from."

Claudia took a drink of water. Then she walked closer to the table where the bishop was seated. "Father Frank went into that room and did not come out. He was never found."

The stage turned silent as those at the tables listened to Claudia's account.

"It is my belief that Father Frank Keller succeeded in his mission and is responsible for the testimonials you have just heard," Claudia said. "It is really our doubts and insecurities that we must deal with in the disappearance of Father Frank. That is what your enemy wants— for you to have doubt. We need to honor him, not mourn him. We must realize he would want us to go on and keep fighting. He'd want us to be strong and set a good example.

"Father Frank hoped that we would quit looking only at the eternal life beyond this one; he wanted us to look also at the eternal life in front of us. He believed that our actions are like drops of water in an endless sea; they send ripples throughout the world, echoing and impacting events around us longer than we could possibly imagine. Our view must change from one that is shortsighted to one that allows positive choices and the growth of our values as a community. The choices we make now will echo through history years after we are gone."

She leaned in to the table and put her hands on it, looking directly at the bishop who had questioned her. "I only hope you don't forget what Father Frank Keller has sacrificed—because he wasn't the first."

The room erupted in applause as the representatives stood. Even the few observers remaining in the far reaches of the room stood and applauded.

Claudia stepped back from the table and looked toward Mark. Kanuik stood and walked over to her. He held out his arm, which she took as he escorted her off the stage and toward another set of doors. Before they could get through them, a young man approached and stood in their path.

"Excuse me," the young man said. "I'm Connor Deitz. Father

Frank Keller was my uncle. I just wanted to thank you for what you've done for him."

"Thank you," Claudia said, and she continued out of the room with Kanuik. "Was Frank's nephew invited as well?"

"He's part of the group," Kanuik said.

"What group?" Claudia asked.

"Didn't Father Uwriyer tell you?"

"We only spoke for a few moments," Claudia said. "I'm sure he wanted more time."

"They are training another group of warriors, and Connor is among them. Jimmie is leading the effort to open the portal and send more through."

"Can this be real?" Claudia said.

"Yes," Kanuik said. "It is real. Frank succeeded. He is fighting for us all."

Printed in the United States
By Bookmasters